THE SNOWS COUNTY

A Novel by

J.A. Snow

Volume One in the Series "An American Family"

Text Copyright by J.A. Snow 2013

All rights reserved. No part of this publication may be reproduced, distributed, or transmitted

in any form without the prior written permission of the author.

Introduction

The fifteenth century was a time of great upheaval in England.

From the very beginning of King Henry IV's reign, the country was torn apart by internal strife. Within three months of taking control, he was forced to flee from Windsor Castle to escape a rebel coup made up of supporters of the deposed King Richard II. The coup failed and most of the traitors were executed by Henry (their dismembered corpses being delivered to London in sacks in a gruesome show of bravado) but the civil uprisings continued across England, Wales and Scotland. Henry's claim to the throne was very weak because of the suspicious nature of his succession. Richard II was still alive, imprisoned in the tower and Henry could not prove with certainty that the king had willingly forfeited his crown in defeat. It was only with much political maneuvering that his claim to the throne was upheld, and he was crowned in 1399.

After his first two years in power Henry's military struggles were depleting the royal coffers. By 1401 the royal treasurer informed him that *"there is not enough money to pay the messengers."* During this time his son, the young Prince Henry had begun to push his way into his father's inner circle. At the age of twenty-two the prince pressured the king's chancellor, Archbishop Arundel, to resign and he assumed the position as the president of the king's council. So headstrong was young Henry there were many quarrels between him and his father. At one point the ailing king temporarily reinstated the archbishop to his former position as a form of parental punishment. This did not last, however. While the king's health continued to deteriorate there were rampant rumors that the prince was gathering forces to depose his father, all of which young Henry denied. The king died a miserable death in 1413, horribly disfigured from leprosy with his son at his bedside. An excerpt from his will reads: *I, Henry, a sinful wretch, ask my lords and true people forgiveness if I have mistreated them in any way.*

The young prince was crowned Henry V and became a warrior-king spending much of his time abroad recapturing French lands that he presumed to have earned by inheritance and making him an often-absentee ruler. By 1415, a mere two years into his reign, he defeated the French forces at the Battle of Agincourt; a most decisive victory in which he lost only four hundred men while annihilating six thousand of the French troops even though most of the success at Agincourt was due to blunders of the French. Henry nevertheless entered Paris triumphantly as Regent of France.

At home throughout his reign Henry V tried to make right the misdeeds of his father, restoring lands to barons that had been previously seized. By extending this olive branch of peace he developed a devoted following. But his ongoing obsession with conquering France was left unfulfilled when he died in 1422 of dysentery in Bois de Vincennes, never to return to his homeland.

Henry VI, son of Henry V and Queen Catherine, was not yet a year old when his father died. As with other "infant kings" throughout English history he was surrounded by an array of unscrupulous tutors and advisors. He soon began to see less and less of his widowed mother; the Queen had begun a love affair with a Welsh squire named Owen Tudor and was otherwise occupied starting a new family. The young king was placed in the care of Richard Beauchamp, Earl of Warwick and a trusted servant of his father Henry V.

He was an arrogant child fully aware of his royal status. At the age of ten he questioned whether it was proper for a king of any age to be disciplined for his behavior for which the high council was severely reprimanded. While England's hold on French lands was slipping away the adults in ten-year-old Henry VI's court were squabbling like children themselves.

In the small coastal town of Porlock in southwest England Lord John Harrington had long been the overseer of the lands in and surrounding the town. Staunchly loyal to Henry V he gathered his able subjects together and enlisted them to sail with him to assist the king in France. With a force of eighty-six archers and twenty-eight mounted lancers he went to fight alongside the king in the Battle of Agincourt leaving his wife Lady Harrington to rule over his estate in his absence.

John Anthony Snow, who was then a mere lad of ten, had been a stable boy on the Harrington estate since the tender age of seven and had captured the heart of the childless couple. John loved his benefactors in return and worked tirelessly to care for their stable of horses, often spending the night in the straw to nurse an ailing horse or assist with the birth of a foal. When Lord Harrington returned home from the war he was extremely pleased to find that his herd of prized broodmares was in excellent condition and he attributed much of it to young John.

A year later, when the Lord fell ill to a nasty fever, the boy visited him daily reporting on the health of his horses and cheering him up with the local gossip. He was so moved by the boy's loyalty one afternoon Lord Harrington asked his wife to bring him his sword and had the boy kneel at his bedside. In his weakened state and barely able to lift the heavy steel weapon he had brandished so bravely in battle, he bestowed on John the honor of knighthood and young John swore lifelong allegiance to his lord, his lady, and to King Henry, a *symbolic* gesture but heartfelt nonetheless.

When Lord Harrington died soon thereafter the boy was taken over with grief and in later years often visited his tomb in the church where he could be seen kneeling down at the foot of his lord's alabaster effigy. Lady

Harrington never remarried and continued to rule the manor for another fifty years, with the boy who grew up and who was to spend the rest of his life in her service.

It is here our story begins in the year 1430 A.D.

Chapter One "The Lord Gives and Takes"

"Go fetch my sister," she said. "It's time."

John was awakened in the wee hours of the morning by his wife gently squeezing his arm.

He jumped immediately from his bed, pulled on his trousers and boots, tucked his sleep shirt under his belt and ran outside. At the pasture gate he awakened the closest horse available, an old mare aptly named Pockets for the two round patches of dark hair on her rump. He didn't bother to saddle her; with just a bit and a bridle he jumped on bareback, gripping the horse's sides with his muscular thighs and clutching a handful of mane with his free hand. With one swift kick they took off in the darkness down the steep Porlock Hill.

By the time he reached his sister-in-law's farmhouse in the valley, the horse was breathing heavily and was lathered in sweat. John dismounted, pulling at his wet, horsehair covered trousers that were clinging to his legs and ran to the door. A lamp was lit inside the house and the door opened.

"The baby is coming!" was all that needed to be said and Mary was ready in minutes, straddling the horse behind John in her long skirt that draped down over the horse's tail.

"Don't ride too fast or I fear you will leave me in the ditch", she said putting her arms securely around his waist. "Besides, babies take a while to come. No need to get excited yet."

Mary was so calm about the situation John's heart slowed a little. She knew much better than he did about such things. This was his *first* baby after all. He allowed Pockets to walk at her own pace back up the hill much to the horse's relief, since the poor beast was exhausted and now carrying two on her back.

When they reached the house, the sisters hugged each other and then sequestered themselves in the bedchamber while John waited nervously in the adjacent room. The first time he heard his wife cry out in pain from behind the closed door it was all he could do not to scream himself. *Such a blessed event as having a baby should not be so difficult,* he thought to himself. He had heard the women in his extended family say it wasn't all that bad. But now sitting nervously at the kitchen table in their little farmhouse he was beginning to think they had misled him.

When he first saw the sun beginning to filter through the windows he tiptoed to the door and whispered through a crack in the wood. "I have to tend to the livestock. Is everything all right in there?"

His wife answered in a soft, tired voice. "Everything is fine, John. You go attend to your chores."

He obliged and went out into the yard trying to focus his mind on something else. Dawn had not completely crept into the horseshoe-shaped valley below and there was a still a blanket of ocean fog covering the marshlands. In the distance the little town of Porlock was hidden beneath the fog too with only the church tower visible poking its steeple up seemingly out of nowhere. The horses were huddled by the gate anxiously waiting for their hay, having already been awakened by the excitement of the morning's events and the cows were beginning to stir further down the road. Pushing a crude two wheeled cart full of hay he pitched separate piles out on the ground for the horses spacing them wide apart to keep Pockets, who was an alpha mare and higher up in the equine hierarchy, from hoarding all the hay for herself. Feeding the cows was less troublesome for the docile bovines never argued over food as the horses did. He fetched his bucket hanging on the fence and went to milking while the cows were otherwise occupied.

 After the milking was done, he scattered some grain across the yard to entice the lazy hens out of their nesting boxes and collected the eggs to put in the larder he had built into the side of the hill behind the house. There he poured enough fresh milk into a pitcher to take back for the day's meals and with the rest he filled a wooden cask and lowered it down into a hole in the cool earth. Pausing in the doorway of the larder, he looked out over the fields contemplating the possibility of getting another short crop of beans in before he planted his winter wheat.

When he returned to the house Mary met him at the door. She had a weak smile on her face, but her brow was furrowed.

"What's wrong?" John asked. He put the pitcher of milk and the eggs down on the kitchen table.

"The baby is *breech,* John. She is having a hard time right now. Maybe you should go into town and bring the doctor. I've never tended a breech before."

John nodded in agreement. He was familiar with the term *breech* from his livestock giving birth and he was horrified imagining the agony his wife must be going through. "I'll go right now," he said.

Pockets was enjoying her hay so much when she saw John coming toward the gate with the bridle in his hands, she pinned her ears to show her disapproval and good-natured John didn't have the heart to take her away from her well-earned breakfast. Instead, he bridled his old gelding, Mr. Colby, and with a little encouragement managed to coax him away from his feed. This time he slapped a saddle on the horse's back and started out on his second journey of the day.

By now the fog had lifted to reveal the thatched roofs and chimney pots of Porlock. The strip of land below the town where the sea had receded had been transformed into fertile fields of barley. John usually brought his bow and quiver slung over his shoulder on his trips to town; he liked to surprise his young wife with a plump duck he had killed in the marshes. Today his thoughts were on more pressing matters. He passed the marsh road and crossed over the river bridge arriving in town just as the townspeople were stoking their fires and getting on with their daily business.

Doctor Nicholas Philby lived with his wife Martha in a small cottage on the main street of Porlock. It was hidden behind a trellis of gooseberry vines that after many decades now covered the entire front of the house. In the yard to the rear were long wooden planter boxes where he grew all the medicinal herbs he used in his practice. John was glad to see a candle through the window but even being accused of having poor manners could not have prevented him from knocking at the door that morning. Martha opened the door a crack and peered out to see who was calling at such an early hour. As soon as she saw it was John Snow, she opened the door wide and invited him in.

"My wife," John began breathlessly. "The baby is breech. Her sister doesn't know quite what to do."

Doctor Philby entered the room and sat down at the kitchen table to pull on his boots. He was a stout man in his fifties with a ruddy complexion that always gave him the appearance of being burned by the sun. "Now, John, don't worry yet," he said." Let me get my horse saddled and we will go straightaway."

Martha had known John most of his life from the time he had been a stable boy on the Harrington estate, and she patted him on the shoulder affectionately. "John surely you have delivered many a calf or foal that got itself turned around! It's tricky but it can be done. Go on now, back to your wife. My husband will deliver you a healthy child."

The two men mounted their horses and galloped over the cobblestone road, the resonating sound of hooves echoing behind them, and headed back up Porlock Hill. When they arrived, John could see his extended family had arrived, as was the custom when a child was born. Agnes and Sarah, his wife's two younger sisters were taking care of morning chores; one was sweeping the floors and the other was preparing food for the men in the kitchen. Their husbands were hitching the horses up to plough John's unplanted field. The doctor was a welcome sight to the women and Mary immediately ushered him into the bedchamber and closed the door.

"Come sit down and eat something, John." Agnes, who was doing the cooking, laid a plate of eggs and two large hunks of bread slathered with butter on the table. Sarah, the younger sister, stopped her sweeping and went to fetch him a stoneware mug of ale from the cask in the larder. John didn't feel hungry; his stomach was tied in knots with worry but after a swig of ale and a few bites of bread he felt a little better. *The doctor is here; everything is going to be all right*, he kept repeating in his mind as he stoked the fire and brought in some more logs to stack on the hearth.

An hour later they finally heard the baby cry. John jumped up so quickly he knocked his chair over on the floor. Mary opened the door and brought him a tiny bundle wrapped securely in swaddling clothes and a woolen blanket, placing the newborn gently in John's muscular arms. The baby looked wrinkled and round-faced, with dark black eyes, not a bit like his father who had an angular face with a short, chiseled nose and silver-gray eyes almost the color of steel. He looked up at his father and his surroundings while squirming within his cloth cocoon.

"Is it a boy?" John wanted to know.

"Yes, John," Mary replied as all the sisters gathered around to admire the newborn. "What are you going to name him?"

"He shall be called *John Anthony Snow the Second* of course!"

"That is a very *large* name for such a *little* boy. Perhaps we should call him *Little John* for now," said Mary and John agreed. He carried the baby outside to show the rest of the family his new son.

When he returned to the house the bedchamber door was closed again and there was no sound from the other side. Mary had disappeared again to assist the doctor. John was sitting in his chair holding his son when she opened the door again and whispered something to her sisters. Assuming they were talking about "women's matters" he went on rocking and talking to his newborn son. Sarah and Agnes started going through the kitchen cupboards and drawers and pulling out rags and anything made of cloth they could find. When they started ripping the material into strips he panicked. "What are those for?" he asked.

"The doctor needs packing material to stop the bleeding. It's all right, John. Don't worry."

He *was* worried. Something was wrong. He *felt* it.

Doctor Philby came into the room and took the baby from John's arms. "You can see your wife now," he said, his eyes drooped, and his lips pursed. "She is very weak so just for a minute."

John entered the room and looked down at his pretty young wife on the bed. Her face was ashen; there was no color in her normally rosy cheeks. She reached for his hand and held it, her fingers gripping his weakly. "We have a son," she whispered.

John sat on the edge of the bed and stroked her hair. "Yes. He is a fine boy."

"We may have to ask my sister to help with him for a while. I am feeling very tired, John."

Her voice got smaller with each word she uttered.

"You've been through a lot. You need to get some rest now," John said.

She nodded and closed her eyes and John felt her fingers loosen and fall away from his hand.

"Margaret?" he said softly.

The instant he touched her face he knew it was over. She looked as if she were sleeping peacefully but his wife's spirit had departed. Tears clouded his eyes and he fought them. He bowed his head in sorrow knowing his son would never know his mother.

Chapter Two "Lady Harrington's Horses"

They buried her on the hill the next afternoon at the edge of the scrub oaks where John said she *"could see all the way to Wales"*. The statement was very true; from her gravesite looking north past the Bristol Channel the rocky hills of Wales loomed like a ragged shadow on the horizon. John held the newborn infant in his arms while Father Clary the town priest said a prayer over his wife's grave and then they moved into the house where plates of food were spread on the kitchen table. The men stood around drinking their ale and the subject quickly turned to farming and politics. They had just come from a funeral and yet there appeared to be no emotion. Death was just a part of life and life went on; John knew this and yet he wasn't ready to bury his wife at such an early age. His family would be expecting him to find a new spouse to care for the babe and to produce more sons to help with the farming, but he couldn't think about that yet. He could just not imagine loving another so soon.

The family stayed on an extra day camping out around the fire and then Mary took the infant home with her bundled in a blanket on her lap in their wagon. She promised John his son would be well-cared for until he was big enough to join his father. John peeked between the folds of the blanket at "Little John" sleeping soundly and thanked her.

"John, you know I will love him like my very own," Mary said, and John knew she meant every word. He knew he had no choice but to temporarily give up his son; it would be impossible to work and care for an infant. With a heavy heart he waved goodbye to Mary and the others as their wagons disappeared down the road.

When the family had all gone home and he was finally left alone, the emptiness of the house was almost too much for John to bear. He put another log on the fire and knelt on his knees in the crackling firelight to finally surrender to the tears that he had kept in check all that day. He fell asleep on the floor near the fire with his head resting on his folded arms; he could not bring himself to enter the bedchamber let alone sleep in the bed he had built for his bride.

It was a sleepless night. When dawn came, he rose from the floor; his entire body was stiff and sore. The fire had gone out and the air was cold and heavy with the aroma of charred oak wood. Walking outside, he could see his brothers had made good progress on ploughing the lower field; the fresh smell of the overturned soil hit his nostrils and he breathed it in deeply. *There is nothing sweeter than the aroma of God's earth* he thought to himself as he went about feeding the livestock and milking the cows. In the larder he packed up the extra food he would not be needing; the milk he would take to Mary for Little John and the surplus eggs he would take to Lady Harrington.

Lady Harrington was a fair and just woman and had always been extremely generous to John and his family and in turn he loved her like his own mother. When John was considered a grown man at fifteen, she had promoted him from his position as a stable boy and bestowed upon him, and later to his young wife's brothers, plots of land on the estate for their own use. In exchange all the men worked three days each week on her estate cultivating her crops and tending to her livestock while their wives spun wool and sewed clothing for her. The rest of the week they were free to cultivate their own parcels or hunt to fill their own larders with a day off for the Sabbath. It was a good life and even though work was hard they rarely wanted for much; John considered it an honor to work for Lady Harrington. Now, with no family to feed, he could offer his surplus to her. He hitched Pockets up to the wagon and started up the road for the Harrington house.

The manor house was situated on a hill, an impressive castle-like rock structure with several chimneys and tall stained-glass windows all around. The house had no walls around it as was customary with most manor houses across England; Lord Harrington had once said that he refused to live in fear and wanted all his tenants to know they were always welcome in his home. *"Walls"*, he said, *"shut people out"*. Indeed, his widow was of like mind; she was a most benevolent woman, going above and beyond to care for the people of Porlock. Not long after her husband's death she had a new larger almshouse built just behind the church to house any poor soul who needed a warm bed, a hot meal or shelter from the elements. After Sunday mass in other churches across England there would always be a ragged and destitute line of beggars asking the exiting parishioners for handouts. In Porlock there was no need for begging; *Lady Harrington* saw to that.

Beyond the manor house with its thick green lawns and rock beds with their sweet- smelling flowers were the stables with the lady's prized horses; tall muscular animals including the black stallion her husband had ridden when fighting alongside King Henry. Lady Harrington employed a half-dozen grooms and was herself an accomplished horsewoman known throughout the land for her love of horses. John pulled in the reins and jumped down from the wagon, taking the basket of eggs from the seat.

"Don't get any ideas" John whispered to Pockets who was watching with much interest Majesty, the lady's stallion, snorting and pawing in his corral at the presence of a new mare.

He made his way to the back door of the house, which opened into the kitchen and knocked politely.

The cook came to the door.

"I've got extra eggs this week," he said handing her the basket.

"I'm so sorry about your wife, Master John," the cook said. "Is the babe doing well?"

John nodded, "Yes. He is strong and healthy, thank the good Lord."

She thanked him for the eggs. "I'll be sure to let Lady Harrington know of your generosity. I can sure use them; I have to bake several cakes today."

John turned and went back to the stable to load the manure and used straw for use in the fields. He pulled the wagon around behind the stable where he and the stable hands picked up their pitchforks and went to work. Majesty was now out of sight, but he continued to call to Pockets.

"Our fellow is interested in your mare, Master John. Better watch out! He's taken down fences before," one of the grooms said, laughing. How well John remembered the day the giant horse in a heightened state of excitement over a mare had pinned him against the stable wall and kicked out, his giant hooves landing only inches away from John's head. John smiled. "Yes. She is behaving like a real wench today. I should have brought my gelding."

When they had filled the wagon to its capacity John walked back through the barn to say hello and scratch the heads of all the horses he had grown up with before he climbed aboard the wagon and snapped at the reins.

Pockets planted her hooves stubbornly in the ground and refused to move whinnying back to Majesty in the barn.

"Get up you!" John yelled at her. "Stop this nonsense."

Pockets fidgeted under her harness and tried to pull sideways under the yoke. John slapped her rump again firmly with the reins. All the while she had drawn the attention of several more grooms who were laughing and enjoying the spectacle. One of them grabbed her collar and pulled her forward while John used the reins and they finally got her moved away from the stable. John took the back road so she couldn't make eye contact with Majesty who was by now losing her scent and had stopped calling. Halfway down the road Lady Harrington appeared riding up beside him on a shiny black mare. He stopped the wagon and greeted her. "Good day, Lady Harrington," he said.

"I hear your mare was enticing my stallion," she said with a grin, pulling off a riding glove to rearrange her hair that was tousled from the wind.

"Yes, M'lady. I would not have brought her if I had known her condition. I will hitch the wagon to my gelding tomorrow."

"Would you like to breed her, John? We would for sure have a beautiful colt! My stallion has the best bloodlines from here to London."

John would never have been so brash as to have made such a request. It was certainly true there was no finer stallion around than Majesty. "That would be most kind of you, Lady Harrington," he said.

"Then bring her back tomorrow morning without the wagon. She will be further along in her cycle by then and be ready. If not, you can leave her here for a few days. It will be my gift to you to celebrate that new son of yours."

John felt himself blush and after all these years he didn't understand why she could always make his cheeks burn. He had decided a long time ago it must have been the way she spoke of subjects like animal husbandry just like a man would without embarrassment or modesty and, try as he might, he could never get used to it. He attributed it to her position; since her husband died, she had to be both lord *and* lady of the manor. Today, riding astride in her manly riding breeches, she was *lord*. The lady never seemed to be concerned about the opinions others had of her; she was as comfortable gracing a ball in a flowing gown as she was now in her masculine attire. Someone had once compared her to Queen Eleanor, the wife of Henry II, who rode horses well into her eighties and had a similar boyish charm and lust for life. "I will. And thank you kindly, M'lady," John replied.

"I am so sorry about your wife, John," she said in parting. "I certainly know what it is like to lose your mate. I've been fourteen years now without my husband. I wish I could tell you it gets easier with time."

John nodded silently. He missed Lord Harrington as well.

With that she rode away up the road at a canter, her mare's long black tail flailing behind her and the lady's auburn locks blowing in the breeze.

Chapter Three "The Empty Tankard"

The clouds were gathering by the time John reached his house and he unhitched Pockets from the wagon stowing the harness and collar out of the coming rain. He hoped for just enough moisture to dampen the road and water his thirsty wheat crop; not a deluge that would pack down his freshly ploughed furrows in the lower field. The weather so near the ocean could be unpredictable and sudden; the sky to the west was rapidly becoming the color of charcoal and getting darker by the minute. John covered the haystack with a piece of sail canvas he had acquired from a ship's captain in town, anchoring it down on four sides with large rocks. The livestock huddled together, their rumps to the wind, as the storm came in and even the chickens knew enough to take refuge in their nesting boxes.

John went inside, started a fire and pulled his boots off to rest his feet on the hearth. He wandered in his socks into the kitchen where he found nothing to eat in the cupboard but a half a loaf of stale bread. He tore off a chewy mouthful to quiet his empty stomach and stood for a moment staring at the bags of flour and sugar and hadn't the vaguest idea how to put them together to make bread. Being accustomed to fresh bread every day and meat and vegetables being prepared for him he never bothered to investigate the preparation of his meals. "I guess I will just have to learn to cook," he said aloud as he put his boots back on and headed out toward the larder where he pulled down a section of salted pork hanging from the rafters, gathered up a half-dozen eggs in his pockets and dipped himself a tankard of ale from the cask to take back to the kitchen. Stoking the fire, he found the iron skillet and anchored it atop the logs to heat up while he sliced the pork and broke the eggs into a crude wooden bowl. Quickly he learned why his wife always used a thick woven mitt when he blistered his hands on the hot skillet handle. He then washed down his dinner of overcooked rubbery eggs and slightly charred bacon with ale mostly to get the taste out of his mouth before he again fell asleep by the fire. He still could not bring himself to go into the room where his wife had died.

It rained throughout the night and John woke up stiff again from sleeping on the hearth. He fed the animals and found that Pockets was off her feed; another good sign that she was indeed in her fertile cycle. He pulled out his nippers from his box of tools and pried off her shoes; while shoes protected the mare's feet from rocks and cobblestones, they had to be removed so she wouldn't kick out and injure Lady Harrington's stallion. After he milked the cows, he saddled her and headed up the hill plodding along slowly her hooves making sucking sounds in the mud. By the time the morning sun appeared over the hills to the east the clouds had moved on leaving a sky painted in shades of pink and blue; the air in the vale after the rain was cleansed and as pure as fresh snowfall on Exmoor. The ride was a pleasant one, up and down the hills. *How often have I ridden this road during my lifetime?* he wondered.

Majesty took immediate notice of their arrival and began pacing up and down in his corral calling to Pockets who answered his call. Lady Harrington came out of the stable doors and greeted him. "I'll have the grooms put him in the large paddock behind the barn. Better keep your mare here until we get him situated," said Lady Harrington. "Did you take off her shoes?"
John nodded. "Yes, M'lady," he said.

The groom led Majesty to the very far end of the paddock and faced him away from the mare ready to release him upon Lady Harrington's orders. John removed Pocket's saddle and bridle and looped a rope around her neck to control her as he walked her slowly through the barn gate.

Lady Harrington called to her groom "Be ready to let him go when I give the signal!"

The stallion could not see the mare, but he knew she was near. With nostrils flared and blood red and giving every physical indication he was up to the task he let out a virile ear- piercing whinny.

"Now!" commanded the lady and both John and the groom released the bridal couple simultaneously. John moved quickly out of danger inside the stable gate knowing from personal experience how unpredictable mating stallions could be. They watched the stallion run toward his mare who squatted and urinated on the ground, a sure sign she was ready to be bred.

"I'm glad she's agreeable to the whole affair," said Lady Harrington. "Mares can sure do some damage if they're not ready for courting."

Again, John was embarrassed by the lady's blunt language, but no one could deny she certainly knew her horses!

The stallion circled around the mare, prancing and arching his powerful neck talking to her in a low guttural voice. He, too, was testing the waters to see if the mare was going to give him trouble. She seemed to be submissive, however, standing totally still. With a squeal he mounted her biting down firmly on her withers and in less than a minute his mission was accomplished. Pockets squealed and Majesty backed away, but this was only the beginning of their courtship.

"You might leave her for a day or so. I will keep them together until she starts getting disagreeable. Just to be sure she is in foal."

"Thank you, M'lady. I will take her home when I return day after tomorrow."

"I'll have the grooms saddle you a horse to ride home on," said Lady Harrington. "It's a long walk down the hill."

"That's very kind of you, M'lady," John said with a slight bow of his head.

"Come up to the house with me first," she answered. "I want to talk to you about an idea I have."

John followed her up the steps of the grand house and stopped at the door.

"I'm afraid my boots are terribly muddy," he said.

Lady Harrington walked through the door. "Oh, not to worry John. Look at *my* boots! You can't hurt these floors anyway. *Good English oak*. They will outlast *me* I am sure of it."

John wiped as much mud as he could on the outside step and proceeded to follow her. She led him into the great hall, with its familiar long oak table and a beautiful woven rug beneath it. He often thought how peculiar it was that the house and the furniture he remembered from his childhood seemed ever so much larger than it appeared to him now through a grown man's eyes. He recognized Lord Harrington's armor which now stood hollow and void of life in one corner of the room and his shield and sword that were hung over the great fireplace.

John stood nervously at the edge of the rug looking down at his muddy boots while Lady Harrington pulled a rolled piece of parchment from a drawer in a sideboard and spread it out on the table, weighing it down on either end with two large, polished rocks. John could see that it was a diagram of some sort.

"Hops!" she blurted out.

"M'lady?" John was confused. He hadn't the vaguest idea what she was talking about.

"*Hops*, John, *hops*," she repeated. "We grow the barley to make our ale. I want to try growing hops too. The last time I was in London we had ale made with hops and it was heavenly! I've never tasted anything like it."

John studied the diagram before him; drawings of a strange framework connected by vertical and horizontal strings. He knew nothing about this "hops" plant; they had always flavored their ale with the bitter herbs and flowers that grew wild on the moors.

"This is how they grow them. They climb, just like ivy, up the strings." Lady Harrington was beside herself with excitement. "I want you to build the framework and we will plant in the spring! We'll make a fortune!"

John was infected by her excitement; Lady Harrington had a way of giving an order that made a man eager to get to work. "May I take these pictures home to study them tonight?"

She rolled up the parchment and handed it to John. "Of *course,* you can! Take tomorrow off to make plans. Do your measurements and make me a list of what we'll need to get started. There will be drying trays to build later after we harvest our first crop. We'll talk when you come to get your mare. And, John," she added as an afterthought, "maybe we should keep our little project a secret for now."

John went back to the stable and found a tall chestnut mare standing tied and saddled for him and he started the ride home. The mare was much taller than Pockets with a chest as wide as most stallions; the Harrington horses were bred to be war horses, crossed with draft breeds to be strong enough to carry heavy armor into battle. Although they usually used only geldings and stallions for battle the mares still had to produce big healthy colts, so they bred them to be almost as big as the stallions. He passed the corral where Pockets was standing side by side with Majesty. John called to her, and she ignored him, nuzzling the stallion's neck instead. With the noonday sun overhead and Lady Harrington's new project rolling around in his head he rode right past his farm and headed for town; a foamy mug of ale and some masculine conversation was what he needed before he went home to his empty house.

When he came to the winding stretch of road that was Porlock Hill he could see that there was work to be done to make it passable to wagons again; deep ruts had formed, and the heavy rain had washed many large rocks into the middle of the road. He maneuvered his horse around the holes and planned for the following day to bring rock and soil in to make repairs. They came upon one of Lady Harrington's herds of slow-moving sheep on the last turn in the road and he reined his horse in to let them pass.

The tide was in bringing with it several ships and the sailors had gathered at the inn drinking and exchanging stories with a few of the town merchants. When John arrived, he was welcomed heartily by the innkeeper who had known him since he was a boy. "What will it be Master John? A drink of ale after a dusty day of farming?"

John smiled, "After that rain there's not much dust, but yes, my throat is parched, nonetheless. And what have you to eat? My stomach is talking to me."

"The mistress just made some fresh meat pies. I will bring you two. I've yet to see anyone eat one and not ask for another!"

John was invited to a table near the door by Captain Tom Hatherly. "How is that canvas holding up for you? Keeping things dry?" the captain asked regarding the used sail material he had sold to John to protect his haystacks from the rain.

"Aye. Best investment I've made. I haven't had to throw out a single bit of moldy hay!" John replied.

The men talked while John ate his pies and drank his ale.

"What do you all know of growing hops?" John asked, his tongue loosening with every swig from his tankard.

The men looked at each other and back at John with blank faces. One said, "I hear it gets a good price at market. But I don't know anything else about it."

"Lady Harrington wants me to grow it in the spring," John said pulling the rolled-up parchment pictures from under his cloak. Forgetting her request for secrecy he spread it on the table. "I have to build these frames to grow it on. I hear it clings just like ivy does on the side of a building."

The men of the sea, knowing next to nothing about farming, soon went on to other subjects more to their liking and the merchants demonstrated only a polite interest in what they considered to be the bizarre notions of a crazy lady. There were still some men who did not know Lady Harrington as intimately as John did and thought her to be eccentric, resenting her unusual manner of dress and direct way of speaking that they felt usurped their manhood. Women, some men thought, should not talk so provocatively and be so openly opinionated especially on matters of business. Knowing what a smart woman Lady Harrington was John knew otherwise but he did not let the opinions of a few ignorant men rile him.

By that time the afternoon sun was flooding through the windows in rays of dancing dust. John was on his third or fourth tankard and feeling the effects quite strongly. The men were getting rowdier, and the conversations had turned to naughty jokes. The innkeeper was about to refill John's empty tankard when John suddenly stood up and staggered for the door. The innkeeper came around and assisted him out to the street where his horse was tied. After he had hoisted John up into the saddle, wrapped the reins securely around the saddle tree and tucked John's papers under his shirt he slapped the horse on the rear. He watched as the horse and rider disappeared up the street and over the bridge toward Porlock Hill. Over the years the innkeeper had saddled many a drunk and sent them home safely on their horses who knew the way home to their own stables. *He had no idea that John was not riding his own horse that day.*

Chapter Four "A Good Dose of Humiliation"

John awoke the next morning in a bed of straw, with Lady Harrington's big chestnut mare standing beside him in the stable, her reins still tethered to the saddle. He immediately knew where he was and panicked in the realization that he hadn't any memory of how he got there. It was still early. The horses were still sleeping in their stalls; some reclined in the straw and some standing on three legs with one hip tilted in rest. John was thankful the grooms were not about yet to taunt him.

When he sat up his head felt like his brain was pummeling the inside of his skull and he immediately lay back down in the straw. He heard footsteps and opened one eye slightly to see a young groom enter the barn with the hay cart. As the boy began feeding the horses, he noticed John on the ground and feared that he was dead. As he approached the prostrate body on tiptoe suddenly John sat up and the startled groom almost fell over backward with surprise. "Master John, what happened to you? Did M'lady's mare pitch you?"

John was sorry he hadn't been clever enough to think of that excuse himself. "Why yes she did! She's an *ornery* one she is! I landed flat on my head, and it knocked me out cold!"

John hated to tell a lie, but he had to save face with the young groom who would undoubtedly tell the story to all the other grooms, and it would eventually get back to Lady Harrington. He stood up and dusted himself off, his head still throbbing with pain. The groom approached the mare and led her to her stall where he unsaddled her and filled her manger with hay.

"I think I will check on my mare," he said to the groom, "Is she still in the paddock with Majesty?"

"No, Sir. The honeymoon was over by last night. Kicking and biting she was," said the groom. "I put her down on the end, see there?" He pointed to the last stall in the very back of the barn. "Would you like me to saddle her for you?"

John started to shake his head but thought it best not to move his aching head more than necessary. "No. Thank you. I will do it myself."

He pulled himself up into the saddle and rode down the pathway that separated Lady Harrington's crops of hay and beans. He stopped at the bottom field which was fallow and bare in a futile attempt to give a reason for his presence at the manor. This would obviously be where he would be planting the hops; in the fallow field that was "resting" in wait for the spring. Without twine he could only estimate the dimensions of the area. In his mind he figured he needed at least a hundred vertical poles to cut. He wanted to get the poles in the ground while it was still soft from the rain, but his head hurt too much to think clearly. Then he suddenly remembered his cows had missed a meal and two milkings and he turned Pockets around and headed for home.

When he reached the farm, he tied Pockets to the fence and threw hay out for the livestock. The cows whose udders by now were swollen and tender were not in a very cooperative frame of mind stomping in the mud and swishing their tails. John proceeded as gently as he could and then had to pour out all the milk when one cow without warning planted her hoof in the middle of the full bucket. He decided at that moment he was *never* going to get *that* drunk again and remounted for the ride down the hill.

As he rounded the first turn of Porlock Hill he found his brothers-in-law were already at work filling in the holes with soil from their wagon, which they were inching up the road a little at a time as they went along. Although he was the elder of the family and considered the foreman by Lady Harrington, John did not consider himself above the other men. They all worked together, doing whatever needed to be done. They all thought alike and pitched in when help was needed; there was no need for supervision. John greeted them sheepishly and apologized for being so late.

Peter, Mary's husband, paused from his work and leaned his arms on the handle of his shovel. "John there is not one among us who has not fought the battle with a mug of ale and lost. At least you had an acceptable excuse!"

John was not shocked that the tale of his afternoon of drinking at the inn had already reached his family. News was slow, but *gossip* spread quickly in Porlock. "Aye, but I fear you haven't heard the worst of it," he replied.

By now he had all three brothers' ears atwitter, and they gathered around him as John relayed his embarrassing story amidst howls of laughter.

"And the nag took you all the way to Lady Harrington's barn?" asked Peter. "John, that is the best one I have heard yet! And what did her ladyship have to say?"

John shrugged. "I don't know if she knows yet. But I am sure she will by tomorrow. Let's get busy so I can honestly report that I did not spend the *entire* day nursing an aching head." He retrieved a shovel from the wagon and began filling holes with ferocity. They worked until the sweat had beaded on their foreheads and had drenched the fabric of their shirts before they rested. By the time the summer sun had begun to wane behind the peaks of Exmoor, and the long shadowy fingers of dusk were creeping across the valley the men were all exhausted and ready to quit for the day.

"Come home with me," invited Peter, "You can see your son and Mary will have something on the table for us to eat."

John reluctantly accepted the invitation, knowing the story had undoubtedly reached Mary and the children as well. His humiliation was temporarily overshadowed by the thought of seeing his son again.

Little John had spent the first few days of his life being the center of attention in his aunt's house. Mary and Peter had three children of their own who were delighted to take part in the care of their little cousin. He was a happy baby and when he wasn't napping he spent his time cooing and gurgling and attempting to find his mouth with his chubby fingers.

"He looks like he's grown already!" John said when he looked down into Little John's cradle.

"I wouldn't be surprised. He has a healthy thirst just like his father," said Mary, smiling at John with a little twinkle in her eye.

At that the entire family had a good laugh at John's expense and sat down for dinner. Mary moved the cradle nearer to the table where he could see the family. Little John stared up at first at the light from the lantern on the table and then focused on John.

"He seems to respond to you, John" Mary remarked.

"I think it is just my beard he likes," said John.

Mary served everyone a helping of hearty pottage and Peter sliced the bread and soon the sound of spoons scraping against the wooden bowls replaced conversation. John was the first to speak. "I've bred Pockets to Lady Harrington's stallion. We should have a nice colt in the spring."

Peter handed his bowl to Mary for a second helping and John continued. "Now she wants us to grow *hops*. Have you ever heard of such a thing?"

"I've heard it's a great bother," said Peter, "building all those frames with strings going every which way. And you can't plough them under; you'll just be on your hands and knees pulling the weeds until your back breaks!"

"We haven't much choice. Lady Harrington says we'll make a lot of money."

"Not if the excise men get wind of it and take all the profit in taxes!" Peter laughed. "But she's a smart woman. She's probably already planned for that."

"I hear those hops put you to sleep. That's the last thing you men need in your ale!" said Mary playfully. "It's hard enough to roust you every morning as it is!"

"I hear it gives the ale an extra kick," her husband retorted. "I'm curious to see what it will taste like."

"Well, we have to *grow* it first. Then we'll worry about *tasting* it," John said and turned sideways from the table. He picked Little John up from his cradle and sat holding him on his lap, tickling his chin with his finger. "I should probably get on up the road. I've livestock to feed and I must see if my cows have forgiven me for neglecting them yesterday. Thank you, Mary, for supper. I haven't quite mastered the art of cooking yet."

Mary walked him to the door. "John you are welcome to come eat with us every night."

"I will come as often as I can," promised John and went home to spend another uncomfortable night on the hearth.

The next day John returned to Harrington Manor to go over his plans for the hops fields and to advise her of the materials he anticipated they would need to start. He went up and knocked hesitantly on the massive oak door of the house, informing the servant who answered that he wished to speak to Lady Harrington.

He heard her call from all the way down the hall. "Come in, John! Let's sit down and talk about our project!"

John had made markings on the parchment plans indicating how much lumber and twine they would be needing, and he unrolled it before her. "My brothers and I can begin cutting the wood this week. That much twine will take a good while to spin."

"What do you think is the best twine?" she asked.

"Hemp would be best, M'lady. It is definitely strongest, but it is a little more costly."

"The ladies will have their hands full with storing the winter meat the next few weeks with no extra time for spinning. Just purchase the twine you need at market and put it on my bill. I can't wait to get started!" she exclaimed.

"I looked at the lower field yesterday. We may have to plough and level it a bit, but I think it will do. It gets the best runoff of all the fields."

"Aye. We'll see how your hemp will hold up once the snows come."

She walked him to the door and patted him on the shoulder. "How is your son?" she asked.

"He is just fine, M'lady. When he is able to sit up in the saddle, I will bring him to introduce you."

"Well," she said, "Don't fault him too harshly if he can't. I hear tell even grown men weave in their saddles on occasion."

She smiled a knowing smile and sent him on his way.

Indeed, gossip in the little town of Porlock was not only swift, it had *God's Speed*!

Chapter Five "A Bittersweet Christmas"

John was glad that everyone in the entire town of Porlock now knew of his sin and he had nothing left to hide. That night he also decided he was ready to sleep in his own bed again; he was tiring of sleeping near the fire and being hardly able to stand up in the mornings from the aches in his bones. He kindled the fire then he went to the bedchamber door and opened it slowly.

The fragrance of heather and wild roses in the closed-up room brought back poignant memories of his beloved wife. She always lined the drawers of the bureau and stuffed the pillow slips with dried flowers; the sweet heather she had gathered from the moor and the wild roses from the riverbanks in the vale. He remembered the day she had dug up one of the rose plants and brought it home to transplant it near the house; how she had watered and tended it so lovingly day after day. The little rose bush never produced any flowers, but she never gave up hope that one day it would burst forth in fragrant blooms.

When he pulled down the coverlet, he could see the bed clothes were stained with her blood and he ripped them off and threw them on the fire. The straw filled mattress had been left too long without laundering and was permanently stained as well; he flipped it over, so he did not have to see the blood; for a man accustomed to butchering animals all his life the blood of his dead wife brought tears to his eyes. He put on his sleep shirt and covered himself with a wool blanket that they normally didn't take out until wintertime, stretching out his arms and legs to the very edges of the bed like when he was a child making snow angels in the snow. The light of the fire flickered from the adjacent room, dancing across the walls, bringing back memories he could not seem to shut out of his mind. His sleep for many nights to come, while without an aching back, would be fitful and filled with nightmares. He realized he was not as strong as Lady Harrington; he didn't think he could spend the rest of his life nursing a broken heart.

During the next few weeks John and his brothers hitched their horses to their wagons and went out every day to harvest lumber for the hops framework. The forested land beyond Lady Harrington's cultivated fields was the perfect source for good strong English oak. After felling a dozen trees, they split and quartered them and loaded them on the wagons. Back at the manor, they laid them out side by side, cut them to matching lengths, shaved off the suckers and honed them to a point at one end perfect for the smooth poles they needed. The men worked tirelessly and by the end of the second week had a hundred poles set in the ground and had constructed the drying trays weeks ahead of the first frost. Lady Harrington was so ecstatic when she inspected the results of their hard work, she gave them all a handsome bonus and a week off from their labors.

It was hardly a time of rest, however. Back home the men had cattle, sheep, and pigs to slaughter to put up in the larders for the winter and they worked together, going from one farm to the next. Mary and her sisters were busy too, salting the meat the men had butchered and harvesting the last of the autumn vegetables from their truck gardens. Christmas was coming and before long the four brothers were again out in the forest hunting for deer to supply venison for the town's most elaborate celebration of the year. It was thirteen days of food and drink and dancing while the church bells pealed, and the children played games in the marketplace; when Lady Harrington opened her home for all the townsfolk and put on elaborate jousting and sporting events in her arena. Even those who gossiped about her behind her back enjoyed their share of her generosity and those who spoke the loudest of her eccentricities had to admit their good fortune at having an overseer who was as kind and compassionate as was Lady Harrington. She was generous to a fault and in a time of wars and heavy taxation by the new boy-king Henry VI and his corrupt advisors she did her best to protect her people from their greedy hands. For most of the residents of Porlock celebrating the beginning of the Holy season at Lady Harrington's was anticipated with great joy and gaiety and although John was doing his part to prepare for the festivities, he did so with a twinge of sadness in his heart having to face Christmas without his wife.

By dusk on Christmas Eve the entire town of Porlock was decked out in garlands and ribbons of red and gold. Branches of mistletoe and fir graced all the doorways; in the marketplace Christmas delicacies were already being prepared and the aroma of spices and simmering fruits wafted in through the town windows. Even the horses had ribbons tied to their manes and tails.

At the Harrington Manor the entire great hall was lavishly decorated in golden braids of spun yarn and holly berries and the tables were draped with beautiful linens and polished silver ready for the rush of townspeople who would be on the road from town as soon as the last word of Christmas Mass was spoken.

John rode to town in Mary and Peter's wagon with the children bouncing and laughing in the back and John holding Little John on his lap. Although there was no snow yet, the air was crisp, and the sky was totally clear; the moon was reflected in a jagged silver trail over the water all the way to the dock where the ships were anchored. Porlock church was filled to capacity and many latecomers had to stand outside the doorway. The narrow streets were blocked with wagons and horses. When the final church bell pealed it echoed up the vale and could be heard all the way to Lady Harrington's front door.

The townsfolk rushed to their waiting wagons and the race was on up steep Porlock Hill with the squeals of the women and children. Every year at least one wagon was dumped over the side of the winding road; they were fortunate on this particular night but there were *still* twelve more days of celebrations!

Lady Harrington was standing in the doorway as regal as a queen with the door opened wide. She was dressed in a long gown of gold brocade pleated down the front with long tapered sleeves and a high starched collar of white lace. On her feet were matching gold slippers and her auburn hair was tied up in a bun covered with golden netting. The servants, dressed in matching doublets stood behind her at the tables laid out with platters of venison, duck and beef, bowls of wassail and fresh fruit and breads of every variety. A small band of troubadours playing lutes and dulcimers and singing Christmas carols stood at the end of the hall. When she saw the first of the wagons coming up the road, she waved excitedly at everyone; nothing gave Lady Harrington more pleasure than to make others happy.

When they pulled up in their wagons, everyone jumped down and took their place in the long line for food and drink. When John finally made his way into the house, he approached Lady Harrington with Little John cradled in the crook of his arm. "M'Lady, may I introduce you to John Anthony Snow the second?"

Lady Harrington smiled and reached for Little John and held him cuddled to her bosom. "Oh, John he is absolutely the handsomest baby I have ever seen! I think I will steal him away for my very own one day when you are not looking!"

With that she was off to show Little John to everyone in the room. If she had been his own natural grandmother, she could not have been prouder. Little John was in awe of all the glittering decorations and very taken by this strange lady who tickled his chin and gave him tastes of wassail from a linen napkin dipped in the bowl. By the end of the evening Lady Harrington had won not only the tiny heart of Little John whom she returned to his father sleeping soundly, but, indeed, the hearts of many a naysayer as well.

The next day was a day for the children; there was storytelling on the lawn and Lady Harrington had hired a troupe of actors all the way from London to perform live enactments of the Nativity complete with animals and musical accompaniment. There were sack races and apple bobbing and plenty of treats for the children. At the end of the day a huge cake was brought out of the kitchen in which a single bean had been added to the batter before baking. The cake was sliced and passed out to the children and the game of King of the Bean (or Queen of the Bean if a little girl found the bean in her cake) began. It took time to pass out all the slices of cake, and the children all ate slowly so as not to swallow the tiny bean. The little girl who finally found the bean was crowned with a paper crown and scepter and she was allowed to rule over the other children for the remainder of the party. And even though most of the children went home that night with belly aches only the fun was remembered by the next day. The rest of the week was filled with music and dancing and more plays performed by the actors.

The final day was the day of the tournaments. Lady Harrington had the stable hands set out dozens of crude benches on which the townspeople could sit and enjoy the spectacle. Knights who had fought with her husband were invited to compete in the hand-to-hand combat and other feats of courage and strength with the final event of the day to be the jousting competition. Everyone got their drinks and when the benches were full the latecomers took their places sitting on the grass surrounding the arena. The sword and archery competitions were first on the program; several pairs of knights were matched in the long sword where they wielded their two-handed weapons at each other with the crashing and sparking of steel. Then came the archery; the knights changed from chest guards and chainmail hoods to slim fitting tunics to facilitate their aim with the long bows and demonstrated their accuracy hitting the targets painted on a long row of straw bales.

The games were enjoyed by all, but it was the jousting that they had all come to see. When the knights first entered the arena, in full armor and riding their warhorses, a hush came over the crowd. Some had never seen such magnificent animals up close and were in awe of their size and ferocity. The knights rode around making a complete circle on the interior of the fence that separated the audience from the arena. With their faces hidden by their helmets and anonymous except for the crests upon their shields, they elicited cheers as they passed by where John and his family sat together on the grass. Little John watched nestled in his father's lap and bounced up and down every time the crowd cheered.

The first pair of knights took their places at opposite ends of the wooden barrier which ran down the center of the arena. Their squires checked the readiness of each knight's armor and handed their lances up to them; on one end was a knight astride a pawing chestnut stallion with a bright blue insignia on his shield and a matching blue plume of feathers decorating the top of his helmet. On the other end was a knight behind a vivid yellow shield with bold black stripes riding a blood bay. The signal was given, and the horses leaped forward, galloping at top speed while their riders kept their lances firmly tucked between their elbows and their ribs. In a cloud of dust, they passed each other, the blue knight struck out at the yellow knight's lance, knocking it out of his grip but failed to unseat him. They switched sides and their squires again straightened their armor; the two stallions were practically sitting back on their haunches in anticipation of the release of the reins. Again, they charged toward each other down the barrier. This time the blue knight's horse stumbled, and he missed the yellow knight completely. The third and final time they came at each other the yellow knight aimed and hit his target and the blue knight was knocked over backward into the dirt. The crowd stood up and clapped and whistled, as he removed his helmet, and everyone recognized Sir Humphrey from nearby Doverhay.

The second pair of knights entered the ring; the first with a black and gold shield riding a gray steed of enormous proportions with the feathered feet of a draft horse; the second knight wore brilliant green insignia and rode a pale yellow colored horse with a flowing flaxen tail. Again, the signal was called, and they charged at each other. On the very first pass the black and gold knight toppled his opponent and whipped off his helmet to reveal himself as Sir Reynolds of Bossington. He galloped a victory lap kicking dust in everyone's ale.

The third and final match of the day began. A knight wearing white and gray entered riding a slightly shorter but very sturdy bay charger and took his position at the end of the barrier. The second knight came through the gate decked out in red and riding a solid black horse. John looked at the horse for a moment before he recognized him; the horse the red knight was riding was Majesty! The two knights squared off at opposite ends of the arena. John took a closer look at the insignia on the shield. It was the armor he had seen Lord Harrington wear dozens of times! John stood up, holding Little John on his shoulders. He realized he was holding his breath when the signal was given and the two rushed toward each other. Majesty's hooves hardly touched the ground so swiftly they flew. The shorter horse was extremely quick and agile as well, every bit as intimidating as the black. At the meeting point the audience gasped as the red knight took aim. He raised his lance and thrust it forward hitting the white knight square on his shield with pinpoint accuracy. The white knight flew into the air and with a crash of crumpling metal landed on his buttocks leaning against the barrier. While the loser's squire ran to collect his horse, the red knight dropped his splintered lance. In a gesture of good sportsmanship, he turned Majesty around and went to the aid of the white knight reaching down a gloved hand to help him to his feet.

By this time the crowd was screaming for the red knight to remove his helmet and reveal himself. Majesty took off at a thundering gallop and the helmet came off to reveal the long auburn locks of Lady Harrington! She held up her hand and blew a kiss to a shocked audience who began to roar in honor of their beloved lady. Surely that day she had won over of the last of her critics.

Chapter Six "Mothers and Mouse Catchers"

The first snows came in early January just as the town was settling back into its daily routine. While the men took down the decorations and the women stored the leftover food in the larders the children were out in their mittens to play in the first snowflakes that drifted through the town and covered the peaks of Exmoor. The masts of the ships sitting in the harbor were laced in icicles and the surrounding fields and marshes were cloaked in white giving all Porlock Vale the soft sleepy look of winter.

Little John continued to grow and with every month seemed to impress his father with something new he had learned to do. Before long Little John knew the sound of his father's voice at Mary's door and would start to wiggle and squirm in his cradle eager for John to pick him up. By the springtime he was trying to stand usually teetering and tumbling down, but he never cried; he would just pull himself back up and try again. By May he was starting to take a step or two and beginning to talk. "Paa!" he would say, stretching out his little arms toward his father. John was beside himself with pride.

When the weather was fair, John would put Little John on his saddle held close to his chest and ride him around the yard. The baby seemed to enjoy that immensely.

"He's going to be a good horseman," John would tell everyone.

"Maybe when he can reach the stirrups" Mary would say with a smile. She was pleased that John was taking such an active role in his son's life, but she worried that John seemed so melancholy most of the time.

John began taking Little John farther and farther away from Mary's house bundling him up in thick woolen clothing and a cap down over his ears if the weather was cold; they would ride along at a slow walk along the wooded cliffs looking up at the snow-covered peaks and out over the channel. As they rode John would point and pronounce each word to him for everything they saw, *mountain, ocean, tree*. After many horse-back rides Little John began to repeat the words imitating his father's voice. One day when they were riding through town, he pointed his chubby baby finger up at the roof of the houses nearby and said "Cow!" clearly and purposefully. John started to shake his head and correct his son but when he looked up at the steep incline behind the thatched roofs sure enough there were the cows on the hill that appeared to be grazing among the chimney pots! His father laughed out loud and Little John jumped up and down at the sound of his father's laughter. "How right you are Little John! Those *are* cows!"

It soon became a game that they played. Little John would point to something and try to say the word, looking up as if questioning his father. John would affirm the word and smile. It wasn't long before Little John began watching the door of his aunt's house, listening for the sound of his father's horse at which he would say "Paa!" Even though they lived in different houses, John was very connected to his son.

That spring John was, however, extremely preoccupied with work; not only with getting Lady Harrington's hops field started but getting all his own crops planted and did not visit as regularly. During his absences Mary could see the same melancholy in Little John as she did in his father.

Growing Lady Harrington's hops turned out to be very labor intensive as John soon found out. Not only did the tiny plants need to be coaxed initially into holding onto the twine some shoots seemed to have a mind of their own and wanted to creep away and spread out in the soil between the rows. There were days when the lines of plants he had to walk seemed endless. He retired each night exhausted and his visits with Little John became weekly instead of daily. By midsummer the plants had finally begun to take hold, however; the hop tendrils had finally begun to cling obediently to the twine and soon the lush green leaves popped out and filled in the naked framework he had built for them in the fall. Lady Harrington could frequently be seen standing at her window in the big house looking down on her hops fields with a smile on her face that reflected the contentment in her heart.

One morning in late summer John arose to start his ritual of daily chores when he sensed that something was different. He pulled on his clothes, took a bite of bread that Mary had recently baked for him and headed out into the farmyard. The sun glistened off the dew on the sheaves of new wheat and the sky was cloudless and blue. He filled his two-wheeled cart with hay from the haystack and rolled it down the road toward the livestock. All the familiar faces watched him from the corrals; the cows chewing on yesterday's cuds, Mr. Colby who was cribbing on the fence and Pockets standing further down the fence line, separated from the others. As John went along pitching the hay and got closer, he noticed something white flickering in the sun beneath the lower railing. He shaded his eyes from the sun's glare expecting to see the white tail of a rabbit running away with a mouthful of stolen alfalfa but when he looked again, he saw the tiny new face of a black foal with a perfect white star on his forehead. Pockets had presented him with an exact replica of Majesty!

"Well, what have we here?" John remarked and patted Pockets on the neck. He leaned on the fence and watched as the colt ran behind his mother at the sight of this strange two-legged creature. Pockets ignored the colt and nuzzled her hay to find the tastiest leaves. The baby decided it was time to eat for him as well and began to bump his nose against her breasts and suckle vigorously when the milk began to flow. John let the colt finish nursing before he opened the gate and went into the corral. In his youth he had handled many a newborn in Lady Harrington's stable but this one was special. He sat down on the ground with his back against the fence boards and calmly waited until the foal's curiosity brought him to investigate more thoroughly, first the soles of John's boots, then the knees of his trousers. John gently extended his arm toward the colt and let him sniff his hands. The colt jumped back and bolted off to hide behind his mother again but in a few moments returned to John. He permitted his face to be rubbed and John let his hand remain putting his fingers into the foal's tiny nostrils to imprint his human scent. It wasn't long before he was able to massage the colt's entire body without him running away and although John would have to work with the colt for many weeks to come, the initial bond had been established. John named him *Morning Star.*

Little John and Morning Star both continued to grow and when John would take his son riding on Pockets, Morning Star would trot alongside his mother nibbling at the boy's feet; it wasn't long before the two became friends. The colt seemed to know instinctively that Little John was a youngster like himself and would leap and cavort at the first sight of him as if saying "Come play with me!"

It went on like that for months and the months inevitably turned into years until Little John and Morning Star were no longer babies. John squeezed as much time for the boy and the colt as he could between his farming chores. Morning Star was coming along well in his training; he had accepted the bridle and saddle with no hesitation. The first time John tried to harness him to the wagon however was a different matter; Morning Star bucked and kicked against the feel of the yoke. Just as it had been with his father Majesty the colt was not going to be a work animal; he was much happier with John on his back galloping across the fields. John knew that horses, like men, were just different in their strengths. John himself, who had worked under one of the bravest knights in England and who could have easily been raised up in the study of fighting if he had shown the slightest interest preferred to be a stable hand working with the horses. So, Morning Star remained a riding horse for the rest of his life.

The boy too had a mind of his own. When Little John was just five years old, he appeared in Mary's kitchen with a small satchel tied to a long stick. Wrapped up in a cloth was a little slingshot, a tiny wooden horse his father had carved for him and a piece of hard candy from the merchant in town.

"Aye and where is it you're going?" Mary asked her nephew to which Little John replied: "I'm going to Paa's house to live."

Mary looked down at the serious expression on Little John's face. "But you haven't had your breakfast yet."

Little John shook his head. "I'll eat later with Paa."

"Well," said Mary suppressing her laughter, "if that is what you want Little John."

She figured he would not lose his way on the road he knew so well, and she let him go watching him from the window until he had disappeared beyond the first turn of Porlock Hill, his satchel swinging from his little shoulder.

John was busy feeding the livestock when something coming up the road caught his eye and he recognized his son making his way up the hill. He stopped and approached the fence. "And where did you come from?" he asked the boy.

"I am going to live with you now," said Little John matter-of-factly.

"Oh, *are* you now? Does that mean you're willing to work to earn your keep?" John asked.

Little John hung his little satchel on the fence. "I can work."

"And what kind of work do you know how to do?"

Little John thought for a moment. "I can tend the chickens and pick beans. Aunt Mary taught me that."

Morning Star ran to up to the fence to greet him.

"Well," replied John. "There's a lot more to do on a farm than that! Can you push a plough? Can you hammer a nail?"

"I can *learn* Paa," said Little John.

"Well, I guess I will hire you then. You can start with the chickens. Their coop needs a sweeping, and the eggs need to be gathered. Do you think you can do that?"

Without a word Little John turned around and headed for the chicken coop. John watched with a smile as his son was shaking the dust out of the nesting boxes. He watched him carry the eggs carefully across the yard to the larder.

Little John returned to his father who was busy milking the cows. "Paa, did you know that the white chickens lay *white* eggs and the brown chickens lay *brown* ones?"

"Is that so?" asked John.

Little John climbed up on the fence and looked as if he was thinking very hard as he studied the cows and watched his father move from one cow to the next filling the bucket with warm milk. After a few moments of concentration, he asked, "Paa?"

"Yes, Son?"

"Why does the *brown* cow not give *brown* milk?"

At that John burst out laughing. "Now that *is* a mystery, Son. I don't know the answer to that one."

It was like that from then on. Little John was one of the most inquisitive boys John had ever encountered. When most boys his age were interested in playing in the dirt or climbing in trees, Little John followed his father around wanting to know the whys and hows about everything. Why did the hay have to be covered when it rained? Where did the rain come from? What made lightning? He wanted to know everything about *everything.* After their first night spent together, he wanted to know what made men *snore.*

One day when John had hitched the wagon to run an errand for Lady Harrington, Little John climbed up on the seat and waited for his father. The boy was not his usual talkative self that morning. Just as John had hoisted a leg up on the wagon Little John blurted out: "Paa where is my mother?"

John fell back and stood speechless for a moment. Until this time, they had never spoken of the subject. Then, with a sigh, he reached for the boy and helped him down from the wagon. Holding his hand, he led the way up the hill behind the house and stopped at the edge of the scrub oaks. He knelt and brushed the leaves from a flat stone that had words carved in it.

"Your mother is here, John. At least her *body* is here. Her *spirit* is with Jesus in heaven."

Little John fell to his knees beside John and touched the stone with his small hand. "Does she know who I am?" he asked.

"Of course, she does! She met you the day you were born."

"She did? Then she remembers me?"

John nodded. After a few moments Little John spoke again. "Aunt Mary had to bury their cat who died. Is her cat in heaven too?"

John thought for a moment before he answered. "Was he a good cat?"

"I reckon he was, Paa. He was a good mouse catcher!"

"Then, I'm sure he is in heaven too."

Little John seemed pleased with that. The two walked back down the hill and climbed up in the wagon and set off for town each one thinking very different thoughts.

Chapter Seven "Amy Anne"

Their task that day was to see Mr. Hartley the town cooper. Lady Harrington had ordered six large casks to be built for her and John was to transport them to the manor. Little John always liked to visit Mr. Hartley's shop because it smelled like the clean pine shavings that covered the floor and he liked to watch how he shaped the wood slats and pulled them together with the bindings. He loved to look at all the different tools hanging on the walls and of course he was always full of questions. That morning Mrs. Hartley brought out a plate of warm nut pies while his father discussed business with Mr. Hartley and offered one to Little John. Their daughter Amy Anne was peeking at Little John from behind the door until he got nervous and hid himself behind his father's trousers.

After a little while, Amy came out from behind the door to stand near her father, casting subtle glances his way. She was a year older than Little John but much daintier in size; a diminutive little girl with honey blonde curls that fell over the collar of her starched dress like spun gold thread from a bobbin and she smelled like sweet soap. The normally talkative boy was absolutely tongue-tied; he could not seem to utter a word in her presence.

As soon as the men had loaded up two of the casks on the back of John's wagon for the first of several trips John jumped up onto the wagon seat and called for Little John to join him.

"Why don't you just leave the boy here?" asked Mr. Hartley. "Amy Anne's cousins are off visiting in Bossington, and she has no one to play with today."

"Do you want to stay, Little John?" his father asked.

Little John and Amy Anne looked each other up and down. Amy Anne was curious about this strange boy and Little John knew staying in the cooper's shop would be much more fun than riding back and forth in a dusty wagon all day, so he nodded to his father. As soon as John was out of sight however, Little John panicked and almost ran up the road after him. The sweet aroma of baked nuts and the mystery of the pretty little girl changed his mind and he decided to stay.

Amy Anne sat down on the bench where Little John was enjoying the last sticky bite of his nut pie. She was holding a cloth doll in her arms. "We can play dolls if you like," she said.

Little John shook his head. "I don't know nothin' about playing with dolls. Have you any horses?" he asked and took his tiny wooden horse from his pocket.

"No," said Amy Anne. She looked at her father. "Daddy, can Little John and I go down to the beach and collect shells?"

That perked Little John's interest. He had never collected shells before! With Mr. Hartley's approval the two ran out of the cooper's shop and down the road toward the shore.

Little John had a hard time keeping up with Amy Anne who ran ahead of him.

"I have lots of shells. Sometimes you can find pretty ones that aren't broken," she said.

John was intrigued by the ocean; he had seen it many a time from the back of his father's horse but never had he walked in the sand and touched the sea bubbles as they came ashore.

"Better take off your shoes or they will get wet, and your ma will give you a lashing,'" Amy Anne said, sitting down in the sea grass to remove her own.

"I don't have a ma," Little John replied and sat down beside her to remove his boots.

"Why?" asked Amy Anne.

"She died a long time ago. She is buried on the hill behind our house. It's just me and Paa now."

"Was she sick?" asked Amy Anne again.

"I don't know," replied Little John slightly taken aback. He didn't know quite how to react to someone who asked more questions than *he* did!

"How old are you anyway?" she continued the interrogation. "I'm seven."

"Six," Little John answered.

Amy Anne left her shoes on the grass and stood up. "Come and I will show you where the best shells are!"

The beach was covered with brown pebbles and Little John's feet, used to the soft earth of his father's farm, were tender but Amy Anne ran over them without any hesitation.

"Do the rocks not hurt your feet?" he called to her from several steps behind.

"No," she said. "Oh, look! Lots of new ones!"

She knelt on the ground where the tide had deposited a cache of fresh shells and began to fill the folds of her apron with them. John followed along and got caught up in her excitement. He never knew there were so many kinds of shells.

"Conch shells are the best but those are hard to find," explained Amy Anne. "So are cockle shells that aren't broken. And if you find one like *this*," she stopped and showed Little John what looked like an ordinary snail shell in her hand, "put it back because it might have a tiny hermit crab living inside of it."

Little John was fascinated. "Show me the crab!"

"He won't come out while I am holding him," she said and set the tiny shell down on the rocks. "Be still and watch and he will get up and walk away."

Little John watched for a moment, and nothing happened. He started to say something when Amy Anne put her finger to her lips, "Shhhhhh," she whispered.

They waited a few more moments until finally the little shell rocked back and forth and a pair of tiny crab legs popped out, hoisting the shell up and carrying it back to the shallow water. It was the most amazing thing Little John had ever seen.

When Amy Anne had pawed through all the shells in that particular pile, she moved on down the beach with Little John trailing behind, tiptoeing over the rocks having filled his pockets with shells to show his father.

"Come John and I will show you something ever better!"

Amy Anne ran up away from the water where they came upon a set of wagon tracks. They followed them up the beach into the shade of some very steep cliffs that were eroding away into the ocean. Little John was glad he could put his sore feet on the sandy earth again. He followed Amy Anne as she went up to the foot of the cliffs and they came to a cave-like hole. "Look at this" she whispered.

Little John walked up and stood beside her and peered into the cave; in it he saw several large bundles wrapped in cloth and lashed together with twine. "What is it?" he asked.

"Daddy said I wasn't to come this far. He said *pirates* would take me away if I did."

Little John's eyes widened in horror. "Then *what are we doing here?*"

"I wanted to show you. I think this is where they keep their treasure." Amy Anne's blue eyes twinkled with excitement as she spoke.

Little John looked over his shoulder, expecting to be accosted at any moment by a band of murderous pirates.

"I'm going *home*," he said.

Chapter Eight "The Last War Horse"

Although she had almost gotten him murdered by pirates, the friendship between Little John and Amy Anne blossomed and grew along with them with every passing season. The Hartley family enjoyed having Little John and his father visit and stay for supper when they were conducting business in town and Amy Anne was occasionally permitted to ride along in the wagon with John and his son on their trips back and forth to Porlock. Lady Harrington herself enjoyed having the youngsters visit and often entertained them at the manor and taught them both to ride horses in her arena. Mrs. Hartley was only mildly concerned when she first saw her daughter riding astride a horse like a young man, when she had been taught all her life that ladies only ride *side-saddle,* but she would never question Lady Harrington on any matter out of respect. When planting and harvesting seasons came, however, and there was much work to be done Little John was now old enough to work alongside the rest of the men in the fields from dawn to dark. Springtime was also the time of sheep-shearing and when Amy Anne wasn't occupied with reading and writing lessons, she had mountains of wool to spin alongside her mother. In years to come Little John and Amy Anne would have to be content with a glimpse of each other at church on the Sabbath.

One sunny spring afternoon Little John stopped his labors in the field to wipe his brow and saw to his surprise Lady Harrington riding up the road. "Paa!" he said and pointed.

She paused at the corral gate watching them planting the last rows of wheat. John quickly put down his spade and went to greet her. "Good afternoon Lady Harrington," he said. "What brings you this far? Are you on your way to town?"

"No, John. I came to speak to you about a matter," she replied.

John went forward and assisted her down from her horse.

"Please forgive my soiled hands M'lady. I would have washed up if I had known you were coming."

"Not to worry, John." Her attention momentarily turned to the horses and Morning Star.

"He is a beauty just like his father," she remarked. "What fine colts he will sire for you!"

"I haven't any plans to breed him yet, M'lady. I am still working on his ground manners. I gave up trying to put him under the yoke; he wants to gallop just like his father. Besides, the three horses I have nearly eat me out of house and home as it is!"

"Well, we can't have that can we? Maybe what I have to tell you will ease your mind in that respect."

"You have good news?" John asked.

Lady Harrington nodded her head. "In a way, John. Let's go sit in the shade. I forgot to wear my hat and I can feel freckles popping out on my nose already!"

John tied her horse to the fence and showed her the way up to the house where they sat down at the kitchen table. Lady Harrington was the first to speak. "John, you know the Lord never blessed me with children of my own. You were the closest we ever had to a real son."

John lowered his head humbly. He did not know what to say.

She went on. "And I am sure you know I am not as dedicated to this infant king they are parading around in his fancy clothes as Lord Harrington and I were to his father; although I am sure I would be strung up on the gallows if they heard me say that. It wasn't until this morning that I knew in my heart that I was going to stop paying the king's ransom."

"M'Lady?"

"I had the pleasure of a visit from the king's excise men yesterday. They have informed me that since we had *fewer* bales of wool to report this year than last, in addition to taxing each bale they now intend to tax me *on the hoof* for every sheep in my flock! Have you ever heard of anything so outrageous? I am so angry I am seeing red!"

John was not surprised. He had heard talk in town that the young king's cronies were coming up with new taxes to support their own lavish lifestyles at court and no one liked the idea. "What will you do?" John asked.

"Well," said Lady Harrington, "I am going to have to separate my herds. I will spread them out over the county. I will hide them in the forest! I will bring them into the *great hall* if I must! But I'll be damned if I am going to pay double tax!"

She stood up and paced back and forth across the floor, her hands on her hips and her eyes blazing. "Furthermore, I am going to re-write my will and name *you* as my sole heir. That way the king and that bishop of his won't be able to swoop down and claim everything I own before my corpse is cold!"

John sat mute and astounded. He had always felt the special bond between himself and the Harringtons but never in his wildest dreams did he expect to be named as their heir. The Harrington lands were vast and their holdings extensive and he hardly felt worthy of such a gift. He stood up and bowed reverently. "I don't know quite what to say, M'lady. I am overwhelmed by your generosity."

"John," she said putting her hand on his shoulder. "I have always tried to care for our people. I fear that when I'm gone, they will be taxed into starvation. I know you will not let that happen for you love the people of Porlock as much as I do."

John nodded in agreement. "I am most honored, M'Lady."

With that, Lady Harrington flung her scarf around her neck and marched out the door toward her horse. "I will have the new will drafted immediately John. You shall have a copy in case there are any objections, of which I am sure there will be. As sure as the sun rises, I expect I will have unknown relatives popping out like knots on an oak tree."

"M'Lady, you have a good long life ahead of you."

"Maybe, if the Lord wills it, John. But we have to be prepared if that is not the case."

She mounted her horse and smiled down at him. "We shall beat them at their own game, aye?"

And off she cantered up the road.

John returned to the field and Little John noticed his father had a dazed and confused look about him. "Did Lady Harrington have news?"

John shook his head and went back to work. *No need to give the boy anything to fuel his youthful imagination,* he thought. John was a simple man with simple needs. He wasn't sure how others would feel about Lady Harrington's plans.

Lady Harrington continued up the road, taking in the view from the crest of the hill that overlooked the town of Porlock, and she reined in her horse looking back at the Snow farm. *Maybe I am expecting too much of John*, she thought, suddenly worried that her decision might put him in mortal danger. She knew that even the most trivial of disagreements could lead to bloodshed. Then she remembered the past and the days when he had been just a boy and she had relied on him when Lord Harrington had been out waging war with King Henry. No, she was convinced he had the *fortitude* to carry on the Harrington principles if not the name itself. "Ha!" she said firmly, and her horse galloped for home.

"Lady Harrington!" She heard someone calling her name as the house came into her sight and she looked and saw one of her grooms running down the road waving his arms. When he reached her, he was quite out of breath. "M'Lady, it's Majesty!" the groom said hoarsely. "Please come see!"

When she reached the barn, she pulled her horse up suddenly and jumped to the ground running into the barn. Two other grooms were standing at the gate to Majesty's stall and the groom who had been with her the longest was kneeling in the straw beside the stallion who lay prostrate and was breathing with great difficulty. She could see yellow fluid oozing from his nostrils as she fell to her knees to examine him more closely. "How long has he been like this?" she asked.

"He seemed fine this morning M'lady. He was afoot but he is off his feed. When I came back to check on him, he was down.

"It is influenza I'm sure," she said. "Go fetch me a dozen bunches of mint from down near the river. And I need a bucket of boiling water," she instructed the grooms. She gathered up several woolen blankets and folded them to make a tent for his head. "We'll get him breathing better so he'll get on his feet."

For the rest of the afternoon, she sat beside him, holding the blankets over his head to keep in the steam off the mint leaves until her own sinuses were draining profusely. The grooms were running a relay back and forth from the manor kitchen to fetch more boiling water as each bucket cooled. By evening he had made little improvement and had still made no attempt to stand. Lady Harrington continued making him breathe in the mint steam trying to encourage him to get up but after a while he would not even lift his head. Lady Harrington took the blankets and spread them out over his massive body, and she sat at his head, stroking his neck. "Come my Majesty," she whispered, "This is no way for a war horse to die. You have survived the battlefields; you can surely fight this sickness!" He looked up at her with his heavily lashed black eyes and blinked as if he understood her words.

The grooms lingered outside the stall, waiting for an order from Lady Harrington.

"Go on to your supper boys," she finally said. "I will stay with him tonight."

As they left the barn, they heard her begin to sing softly to him the words of an old folk song:

"Old apple tree, it wassail thee,

And hope that thou will bear,

For the Lord doth know where we shall be,

To be merry another year."

She fell asleep on the straw with her arms around the neck of this most regal of all animals; her beloved knight's protector, sire to so many handsome colts, until the only breath heard in the stillness of the stall was her own.

Chapter Nine "Singing Like Canaries"

It was as if the day could not decide what it wanted to do; while thunder clouds hung over the peaks of Exmoor, what remained of the afternoon sun bounced off them, creating shifting rays of light and rainbows that arched gracefully over Porlock. April was always a surprise when it came to weather. Sometimes there would still be snow in the shady corners and a chill in the air; other years April would be warm and fragrant with the early bursting of apple blossoms. This particular Sunday Little John stayed behind after the morning mass sitting atop the rock pillar at the end of Porlock Bridge watching the parishioners mingling in the street outside the church. Amy Anne slipped away from her parents and hurried to meet her sweetheart.

They had matured since their first day spent collecting seashells; although "Little" John could no longer be considered *little* by the wildest stretch of anyone's imagination, towering over his father by almost a foot and outweighing him by at least twenty pounds, still the nickname remained. Amy Anne was still petite but womanly curves had replaced the flat bosom and narrow hips of a seven-year-old. She wore her hair differently now; braided down the back and tied with a bow and no longer were her knuckles and knees skinned from too much boyish play. Although they had never made official their betrothal everyone expected the inseparable pair to wed someday.

Amy Anne jumped up and sat beside Little John on the rock wall letting her skirt dangle over the edge. "Did you see the rainbow?" she asked.

"Yes," answered John.

"Do you really think that is God's sign to Noah?"

John had never had the advantage of having a mother to read Bible stories to him while he was growing up and he was always impressed by Amy Anne's knowledge of scriptural subjects. His quizzical expression prompted an explanation from Amy.

"It's true, John!" she said, her blue eyes dancing as she spoke. "God felt sorry for the flood and the rainbow was his promise to Noah to never destroy earth again. Didn't your father ever read that story to you?"

Little John was silent for a moment. "Paa can't read, Amy."

Amy Anne realized she had embarrassed him, and she took his hand. "I'm sorry John. I didn't mean to hurt your feelings. Your father is far too busy with farm work to worry about such things anyway. When *we* have children ......"

She stopped herself and a blush crept up her neck to her cheeks.

Little John smiled. Amy Anne's words gave him courage to carry out his plan. "Amy, do you think your parents would mind if I visited this afternoon?"

She smiled "Of course not, silly. They always love to have you. My mother is roasting a duck and she made an apple cake for dessert. Do you think your father would like to come too?"

"He has already left for home. I told him I wanted to stay in town for a while."

"Can't we sit here for a little longer? I don't want to go in just yet."

Little John's mind was going in two directions. He wanted to remain there holding Amy Anne's hand and talking together without the scrutiny of her parents and yet he wanted to get his difficult task over and done with; he had decided that day to ask Mr. Hartley for her hand in marriage. The weather had its own say in the matter however and soon raindrops were falling on their heads, forcing them to run for the shelter of the Hartley house.

Talk was always lively, and laughter was abundant in the Hartley household. Although it wasn't much larger than his father's farmhouse it had a warmth that came from more than just the crackling fire; it was the woman's touch that made it cozy and welcoming. While Little John and his father would sit in the evenings after work resting their feet on the hearth, the Hartleys would be playing board games and singing like his Aunt Mary and Uncle Peter did with their children.

After dinner, Little John and Mr. Hartley remained sitting at the table while Mrs. Hartley and Amy Anne cleared the dishes and put the picked over duck carcass in a pot to simmer for the next day's soup.

"How is the planting going Little John? What does Lady Harrington have you growing this year?"

"Paa and I are setting out wheat again. The blight got most of last year's plants and we had to pitch 'em in the fire."

Mr. Hartley got up and went to the fireplace to warm his hands and then turned his backside towards the fire as he continued to talk. "How're those hops doing? I don't hear much about them."

"Paa says the first year was the hardest, getting the plants started. Now he just gives them a little horse manure and keeps the weeds down."

"Lady Harrington must be scooting them out by the back roads. I never see any at market."

"Aye," said Little John. "She is so mad about them taxing her sheep she says she'll *die* before she gives them a double share on the profit of her hops too."

Mr. Hartley laughed. "She is a smart old lady; every bit as shrewd as Lord Harrington himself."

"Aye she is," said Little John. "I just hope she doesn't get herself hurt. Paa says those revenuers can get mighty nasty when they're crossed."

The conversation lagged long enough to make a change of subject and Little John was not about to lose what might be his last chance before the ladies joined them. "Mr. Hartley I would like to ask you for Amy Anne's hand in marriage," he blurted out.

There! It was out there! There was no taking it back now!

Mr. Hartley rubbed his chin and thought a moment before a smile broke from his lips. "Well, it's about *time* John Snow! That daughter of mine has been pining away for you since she was seven years old! And I can't think of a better match for my Amy!"

Just as Mrs. Hartley and Amy Anne entered the room he added, "Welcome to our family son!!"

They all hugged each other and had their apple cake for dessert.

Little John left for home walking alone up Porlock Hill in the dark. What was normally an exhausting climb up the steep road seemed to dissolve under the lightness of his steps and he was singing as he neared his father's house. John went to the door to greet him. "Aye, you've been to the inn, have you?" he inquired of his son.

"No, Paa. I'm not drunk," said Little John.

"Then pray tell what has turned you into a canary?"

"I have asked for Amy Anne's hand, Paa! And Mr. Hartley has agreed!"

Little John burst through the door and John closed it behind him returning to his chair by the fire. He sat silent for a moment remembering suddenly the day he had become betrothed to Little John's mother and a strange sadness fell over him. Little John noticed his father's demeanor and knelt beside him. "Paa, that is all right, isn't it? You *approve* of Amy, don't you?"

"Son, I have no objections. Amy is a fine girl and the Hartleys are good people."

Little John sighed with relief. For a moment he thought his father was not happy about the news.

"We will have to get busy adding a room to the house I expect and be building some more furniture. Let's see we'll need another bed frame and chest of drawers. Perhaps your Aunt Mary will sew you a new mattress cover. I am sure Amy will want her own things in the kitchen. Tomorrow I will ask Lady Harrington's permission to cut some lumber."

Little John nodded absent-mindedly; being betrothed had seemed so simple that afternoon. There was much more work to this marriage business than he had thought about!

John sat for a moment and thought about the conversation he had with Lady Harrington when she had informed him of his inheritance. He had never spoken of it to anyone, even his son. *Now*, he thought, *might be the time.* He dwelled on it a bit longer but decided against it. *No point getting the boy excited about something that might be years away from happening. No*, he thought, *we will just carry on as if nothing has changed.* They both went to bed with marriage plans in their heads, Little John with the anticipation of romance and passion and his father with the cutting of lumber and the hammering of nails.

The next morning the sun gained no advantage on either father or son; both awoke in the shadows just before the dawn eager to be done with the regular chores at hand and on to the new project. As Little John was fastening his boots near the door his father approached him with a small velvet pouch in his hands. "I doubt you have had time to think about the things that are important to a woman," he said, handing Little John the pouch.

Little John pulled the strings of the pouch and shook the contents out into the palm of his hand; a small plain silver band rolled out that he had never seen before.

"It was your mother's wedding ring," said John. "I am sure she would be pleased for Amy to wear it."

Seldom had Little John shared an emotional moment with his father, not since the day at his mother's grave.

Now, his eyes misted with tears. Little John stood up and the two men embraced each other. "Thank you, Paa. I was wondering what I would do for a ring. I wish my mother could be here for the wedding."

John had to wipe tears from his own eyes. "Yes, Son, I wish that too. But she is somewhere looking down on us and I'm sure she is pleased."

Lady Harrington was also happy with the news later that morning when they arrived at the manor in their wagon. "Of course!" she replied at John's request to cut lumber from her forest. "You take whatever you need! And I hope you will let me give the wedding feast here in my home, Little John!"

Little John was flattered with her offer and couldn't wait to tell Amy Anne. "Thank you, M'lady," he said.

"And, Little John, tell Amy and her mother I have some bolts of silk I have been saving for a special occasion. It would make a beautiful veil for the bride!"

The men took the wagon into the forest and began the labor of felling and cutting enough wood for the new room. Side by side they worked at it until the shadows overtook the rays of the setting sun and it became too dark to see amongst the trees. They drove toward home in a jovial mood with the wagon filled with wood; this time both father *and* son were singing like *canaries*.

Chapter Ten "With His Mother's Ring"

The day of the wedding was suddenly upon them. With Lady Harrington taking part in the planning of the festivities, the affair was to be far more elaborate than the townsfolk had seen in a long while. While most brides could not afford to wear anything more elegant than their Sunday church clothes, not only did Lady Harrington supply the silk for the veil, she insisted on buying additional material so that Amy Anne could have a brand-new dress for the occasion: yards of blue and green linen. "Green is the color of young love," she said, "and blue is the symbol of purity. So, we shall have *both*!"

This pleased Amy Anne immensely as blue and green were her favorite colors. On that morning she with her mother and Little John's aunt Mary were busy in Lady Harrington's upstairs dressing room getting the bride ready for her special day. Amy Anne had never seen a full-length image of herself before; the only mirror in the Hartley household was a small hand mirror her mother kept in her bureau. Now she stood there looking at herself decked out in yards of soft blue and green from head to toe; her veil of white falling gently from a woven crown of wildflowers picked that very morning. Lady Harrington and Aunt Mary were both in awe of her youthful beauty. Mrs. Hartley began to cry.

"Little John is just going to faint on the spot!" said Lady Harrington. "Here, we mustn't forget your blue garter!"

Amy Anne blushed as she pulled the garter over her knee. "I can't thank you enough, M'lady."

Lady Harrington took her hand. "Amy, it gives me so much happiness to share in your joy, especially since I will never have a daughter of my own to indulge!"

Downstairs the great hall was being prepared for the wedding feast and Lady Harrington had instructed her grooms to hitch her two finest mares to her carriage. They had decorated the carriage windows with flowers and made bows of the remnants of linen so that when Amy Anne came down the walk from the house, she felt like a queen being escorted to her coronation. The ladies helped her climb aboard the carriage then they all joined her for the ride to town, giggling and whispering all the way like little girls.

The rest of the family members and almost the entire town had gathered outside the little church in Porlock. Little John wore his father's best shirt and he had polished his boots. This was the first break from the work of adding the new room to his father's house and they had completed it in record time with the help of many of the men in town. The carpenter helped with the framework and the thatcher had supplied the new roof while their womenfolk sewed a colorful quilt for the bed and linen curtains for the bedchamber windows.

"I wish they would get here, Paa," said Little John. "I'm as nervous as a cat."

John laughed. "You'll get over it," he said and paused, thinking about Little John's mother, and added, "It will be good to have a woman in the house again."

"What you don't like my cooking, Paa?"

Mr. Hartley joined the conversation then. "Oh, I remember those days when I was a bachelor! Scrambled eggs were all I knew how to cook. The first time I smelled meat and vegetables simmering on the fire I thought I'd surely died and gone to heaven!"

"Aye and making that trip to the larder was too much work after a day in the fields. Most nights chewing on stale bread I was!" said John.

"Well, I'm not nervous anymore. Now I'm *hungry*!" said Little John.

"I am sure Lady Harrington has prepared a fine spread! We'll all be going home tonight with bulging bellies!"

At that moment Lady Harrington's carriage appeared on Porlock bridge, the hooves of the horses clattering on the cobblestones. The crowd parted and made a passageway for the arrival of the bride. The driver secured the horses and jumped down to open the door for the ladies.

First to exit the carriage was Lady Harrington in a long-sleeved velvet tunic and a peacock feather in her hat.

Next Aunt Mary stepped down from the carriage in her best Sunday dress and a bright blue scarf around her neck and followed Lady Harrington into the church. The driver reached out his hand as Little John held his breath and out stepped the most beautiful girl he was sure he had ever seen; his bride in her flowing linen gown and the veil so thin and fine it fluttered in the air as she approached him. He was speechless at Amy Anne's radiance. Words were not necessary; Amy Anne understood and reveled in his unspoken expression of love.

Father Clary came forward and asked the bridal couple to step into a small room off the sanctuary where they met behind a closed door for a private blessing. The rest of the wedding party entered, passing first by the crypt of Lord Harrington along the east arch of the arcade to pay their respects before they took their seats on the church pews. The bride and groom emerged again and took their places at the altar. When the final vows were spoken, Little John placed his mother's silver ring on Amy Anne's finger and lifted her veil. He then kissed his bride for the first time in view of others; not his usual light kiss across her cheek; for the first time he kissed her firmly on the lips.

As soon as everyone had wished them well Amy Anne and Little John escaped to the carriage to exchange the rest of their kisses in private. "I love you *John Anthony Snow*!" she said laying her head on his shoulder.

"And I love you too, *Amy Anne Snow*!" Little John replied.

Lady Harrington appeared and spoke to the driver. "Take them on to my house. I will ride along with John and the others."

And off the entire town went to the wedding feast which lasted well into the night. Lady Harrington had her grooms put out hay and water for all the guests' horses and was not the least surprised in the morning to find several wagons still on the manor grounds with their owners asleep in the back. It had been a wonderful party and she was pleased even though her own head ached a little from too much wine.

John had risen with the sun; ever since his embarrassing experience at the inn, he was careful not to imbibe too much. He awoke the day after the wedding party with a clear head and was out working in the field when Amy Anne stepped out of the farmhouse door and called him in to breakfast.

It had been a long time since he had eaten such a meal. Amy Anne had baked fresh bread, fried a slab of bacon without burning the edges and prepared stewed apples with cream. She was busy in the kitchen with her dowry to the marriage, the kitchen utensils and dishes given to her by her mother, and she served Little John and his father their food beaming with pride.

"I never knew you could cook so well," said Little John.

"My mother has been teaching me since I was little," replied Amy Anne. "Did you think I only washed the

dishes in my father's house? You've been eating my cooking for years now and didn't even know it!"

Chapter Eleven "Smuggler's Cove"

There was no time off for a honeymoon. Even the summer months were busy for the farmers. If the temperatures were favorable and they had ample rain, they could harvest and get another crop in before the fall frosts. Amy Anne was occupied in her vegetable garden behind the house and Little John was given the responsibility of transporting the last of Lady Harrington's dried wool to the landing in Porlock. He had been working at it with his father and his uncles for weeks and they were finally down to the last load scurrying to get it to town before the sun set.

"Take it slow down the hill son. It's a heavy load you're carrying," said John. "And don't take any detours on your way. Go straight to the dock and wait until the king's men tell you to unload the bales."

"I will, Paa. I've been with you on enough trips to know what to do."

"Just don't give them any reason to suspect you're doing anything illegal, or they'll tie you to the pier pilings and leave you there for the tide to rise."

Little John laughed, but he knew his father was dead serious. There was no point asking for trouble. The king's men had come to town a month before and had long since overstayed their welcome in Porlock watching every shipment of goods in and out of the town. They had immediately tried to intimidate the townsfolk, but their threats were empty and falling on deaf ears. The two that were assigned to the Porlock docks turned out to be lazy and ignorant so that no one paid much attention to them, and the smuggling went on uninterrupted. They were still dangerous, however, for they had the authority to hang suspected smugglers.

Little John approached Porlock Bridge just as candles were beginning to flicker in the town's windows. He steered the wagon down to the pier and took his place in line behind two other wagons: a shipment of tools on their way up the coast to Bristol and a wagon serving as a makeshift hearse with a coffin in the back. The king's tax men were standing at the bottom of the gangway taking inventory of every load.

When the last box of tools had been carried onto the ship, the hearse pulled forward.

"Aye and what have we here?" said the tax man strolling around the back of the wagon and peering inside.

"Is the king now taxing *corpses* too?" asked the driver sarcastically.

"Well, I don't know. How much gold do you think he is taking with him?"

"He has nothing but his best Sunday suit I assure you. I'm sending him home to be buried with his family," replied the driver.

The man stepped back and motioned to his comrade. They whispered something to each other and then gave the signal to the seamen on the deck of the ship.

"Get this out of here," one of them yelled.

The superstitious deck hands stood still at the top of the gangway frozen with fear at the thought of touching a dead man's coffin. Finally, the captain had to *order* them to step forward. The two unfortunate sailors chosen hoisted the dreaded cargo out of the hearse with the utmost care, silently carried it up the gangway and set it gently down on the main deck, backing away from it as if it were a wild animal.

One of the king's men remarked under his breath, "I'll not be searching *that* cargo!" and the two of them laughed as they turned their attention toward Little John.

The first man walked around the wagon pushing his hands between the bales of wool and shaking them back and forth as if he expected to loosen a hidden cache of gold.

"I count eleven bales. Is that right mister?" he asked with a crooked smile revealing teeth that were as yellow as corn kernels.

Little John knew he wasn't supposed to question the men, but his father had also warned him that they would try to cheat him to collect more taxes for the king's coffers. "I *do* hope I only have *ten* bales, Sir, or I will be a cooked goose when I bring the receipt back to Lady Harrington."

Little John jumped down and circled the wagon pretending to recount each bale carefully while the man with the yellow teeth stood by staring at him.

"I believe there are *ten,* sir. But I haven't a head for numbers. Would you mind counting them again?" asked Little John.

"Are you saying I can't count?" the man snapped.

"Oh, no Sir! I'm just a dumb farmer but since Lady Harrington counted the bales *herself* when I left, she'll be expecting a receipt for that *exact* amount when I return!"

The other of the king's men approached and looked at Little John. "So, you work for Lady Harrington, do you?"

"Yes, Sir. She is a fine lady."

"She certainly is!" the captain, who was listening to their conversation from the deck of the ship, called out. "And how is your family, Little John?"

Little John was happy to see a friendly face. "They are very well, Captain!" he called back.

The king's men whispered to each other again. "I remember Sir Harrington. A gallant knight he was!" said one of the men. "Go ahead and unload your wool mister.

I will sign your receipt for ten bales, so you will please your lady."

Little John swallowed hard and began to unload the bales as quickly as he could while the one with the yellow teeth watched and scowled at him. He knew his heart would not stop pounding in his chest until he was safely out of town and on his way home.

"Is this your last load today?" asked the friendlier of the two men. "It's been a long day and we're tired and ready for the kip."

"Aye, Sir. This will be the last."

While the sailors were unloading his wool, Little John took the receipt from the man and thanked him politely. He watched them as they walked away toward the inn. As soon as the last bale was removed, he reached over and shifted the boards on the bed of the wagon to reveal the hidden compartment beneath. Quickly the men unloaded the bags containing Lady Harrington's dried hops carrying them up the gangway in the darkness and hiding them safely in the captain's cabin while Little John watched out nervously for the king's men. As soon as the last of the hops had been safely stowed away Little John jumped up on the wagon and whipped the team of horses to a gallop. The empty wagon bounced wildly and squeaked all the way to the foot of Porlock Hill where he finally stopped to let the horses rest. At that moment in the darkness, he looked down and realized he was *literally* shaking in his boots. He took a deep breath and steered the horses slowly up the hill, trying to calm his heart that was still beating rapidly; he did not want Amy Anne to suspect what they were doing.

John met him at the corral gate and helped him unhook the horses, putting them out for the night. He slapped Little John's shoulder. "I'm proud of you, Son. You did all right."

"I don't think I have ever been as scared as I was tonight, Paa," replied Little John. "I guess I wasn't cut out to be a smuggler."

"None of us were, Little John. It's just the times we live in. Lady Harrington is keeping what she can for *all* our benefit."

"I know, Paa. I know. I just don't like it much." Little John knew Lady Harrington wasn't the only one doing it; most of the town of Porlock was engaged in some type of underground buying and selling of goods to avoid the high taxes.

The two men went inside where Amy Anne had supper waiting for them.

As they climbed into bed that night, Amy Anne snuggled up next to Little John with her hand placed squarely on his chest. "I know what you and your father are up to John," she whispered. "You can't keep secrets from me. You should know that by now."

"I don't know what you mean, Amy Anne. I have no secrets."

Amy Anne smiled back at her husband. "No?" she said with that little twinkle in her eye that had the same effect on him as butter melting on warm bread. When he didn't answer Amy Anne went on. "It doesn't matter. I just want *you* to know *I* know, and I think it's silly not to trust me," she said. "Besides I have an even *bigger* secret! And it's much more exciting than your old secret anyway."

Little John was glad she had changed the subject. "What?" he asked. Ever since the day she had shown him the hermit crab on the beach she never failed to surprise him.

"Goodnight, John," she said sweetly, kissing him on the cheek.

She rolled over on her side of the bed and closed her eyes pretending to go to sleep.

"No, you don't!" said Little John, tickling her ribs playfully. "Tell!"

"Oh, all right. I will tell you. It's a gift I have for you. But you must wait until the fall. It won't be ready until then."

Little John looked puzzled. Then he realized what she was saying. "A baby? Are you sure?"

Amy Anne nodded, and Little John took her in his arms holding her gently as if she were made of eggshells.

"I'm not going to *break* John!" she giggled and wrapped herself tightly around him, giving him a deep kiss.

Later, just as she was falling asleep with her head on his shoulder, she whispered in the same girlish voice she used when they were children. "See, I told you *my* secret was better than *yours*!"

Chapter Twelve "A Ghostly Cortege"

As soon as the last of Lady Harrington's hops were loaded and tucked away in his cabin, Captain Tom Hatherly gave the order to untie the lines and prepare to shove off. He wasn't taking any chances of the king's men returning in a drunken stupor and coming aboard which they had been known to do. *Better,* he thought, *to be halfway up the channel and out of their reach before daylight*.

In the darkness the small two-masted caravel drifted away from the dock and floated lifelessly for a few minutes before the strong current pulled it in. Not much larger than a fishing vessel, the *Dove* was slim and fast, perfect for slipping in and out of the tiny inlets and coves along the southwestern coast of England. It was light enough to be swift yet strong enough to carry a decent load of cargo. As soon as the sails were set the crew waited anxiously for the limp canvas to stiffen still tiptoeing around the coffin that sat ominously in the middle of the deck. It didn't take long before the topsail caught the wind and filled out with a snap, and they were on their way northeast to Bristol.

Captain Tom retired to his cabin where Lady Harrington's hops were stacked leaving his able first mate Mr. Wallace to navigate while he got some sleep. He squeezed his way through the maze of bags and found his way to his bunk where he opened a bottle of brandy and took a few long-awaited sips, all the while keeping a vigilant eye through the stern porthole for any vessels that might be following them. Pirates regularly traveled the route up and down Bristol Channel to raid merchant ships and make off with their booty. When he was satisfied no ships were following them, he closed his eyes, lulled to sleep by the rolling of the swells and the slapping of the wake against the hull of the ship.

He had not started out to be a smuggler; in the beginning when his father had taught him to sail, he had gone out on fishing boats to "*get his sea legs*" as his father called it. Then, he began to travel with his father on legitimate merchant runs up and down the coast of England and Wales. That was before smuggling became a way of life for people who were being taxed so heavily on their goods, they could barely support their families. And if smuggling wasn't bad enough, some became pirates, loyal to no king, not even loyal to their own countrymen.

Captain Tom had left his young wife Maggie back in Barnstable in the house they shared with her parents; he did not like his young wife to be alone while he was out at sea. The ports on the Devon coast had become such hotbeds for confrontations between the king's men and the smugglers, he was seriously thinking of moving to another town; maybe Minehead or Porlock. And while they too had their share of king's men snooping around on the docks, the men weren't as ruthless as the southern ports where hangings over smuggling were common. He wanted to raise his family in a safer place. If smuggling didn't pay such a good wage, he would have gone back to fishing long before.

He awoke at midnight and relieved Wallace at the helm of the *Dove*. The wind was behind them and had carried them swiftly all the way to the mouth of River Avon. It was there, under the cloak of darkness, that he maneuvered the ship as close into the shallows as was safe and ordered the men to drop the anchor. He lit a lantern and hung it over the starboard side of the ship and waited. In a few moments another lantern was lit on the shore; the signal the smugglers had arrived and that the coast was clear of the king's men.

The crew lowered the longboat and began to unload Lady Harrington's bags of hops into it. It took less than an hour to exchange the cargo for a hefty bag of gold coins. The captain tested a few coins with his teeth to be sure they were genuine gold and then stored the bag in a lockbox in his cabin. The light on the shore went out and the wagon drove off in the darkness. The captain gave the order to raise the anchor and they were on their way upriver before the sunrise to deliver their *legal* cargo.

The crew stacked the boxes of tools and the bales of wool on the dock under the watchful eye of the king's men. Captain Tom showed them his bills of lading. Neither the crew nor the king's men were willing to touch the coffin. The captain understood their hesitancy although he was not as superstitious as was his crew who considered it unlucky for a ship to carry a corpse. The buyers of the wool and the tools arrived in their wagons and paid the captain for their purchases and the king's men moved down the dock to other ships but as yet no one had appeared to retrieve the coffin. He checked his manifest; someone by the name of James Wilson was supposed to accept the shipment. Captain Tom decided he would wait a decent amount of time before they shoved off again.

"What if nobody comes for it, Captain?" Wallace asked, his eyes wide with fear.

Captain Tom scratched his chin. "Well, we can't just go off and leave it on the dock, now can we?" He knew the crew was anxious to go to town in search of a hearty breakfast and he thought it would temporarily calm their fears. "You lads go ashore. Ask around about this *James Wilson* fellow. I'll stay behind in case he comes to pick it up."

The crew scrambled ashore still terrified at the thought of turning the *Dove* into a floating hearse. A couple of hours passed. Captain Tom was sitting on the quarterdeck studying his charts when they finally returned to the ship; Wallace was not surprised to see the coffin still sitting there. "We asked everyone at the inn Captain. They say the king's men hung this *James Wilson* last week when they caught him hiding a trunk full of undeclared brandy."

The captain thought for a moment and looked at the coffin. "Someone fetch me a hammer," he said.

The crew looked at each other in disbelief; several took a step backward.

"Captain, you can't!" Wallace pleaded. "Please don't open it! It will surely be a curse on the *Dove* if you do!"

Captain Tom stepped forward and inspected the coffin more closely. There were no marks on the outside of it to render a clue who or what was inside it; it was just a plain, ordinary pine box. He lifted one end to ascertain the weight of it; it definitely wasn't empty. "Are you all *deaf*?" he said. "Get me a hammer!"

Still, no one moved, and the captain was losing his patience. "*Superstitions be damned*!" he yelled. "Get me a hammer or I'll be going ashore and hiring myself a new crew!"

Wallace went below and returned reluctantly with the captain's request.

As the captain began to remove the nails holding the lid of the coffin down the crew huddled a good distance away and watched in horror. After he had loosened the last nail, he took hold of the lid and gave it a yank. There, packed tightly in a cozy bed of straw were two dozen bottles of fine brandy. The captain laughed heartily at the crew.

"There's your corpse, Boys!" he said to the astonished men and added, "And I'll wager he will be fetching a handsome price for us when we get back to Barnstable!"

Chapter Thirteen "Good Friends"

As soon as they were down the coast a few miles the captain had the crew transfer the bottles of brandy to a trunk in his cabin then they broke up the coffin and pitched the wood over the side of the ship. He was still laughing at how this James Wilson fellow had hoodwinked the king's men and his superstitious crew, but it gave him pause for thought; it *was* the perfect ruse and one that might be useful in the future.

They arrived in the port of Porlock at noonday to find several pallets of cargo waiting for them on the dock. Leaving Wallace in charge, Captain Tom set out to find the livery stable. He found it situated directly behind the inn. "Have you a horse for hire?" he asked of the stable hand.

"Aye, there is a good one already saddled there," the man said, pointing toward a mare tied to the corral fence. "How long will you be needing her for?"

"Just the day," replied the captain. "I have business with Lady Harrington."

He gave the man two shillings for the horse and climbed aboard reining her up the road toward Porlock Hill. He felt clumsy; he was a sailor not a horseman. His body was balanced for sea winds and rolling waves, not the bouncing trot of a horse and he knew his backside would be aching by the end of the day. He had no other choice;

he certainly wasn't going to *walk* up steep Porlock Hill to get to Lady Harrington's estate. As he reached the crest of the hill and the road passed through John Snow's farm, he saw John and Little John in the fields and waved to them from the road. "I am off to Lady Harrington's," he yelled. "I will stop for a chat on my way back!"

"You can join us for supper!" John called back, and Captain Tom waved in agreement.

By the time he reached the Harrington estate and tied his rented horse up in the barn, the lady herself was already coming down the rock pathway from the big house to greet him and invite him in. "How did it go?" she asked as they entered the house. "Did the king's vultures give you any trouble?"

He smiled and handed her the bag full of gold coins.

"You are amazing, Tom," she said, peering into the bag. She reached in with her hand and gave him back a handsome share of the profit. "I don't know what I would do without you!"

They sat and talked, and the captain told her the entertaining story of the coffin full of brandy.

"I would never have thought of that! Imagine smuggling in a coffin!" she replied laughing.

"I daresay it borders on heresy, but genius as well," said the captain. "Even though the poor bugger paid for it with his life."

"Aye, it gets more dangerous every year. I worry about sending Little John to town now that he has a young wife to care for."

"I will watch out for him, M'lady," the captain assured her. "The docks here are not that bad; it is a hundred-fold worse down south. I am seriously thinking of moving here with my wife just to get her away from the bloodshed."

"Oh, I hope you do, Tom!" Lady Harrington exclaimed. "You'll be looking for a place in town to be close to your ship?"

"Yes. We would like a place of our own, but she is still staying with her parents. I fear her being alone so much when I am at sea."

Lady Harrington smiled. "There is an adorable little cottage that is, at the moment, unoccupied just on the outskirts of town but still close to the harbor. Our town cobbler moved off to London last month and I haven't had anyone interested in it yet. I could have it cleaned for you if you like. Why don't you bring your wife up and see what she thinks! You both can come have dinner with me. I get lonely in this big old house!"

"You are most kind, M'lady. That is what I like about Porlock the most; everyone is so friendly here."

"Aye," said Lady Harrington with a smile. "We are like family. When my husband was alive, I do believe just his presence shielded us from the king and his men. It is a wonderful place to live but I fear it will not always be so."

Captain Tom nodded. "Barnstable used to be like that, when I was growing up."

He paused in thought.

"Would you like to stay for supper?"

"On my next trip I promise I will, M'lady. Tonight, I have been invited to eat with the Snow family. And I must get back to my ship. I daresay I would be terrified of riding that animal down the hill in the dark."

Lady Harrington laughed out loud. "I forget you are not a horseman! But rest easy Tom; horses see better at night than we do!"

"Yes, I must admit I am much more at ease on the sea!"

"Aye, well you go on and have a good time. And let me know about the house. I won't let it go to anyone else until I hear from you!"

He climbed on his horse and steered the beast down the road again, waving goodbye to Lady Harrington. *It would be a nice place to live, this Porlock place*, he thought to himself as he rode along, wondering if Maggie would feel the same. He and his wife were close in age to Little John, and he knew she would find Lady Harrington delightful. Their hometown had become a miserable pit of smuggling and retribution under the brutal hand of the king's watchdogs. In addition, it had become dangerous entering and leaving the harbor due to the gang of pirates that waited just beyond the bay and the boat captains frequently had to do battle with them to protect their cargoes. He knew personally how dangerous it could be, carrying the scars of a pirate's knife on his own torso.

When he arrived at the Snow house, John and Little John were just finishing up in the fields and they all went inside. Amy Anne had the table neatly set and decorated with a small vase of tiny white roses and beef and vegetables simmering in a pot over the fire.

"This is my wife, Amy," said Little John.

"We are proud to have you, Captain," said Amy Anne.

"Thank you, Mistress. Your kitchen smells just like my mother in law's kitchen at home! How I miss it when I am at sea!" Captain Tom replied.

"My new daughter in law is a very good cook," John added, surprised to see flowers once again on the table. "Wherever did you find the roses, Amy?"

"From the little bush just behind the house," she answered smiling proudly as they sat down at the table.

"That is remarkable! Little John's mother could never get that bush to bloom at all!"

"I must have a green thumb," Amy Anne said laughing. She ladled out their dinners as John sliced the bread. Amy disappeared and came back a few moments later with a pitcher of ale and a pitcher of milk. "Would you prefer milk or ale, Captain?" she asked.

"You know a drink of fresh milk would be a welcome change. That is another thing I miss when I am at sea."

She poured the captain's milk and ale for John and Little John then filled her own mug with milk.

"I see you prefer milk too," said the captain.

Amy Anne blushed, and Little John answered for her.

"Aye, she does especially now that we have a babe on the way!"

John was silent. The memory of the day Little John was born flashed before him; the same confusing emotion he had felt at hearing of his son's betrothal. *It can't happen again*! he told himself and forced a smile.

"This is the first I am hearing of it as well, Tom!" said John. "I suppose that since I already have the *gray hair* of a grandfather, I guess it's time I had the *title* as well!"

They had a good supper, laughing and telling stories. John especially enjoyed the story of the coffin full of brandy. An hour passed before they realized it.

"I must be getting back to my ship," Captain Tom said with obvious disappointment. "I've truly enjoyed the supper and the fine company."

"We are glad to have you, Captain! Please visit us again!" said Amy Anne.

The captain smiled. "You may indeed see more of me in the future. I am thinking of bringing my family to Porlock! The Devon coast, I am sad to say, has become an unpleasant place to live."

"That is great news, Tom!" said John. "Where did you have a mind to live? Will you be looking for a farm?"

"Oh, no," laughed the captain. "I will leave the farming to you, John. I will always have saltwater running in my veins. Lady Harrington has a cottage in town she says she will rent to me so that I will be near the harbor."

"I would love to meet your wife, Captain. Please bring her to dinner with us soon!" Amy Anne said, beside herself with joy at the thought of having a new friend her own age.

"I will tell her, I promise. And thank you all again for the pleasant evening!"

At that he went outside and climbed on the stable horse who was already halfway down the road toward her hay in Porlock before he could get both feet in the stirrups.

After the captain had departed, John collected his lantern and went outside to make his nightly pilgrimage to his wife's grave on the hill. When he rounded the corner of the house, he saw the little rose bush his wife had planted so many years before; shining his lantern he could see that it had indeed brought forth blooms from branches that had for years been barren. He picked some of the tiny open faced white roses and took them to the gravesite where he laid them over her headstone whispering, "Your little rosebush has finally bloomed for you, my dear."

Chapter Fourteen "Charting a New Course"

Captain Tom returned the horse and set out for the docks rubbing his aching backside and walking slightly bow-legged. It was barely dusk and yet the king's men had already retired for the evening; he chuckled to himself wondering what the king would do if he knew the amount of smuggling that was going right under their noses! His crew had loaded their cargo and was sitting around a cask playing cards awaiting his orders to shove off for Barnstable. The captain, however, had decided to wait until morning to sail. He preferred not to travel at night unless he had contraband to hide and although there were two dozen bottles of undeclared brandy in his trunk, the king's men had yet to search his private quarters mostly out of laziness he suspected. He just didn't see any reason to take the additional risk of encountering pirates in the dark. In addition, he wanted to go have a look at the cottage Lady Harrington had spoken of; after his pleasant visit with her and equally enjoyable supper with the Snow family he was beginning to be persuaded that moving to Porlock would be a smart decision.

"We'll sail at first light," he told the crew who immediately jumped up and began to disembark for the inn.

"I need one of you to stay," added the captain. "I have one more errand to run. It shouldn't take me very long."

"I'll stand watch, Captain," said Wallace. "I'm not much in the mood for drinking tonight anyway."

Porlock had only one street so the vacant cottage on the outskirts of town was not hard to find: a quaint wooden frame structure with walls of whitewashed wattle and daub at the west end of the town. It had one fat round chimney running up the front and was tightly thatched with the thick rushes that grew in the marshes. He stepped into the yard and opened the front door; with only the remnants of the setting sun he could see the house was in good shape; its floor was of sturdy oak and it even had *glass windows* instead of wooden shutters; hardwood floors and glass windows were considered a luxury back in Barnstable. It was a testimony to its landlady's generosity and compassion for her tenants. He liked the scent of the salty sea air that was blowing gently up off the channel and the sound of the river water as it gurgled pleasantly under the nearby rock bridge before it emptied into the bay. Most of all he liked the fact that he could see the masts of his ship just over a nearby hill so close he could almost reach out and touch them. Closing the door, he wandered a bit back down the street, passing the quiet little rock church and livery stable where the horses were bedded down in their stalls. Even now when the inn was packed with rowdy men their muffled laughter was a friendly welcoming sound. Porlock was indeed a nice peaceful place, and he was eager to tell Maggie about the house. He was sure she would love it too. He returned to the *Dove* and relieved Wallace from his duty having made up his mind.

At dawn he was again at the helm of the *Dove* and the crew had to forget their hangovers and tend to business. It was a typical overcast morning in Porlock; the fog bank hovered out over the channel like a long roll of white wool on a shearing floor and the air was thick with mist that dripped from the yards and made slippery the work of the crew unfurling the sails. As the *Dove* drifted out into the channel it was enveloped quickly and disappeared; it was even difficult to see from bow to stern. It didn't worry Captain Tom; he often boasted that he could sail the channel blindfolded having traveled it for so many years as a lad under his father's tutelage and then when he got his own ship. They floated along stagnant on the water for quite some time before the wind finally filled the sails, blowing directly against them from the southwest. The captain began tacking in a zig zag maneuver, attempting to make use of the wind that was fighting him and making the current very choppy and rough. Instead of dissipating however the fog was just being swirled around while the wind continued to impede the *Dove's* forward motion. The wind was sporadic, gusting and resting at odd intervals keeping the crew scrambling from port to starboard to adjust the sails and accommodate the captain's erratic course. Yet there was not sufficient wind to clear the fog away. Wallace joined him on the bridge looking concerned. "We should be nearing Ilfracombe Captain," he said.

"Aye," Tom replied. "If only this bloody fog would lift! It's bad enough we are on a windward course."

He understood Wallace's concern; the rocks off Ilfracombe could be treacherous in the fog. He was confident he was steering the ship far enough to the west toward the center of the channel; the trick was not to go so far as to be propelled out to the Celtic Sea! He knew he would clear the rocks. In a strange way these were the conditions he loved, maneuvering the *Dove* against the sea, feeling her swaying back and forth at his fingertips. He loved the sea despite its dangers; as he had told the Snow family – *saltwater ran in his veins*.

Finally, the fog began to lift enough for them to see; they had indeed steered clear of the rocks and the mouth to Barnstable Bay lie ahead, clearly marked by Hartland Point. As the Captain changed course eastward the crew knew they were as good as home, just a short stretch across the bay and up the River Taw to the port at Barnstable.

"You all have a week's leave," Captain Tom told the crew as they docked. "I have some business to attend to ashore."

Maggie was happy to have her husband home again. She had become accustomed to his absences, and she knew his stay would be brief however, so her excitement was always somewhat tempered. She and her mother were sewing at the kitchen table when he came through the door. He dropped his sea bag and crossed the room to give his wife a kiss on the cheek.

"Hello, Mother Hanfield," he said and kissed her also.

"How was your trip, Thomas?" his mother-in-law inquired without taking her eyes off her sewing.

"Quite profitable it was!" said Tom. "And an interesting trip as well."

He sat down across from the ladies at the table and began recounting the events of the last few days. His story about the coffin full of brandy didn't even elicit a smile from either of the women.

"I never have approved of smuggling, Thomas," said his mother-in-law shaking her head. "It's a shame people can't earn an *honest* living these days."

"I know, Mother Hanfield. But the taxes are outrageous. The men only want to feed their families."

What he *wanted* to say to her was "Do you know where *your* husband is right now? Do you know that Father Hanfield is at this very moment packing away illegal goods in the livery down the street to keep *you* well-fed and warm through the winter?" He was never quite sure whether his mother-in-law was actually clueless as to her husband's underground activities or if she simply was in denial. Instead, he stood up and took his bag into the bedchamber and Maggie followed a few steps behind.

"I wish you would not tell those stories to Mother. You know how she gets, Tom," she said, turning the bag upside down and emptying the soiled clothes on the floor.

"I'm sorry, Maggie. I just thought that story was amusing!" said Tom. "I promise not to mention the subject ever again."

He took her in his arms. "I saved the best news for you," he said between kisses.

"News?" asked Maggie, "What news, Tom?"

They sat on the bed and Tom told his wife of Lady Harrington's offer and of the little house in Porlock.

"You will love the Snow family. And Lady Harrington! She is a most amazing woman!"

Maggie's mouth was smiling but her eyes looked sad. "You know my parents will never move there. Barnstable is their *home*, Tom."

"It wouldn't be like we were moving to the other side of the world. We can visit often."

Maggie had never been separated from her mother and father. As much as she loved Tom, the thought of being away from the home she grew up in and the streets she knew so well weighed heavily on her heart. Tom took her by the shoulders and cupped her chin in his hand. "I want my wife to have a home of her own. I want our children to grow up in a safe, happy place. I am taking you to Porlock tomorrow to see it for yourself!"

He was sure she would change her mind once she got away from her mother's influence. Tom was so excited he could hardly wait until morning!

Chapter Fifteen "Porlock Adventure"

Tom had rented a wagon and a team of horses for the trip to Porlock intending to make the trip by land because Maggie had, surprisingly enough, a fear of the sea, quite contrary to her husband. His secret motive was to let her see the beauty of the Exmoors and the countryside surrounding Porlock since she had never been anywhere but Barnstable. He was up early, bringing the wagon back from the livery and parking it directly in front of the Hanfield gate. Father Hanfield, who had returned from his work late the night before, was already up sitting on the porch step out of the earshot of his wife. "Tom" he said quietly, laying his hand on his son in law's shoulder, "I support you in what you are doing even though my wife will no doubt be distraught at losing her daughter."

"Maggie may not even *like* Porlock, Sir," Tom said. "And, if she does, I have promised we will visit often."

"You are the head of your own family, Son. You must do what is right for you and Margaret. You'll get no opposition from me, Tom, however difficult it might be to console her mother."

Maggie had packed a bag and was sitting at her mother's bedside while her mother sniveled into a handkerchief. "Mother, we are only going for a visit. I'm not moving away just yet. Tom wants me to just see the house in Porlock, that's all. Please don't cry, Mother."

The older woman blew her nose and dabbed at her red eyes. "I just never thought you would go away. Whatever will I do without you?"

Maggie stood up and took her mother's hand. "No decision has been made yet. You must think of this as just a holiday for us. Tom needs a break from his work. Surely you won't deny him a relaxing holiday!"

She bent over and kissed her mother on the cheek. "I will see you in a few days," she said and reluctantly left the room to join her husband.

Father Hanfield hugged his daughter tightly and whispered in her ear, "Don't worry about your mother, Angel. I will cheer her up somehow. Go now and enjoy your trip."

Tom helped her up onto the wagon seat and climbed up beside her and they were off on their Porlock adventure.

They drove through town without conversation, waving mindlessly at their acquaintances as they went. Tom took the reins in one hand and put his free arm around Maggie's waist. "Come now, Maggie," he said, "at least *try* to enjoy our trip."

"I am trying, Tom. I just feel so badly for my mother," replied Maggie and fell silent again.

The horses plodded along slowly and soon the dirt road became much smoother than the cobblestoned streets of Barnstable, rising above the town and onto the high moor. The view of the channel below was indeed breathtaking; they could see westward over the cliffs as far as Lundy Island, famed for the pirates who frequented it and to the north and east were the towering peaks of Exmoor still capped with snow. The wind that blew off the mountains had a strange invigorating sting to it; so pure and cool it was. Maggie remembered as a child looking up at these very mountains from town and wondering what it would be like to look down from them. "*Is that the top of the world?*" she had asked her father at the age of six or seven, to which he had replied, "*Not quite, my child. Those are baby mountains compared to others in the world.*" Now, looking up at them she couldn't imagine mountains higher lest they touched the very feet of angels.

She was glad she had dressed warmly for soon the wind carried with it a mist caused by the rising of the damp Atlantic air and it was quickly turning it into a light rain. It lasted only a few minutes however and then the sun came out again sparkling on the mountain peaks. "The weather changes so quickly here," she said, pulling off her scarf and shaking out the raindrops. She raised her face to the sun and closed her eyes for a moment.

"Aye, it does indeed," replied Tom, pleased that she was beginning to take a little interest in her surroundings.

"Wait until we get into the woods. I think you will like that."

Maggie had a usually quiet nature, somewhat on the serious side. Tom had fallen in love with her striking beauty, her coal black hair and equally dark eyes that reminded him of a doe's eyes, soft and deep. When he first began to court her, he was hopeful that marriage would transform her into a happier person, so he proposed. Since then, however, living with her parents and with Tom at sea so much of the time, she seemed to become even more withdrawn within herself and Mother Hanfield's negative and suspicious nature seemed to dominate the mood in the household. He was encouraged now, seeing her eyes looking with interest at the beauty of the Devon countryside.

"Oh, look, Tom! Wild ponies!" Maggie exclaimed, pointing to the fields ahead.

"Yes, they are everywhere up here I'm told," said Tom. "They say they have been here since before man."

"Really?" asked Maggie, enthralled by the fuzzy little beasts grazing on the grassy slopes. As they got closer, she put her hand on Tom's arm so that he would stop the wagon. "They are as woolly as sheep! And so tiny! Aren't they *adorable,* Tom?"

Tom pulled up the team of horses and they sat for a few moments watching the ponies. "I hear they have special coats to keep them warm in the winter," he said. The information he had gained by many nights spent at local inns was suddenly becoming useful. "They have an undercoat very much like wool and a longer oily topcoat that repels the water. I hear tell they can have a layer of snow on their backs and still stay warm underneath."

"How I would have loved to have had animals when I was a child," she said sadly. Tom knew that Mother Hanfield had forbid her daughter to ever have a kitten or a puppy while she was growing up and that Maggie was never allowed to go near the livery stable. Not long after they were married, she had confessed to him that she used to sneak down to the livery in Barnstable and climb up on the fence to pet the horses there. It was a secret, she said, she would take to the grave with her.

"When you have your own house my dear you may have as many animals as you like," said Tom. "Wait until you see Lady Harrington's stable of horses! If ever I lose you, I will surely know where to look!"

He snapped the reins and moved the team ahead, wanting to reach the town of Lynmouth by nightfall, while Maggie kept straining her neck to look backward at the ponies. Soon they were on the high coastal hills looking out over the sheer cliffs of Great Hangman and upward toward Culbone Hill. When they had reached the crest, the road turned away from the cliffs and the scenery changed dramatically as they entered a dark forest of white beam trees. They came to a shallow stream of clear mountain water that sparkled with the points of sunlight filtering through the canopy of leaves above them. Maggie put her hand in the crook of Tom's arm and snuggled against his body. With eyes wide, she took in the sensual sounds and sights of the woods around them; the soothing trickle of water, the chirping of birds in the branches above, the silver slivers of sunlight and the thick greenery off which the sounds of the forest bounced softly. "Please stop, Tom. I want to touch the water."

Tom reined in the horses and helped Maggie down from the wagon. She found a pathway and tiptoed over the moss-covered river rocks to kneel beside the stream where she cupped her hands in the cold water and lifted them to her lips. "It is safe to drink this water, isn't it Tom?"

Tom nodded. "It is only the water in town that is bad, Maggie, from the waste that gets dumped in it. The water coming down from Exmoor is pure, the way God intended water to be."

"How I would love to wash my hair in it!" exclaimed Maggie. "I'll wager it would make it soft!"

"Then we shall take some home with us for your hair," he promised.

"I would like a house right here!" she said. "Right on the banks of this stream!"

Tom laughed happily. He had travelled this road many times growing up, but he felt, somehow, he was seeing it for the first time through the eyes of his wife. He watched her as she made her way along the shore, hiking up her dress and leaping from rock to rock, looking like a little girl seeing these things for the first time.

"And look, Tom! Cranberries!!! Growing wild! Please get me something I can put them in!"

Tom went back to the wagon but all he could find was her scarf.

"Will this do?" he asked.

"Oh, I don't care about that old scarf anyway. Dying it cranberry red would be an improvement," Maggie replied taking the scarf and filling it with the wild berries and tying it up like a knapsack. She picked a few more to pop into her mouth and she returned to the wagon where Tom was standing and put one in his mouth also. Tom winced at the tartness of it and made a sour face.

"Maggie, I don't know how you can eat those things without sugar on them!" he said. "They make my teeth ache!"

"I think they're delicious!" Maggie said happily smiling with lips that were already stained purple.

When they had climbed back aboard the wagon Maggie leaned over and with her cranberry-stained lips kissed

Tom on the cheek to which he responded by cupping her chin and moving her lips to his. He kissed her deeply and memories of their first night together as man and wife came vividly to his mind.

"Tom, if Porlock is half this beautiful I know I will love it there!" she whispered.

"Onward horses!!" Tom called out laughing. "We have to make Lynmouth before the livery closes!"

From there the road ran along the coastal cliffs for a while. They passed through a place called the Valley of the Rocks at the foot of the western tip of the Exmoor mountains. It was a peculiar little valley with a rocky hillside on the east and nothing but smooth green grass on the west as if God had swept the rocks off into the ocean. The little coastal town of Lynmouth turned out to be closer than he had remembered. It came into sight as soon as they had emerged from the valley; a small fishing village very much like Porlock sitting at the foot of the highlands. They pulled the wagon up in front of the livery stable at the east end of town with daylight to spare.

"I will have them hitched and ready for you in the morning mister," said the stable hand.

"Do you not remember me, Lad? Captain Hatherly of the ship *Dove*?" asked Tom.

"Oh, I do indeed, Sir! I'm not used to seeing you driving a team of horses. It's good to see you again and greetings to you too, Mistress Hatherly."

"I see that my husband is very famous," commented Maggie as they made their way through the streets toward the inn.

"Aye, but only along the coast where my work takes me and only with the men I meet in doing so. I have never stayed overnight at the inn, so I know not how soft their beds are but their food here is quite good."

Their dinner was indeed tasty; chunks of tender pork and fresh vegetables with hearty dark bread with which to sop up the broth. They lingered over dinner, drinking brandy while they watched two men playing chess at a nearby table and shared pleasant conversation with the innkeeper and his wife. Later they discovered the beds at the inn were quite comfortable and for the first time since their marriage Tom felt he had his wife completely to himself away from the prying eyes and ears of her parents and he wasted not a moment of the opportunity to convince her of his undying love. The next morning, they lingered in each other's arms until half past nine before they were on their way again, having retrieved the wagon from the livery.

"I like it here too," said Maggie.

"One in the forest and another in Lynmouth, and you have yet to see the cottage in Porlock! I fear I have opened Pandora's Box, my dear! Are we to have more houses than the king himself?"

Maggie blushed which pleased Tom immensely just to see the color back in his wife's cheeks. They rode out of town crossing a bridge that spanned a deep gorge over the fast-running River Lyn far below.

"The salmon spawn up this river," said Tom. "We shall have to come here when salmon are in season. It is delicious."

Maggie was afraid to look over the side of the narrow rickety bridge and hid her eyes in the folds of Tom's shirt sleeves until the wagon made it safely across. Then they were traveling upward on a steep incline to the high moor again, this time through herds of red deer grazing alongside the road. The road turned into a bit of a seesaw as it went along for miles rising high up on grassy plateaus and dipping down into peat mires and bogs until at long last they rounded a bend and the town of Porlock came into view. Tom looked at his wife. This was the happiest he had ever seen her since their marriage. "We're here, Maggie!" Tom said pointing down at the little cove beneath them. "That is Porlock."

She studied it; this tiny hamlet on the edge of the Bristol Channel that was to be her new home. The scent of wood burning drifted up in spirals of smoke from the town's chimneys and combined with the familiar smell of mud and saltwater at low tide. It almost *smelled* like

Barnstable, she thought. But there was no other resemblance. Porlock was as quaint as a painted picture from the tiny, thatched cottages and shops that lined the main road to the pointed steeple on the little rock church and the fishing boats bobbing up and down in the harbor. The town was cradled in the arms of the steep hills that encircled it like the protective walls of a castle: quiet, sheltered and at peace.

It looked inviting.

But was it *home*?

Chapter Sixteen "The Cursed Bed"

The day the Hatherlys arrived in Porlock just happened to be Little John's name-day and Amy Anne had decided to give him a party. The entire family had gathered that afternoon at John's farm; the Hartleys had arrived from town. Mary, her sisters, and their children came up the hill, piling into the back of her wagon to join the men who were still working in the fields. It had been a bad season; John's wheat crop had succumbed to blight and there was nothing left to harvest. While the sisters helped Amy Anne with the supper chores, their husbands finished cutting down the last of the bad wheat stalks. To keep the disease from spreading to the other crops, they had piled them up in the field to burn and the children had climbed upon the fence to watch the fire. Eating outside seemed like so much fun, Amy Anne and her sisters brought their supper out and set a "table" on the back of one of the wagons for everyone to help themselves. As the sun went down and the air cooled they were enjoying themselves too much to go inside.

"It's just like a picnic!" said Amy Anne happily. "I think we should just stay out here! Put some wood on the fire John to keep it going!"

It *was* fun; *Amy Anne always made things fun*, thought Little John as he retrieved logs from the woodpile. They overturned buckets to sit on and gathered around the fire to eat their supper balancing their plates on their knees. One of the children started to sing a song and soon they all joined in, laughing and singing and eating in the twilight and hardly noticing the wagon coming up the road.

Tom pulled the team of horses to a stop and Maggie stared at the fire and the gathering of people and children dancing around it, looking like some type of pagan ritual. Never had she seen such an event. Then Amy Anne saw them and ran to greet them. "Captain Tom! Welcome to Little John's name-day party!"

Tom helped Maggie down from the wagon. "This is my wife, Margaret," he said. "But you can call her Maggie."

"Please help yourself to some food," invited Amy Anne. "We're having a picnic!"

"Thank you, Amy, but we ate supper in town. We are on our way to Lady Harrington's. We have decided to accept her offer. Maggie likes the cottage in town."

"You might as well stay, Tom," said Little John. "Lady Harrington is off to Bristol trading horses and won't be back until tomorrow."

So, they decided to stay for the party.

"It is so exciting, Tom! We'll be neighbors!" said Amy Anne. "I am very glad you came." She took Maggie's arm. "I think you will like Porlock."

Maggie looked around. "You have a very large family!"

Amy Anne chattered away. "Yes!" she said and then she patted her stomach. "But Little John and I haven't had *our* family yet!"

"You're expecting?"

"Yes, in the fall," replied Amy Anne as she took Tom and Maggie around introducing them to everyone. Tom watched as Maggie's usual shyness seemed to dissolve under Amy's outgoing nature.

"It's time for cake!" said Amy Anne and took Maggie by the hand. "Come and help me, Maggie!"

The two retreated into the house hand in hand like little girls. Amy Anne brought out the cake and retrieved a stack of plates from the shelf.

"I was so happy when Tom said he was considering moving to Porlock. I think you will love it here, Maggie. I hope we can become good friends."

Maggie smiled. "Never would I have dreamed of living anywhere other than Barnstable. But I have discovered there is a whole new world outside. Our trip here was wonderful. I never imagined such beauty!"

"Yes," replied Amy Anne. "And you will like the people. It's like one big extended family. Wait until you meet Lady Harrington!"

"I have heard much about her from Tom."

"She is a great lady. So kind and generous. You will see!"

Amy Anne lit a candle in the fireplace and placed it on the cake. "Lady Harrington says they put candles on their cakes to celebrate name-days in the royal palace! She has had supper with the king, you know!" she said as they went back outside.

They all cheered as he came forward and blew out the candle.

Amy Anne sliced the cake and Maggie passed out the plates to everyone. When John had finished his cake, he excused himself to go feed the livestock.

"Do you have horses?" Maggie asked.

"Aye, we have. Do you ride, Maggie?" John asked.

She left Amy Anne and followed along behind him. "No, but I just *love* horses. May I watch you feed them?"

It seemed like such a silly thing, he thought to himself, wanting to watch horses *eat.* But then he remembered when he was a child and how everything about Lady Harrington's horses interested him. Tom's wife seemed almost childlike in that way.

She leaned on the fence while John retrieved the hay. Morning Star was standing aloof. *It is not like him to shy away from strangers*, John thought to himself. *Maybe it is the crowd and the bonfire that troubles him.*

"What a beautiful horse!" she said.

John nodded. "Yes, he looks just like his father who was a great warhorse. I used to care for him when I was a child."

Maggie was intrigued. "So, you grew up around horses?"

"Aye," said John. "They were pretty much my life until I started farming."

John went on to feed the cows and Maggie lingered, especially impressed by Morning Star. When he returned, she was still at the fence, watching him. Morning Star had wandered away from his feed and was standing down in the lower pasture. Maggie couldn't take her eyes off him. She seemed more at ease with horses than she did with people. They stood there for a moment, listening to the other horses snort and chomp their hay.

"Come, Morning Star!" yelled John. "Aren't you hungry, Boy?"

"I tried to feed a horse a radish once," Maggie said smiling. "I think he took it because it looked like a little apple. He sure spit it out in a hurry though!"

"Aye. They don't much take to radishes, I'm afraid. They love apples and carrots. Can't feed 'em too many though or they can get colicky."

"Clickety?" asked Maggie.

John chuckled. "Not *clickety*.... *colicky*. It means they get a stomachache."

"Oh," said Maggie.

"That can be death for a horse. They can't spew it up, you see."

"Really?" asked Maggie. "How queer!"

"Yes. For big, strong animals they have very delicate stomachs," said John.

By that time Tom had come looking for his wife.

"There you are!" he said. "I should've known I'd find you here with the horses! John, you should have seen her when she saw the wild ponies on Exmoor! If I hadn't pushed on, we'd still be there!"

John nodded. "I can certainly understand that. I love horses too."

"It's getting dark, Maggie. I think we should be making our way back into town. We will have to visit Lady Harrington tomorrow."

"Go slow on the hill, Tom. Try to keep the wagon to the inside of the road," John cautioned.

"I will. And I thank you for having us."

They said their goodbyes to everyone, and Amy Anne gave Maggie a hug. "Please come see us again very soon."

By the time they reached the top of Porlock Hill darkness had already fallen. Tom reined in the horses tightly and made them walk very slowly, hoping Lady Harrington was right when she said horses could see better in the dark than men. Maggie had closed her eyes and was leaning peacefully on his shoulder. The incline itself was bad enough but the road also jackknifed back and forth tilting the wagon at odd angles with each turn and Tom struggled to keep the wagon on the hillside away from the cliff. On the last bend it seemed as if the road narrowed, and Tom could feel the wagon listing a little more than on the other turns; it felt as though the wagon wheels had hit soft sand. When he tried to correct it by steering the horses inward toward the hillside the back wheel only sunk in deeper, and he felt the wagon start to roll backward. The horses felt it too and began to heave, pawing at the dirt. Tom urged them on with the reins, suddenly panicked that they were going to go over the edge. The more he whipped them, the more the wagon slipped, and Maggie started to scream as they all rolled off the road and down Porlock hill.

They were both thrown from the wagon while the horses landed with a thud in the brush, thrashing and squealing still pinned underneath the wooden yoke. Tom picked himself up and frantically searched in the dark for his wife. He found her lying in the grass.

"Maggie!" Tom said. "Maggie, are you hurt?"

There was no reply. He picked her limp body up in his arms and tried to climb back up to the road, digging in with his knees and repeating "Maggie! Maggie!"

Suddenly he heard voices and a wagon coming from up the road. "Help!" Tom yelled. Someone must have heard him for the voices stopped then he heard footsteps running toward them. "Please help me! My wife has been hurt!"

Peter appeared out of the darkness and reached down taking Maggie in his arms. "Are you all right, Tom?" he asked.

"Yes, I'm fine. It's Maggie. She has fainted or something."

Peter took Maggie from Tom's arms and carried her motionless body to the rear of his wagon where he placed her down gently next to the children. He felt for the pulse in her neck. Tom jumped into the back of the wagon and cradled Maggie's head in his lap.

"She's alive. Just a bump on her head I suspect. Mary can take you both back to John's house. It's the closest. I'll free the horses and go fetch the doctor."

Mary turned the wagon around and headed back up the hill.

There were still a few others at the party standing around the fire when the wagon appeared. Amy Anne was the first to run to them. "What happened?"

Tom jumped down. In the firelight his wife's blood on the sleeve of his shirt was visible.

"Bring her inside. I'll care for her," said Amy Anne.

John instructed them to put Maggie in his bed. "I can sleep by the fire tonight," he said.

"Should I go to town for the doctor?" asked Little John.

"No," said Mary. "Peter is fetching the doctor and helping the horses."

Tom was beside himself with worry sitting in a chair in the corner of the room wringing his hands. Amy got a basin of cool water and a cloth and sat on the edge of the bed sponging the blood from Maggie's forehead. "She's got quite a bump, but the cut doesn't look too bad. Don't worry, Tom. Peter will bring the doctor. She'll be all right."

Hours passed before Peter and Doctor Philby returned from town.

"I stabled your horses, Tom," he said. "One was favoring a front leg a bit, but I think he will be all right. I will get your wagon repaired tomorrow."

Doctor Philby took over for Amy Anne. After he had examined her for broken bones, he pulled the covers up around her and stood up. "All we can do now is wait. Keep her body warm but keep applying the cool cloths to her head. It is most likely a concussion and there is some swelling that must go down. She will probably wake up in a few hours."

Tom shook his head, "I never should have tried to drive that wagon. It's *my* fault."

The doctor smiled, "It's not your fault, Son. Porlock Hill isn't made for wagons, especially in the dark."

Tom remained in his chair and Amy Anne sat stroking Maggie's forehead with the wet cloth.

Peter and Mary's family said their goodbyes and were ready to leave in their wagon.

"Where is your father?" Mary asked.

Little John looked around. "I think I know where he is," he said. "You all go on home."

"Poor John," said Mary sadly. "He is at the grave, is he not? I doubt if he will ever get over your mother's death."

"I will fetch him, Aunt Mary. I will cheer him up."

Little John waved to them as they disappeared down the hill then he took the spare lantern from the kitchen and went outside. With the light of the moon and the lantern beam he made his way up the hill behind the house, past the larder, to the edge of the trees. There he found his father kneeling at his mother's grave.

Little John sat the lantern down illuminating the epitaph on the tombstone. Since Amy Anne had been teaching him to read, he could finally make out the words inscribed there:

BELOVED WIFE AND MOTHER

MARGARET ELIZABETH SNOW

DIED FIRST DAY OF AUGUST

YEAR OF OUR LORD 1430 A.D.

He had never asked how his mother had died. Now, he realized she had died giving birth to him. Now, he knew why his name days had always seemed to make his father a little sad. He put his arm around his father's shoulders. "I'm sorry, Paa. I never knew."

"You needn't be sorry, Son. 'Twasn't your fault."

"Come. Let's go home."

"Morning Star is dead," John said quietly. "I knew something was wrong with him when he didn't eat his supper. I found him in the lower pasture after all the excitement."

Little John knew how much his father had loved that horse. "He lived a good long life, Paa. We will take care of burying him tomorrow."

"This has just not been a very good day all around," John replied rising from his knees.

They turned and began to walk back down the hill together.

Old superstitions were hard to shake once they took hold and John's mind was troubled.

First the terrible accident, then the death of Morning Star. And now another named Margaret was fighting for her life on the very same day in the very same bed in which his wife had died. Was the bloody bed cursed? he couldn't help but wonder.

Chapter Seventeen "A New Home Port"

Amy Anne sat with Maggie through the night and Tom fell asleep in the chair beside the bed. At midnight, Little John came to the door in his sleep shirt, passing his father who was asleep by the fireplace. "How is she?" he whispered.

Amy Anne shook her head. "I don't know. She hasn't moved. It's like she's just sleeping. You go on back to bed, John." She tiptoed across the room and kissed him.

"I miss you," said Little John.

"I just want to stay with her until she wakes up."

As it turned out Maggie slept on and was still sleeping when Doctor Philby came back the next day to check on his patient. He came in and felt her forehead then he pried open her eyelids to look into her eyes, while Amy Anne and Tom stood nearby. "The swelling has gone down a little. She should be waking up any time now," he said. "Have you any smelling salts?"

Amy Anne said they did not.

"Get me anything that has a strong odor," said Doctor Philby. Amy Anne returned with a clove of garlic and a sharp knife. "Will this do?" she asked.

"We shall see," he said, slicing the clove open and holding it under Maggie's nostrils. At first, there was no reaction. Then her nose twitched ever so slightly, and she turned her head, but she remained sleeping. One more time he put the garlic under her nose. Her hand came up to brush it away. Then she opened her eyes and Tom rushed to her side.

"Maggie! You're awake!"

Maggie blinked and looked around the room which was fuzzy and unfamiliar. "Where am I?" she asked.

Tom took her hand and sat down on the bed as the doctor moved away. "You are in the Snow house. We had an accident in the wagon. You've been asleep for a day and a half."

Maggie attempted to sit up, but the doctor objected. "Don't try to sit up just yet. You've got a pretty good bump on your head. I want you to just rest for a while more."

Amy Anne was smiling from across the room.

"Amy Anne sat with you the whole time," Tom told her.

"Thank you, Amy," she said. "You must be exhausted."

"Now, that you are awake, I might take a little nap. I will be fine."

Amy Anne escorted Doctor Philby to the front door and thanked him.

"Amy, I want you to keep her in bed. She needs complete rest right now. Blood clots near the brain are very serious and I don't want to take any chances," the doctor said. "I'll be back tomorrow."

"I'll keep her in bed if I have to *tie* her to it," Amy Anne said with a tired smile.

"Don't forget to take care of yourself too, young lady. Remember *your* condition as well."

The next few days Amy Anne supervised the rearranging of the Snow household making it into an infirmary of sorts. Mary brought extra mattresses and they prepared makeshift beds for John and Tom near the hearth. Amy Anne tended to Maggie day and night, bringing her meals in bed, and helping her with her personal needs then sitting with her until she fell asleep every night while Tom worried and waited in the adjoining room and Little John grew melancholy from lack of attention. By the end of the week John convinced Tom he should return to his ship in Barnstable and to let Maggie's parents know of her condition. "My daughter-in-law has things well in hand, Tom," said John. "Between her and the doctor she will be fine in no time. No need to be bouncing her around in a wagon on the roads."

Tom knew it was best. Her mother would be worried if they did not arrive back in Barnstable on schedule and his crew would think he had deserted his ship. With mixed emotions he bid goodbye to Maggie. "I hate to leave you," he said sadly.

"You must go, Tom. Don't worry about me. The doctor says I should be good as new in a week or so."

He kissed her goodbye and John saddled a horse for him to ride into town. "Just leave him at the livery when you retrieve your wagon, Tom. I'll fetch him later."

Tom rode off carefully and slowly down the dreaded hill he had begun to loathe. When he reached the livery in Porlock, he was pleased that the wagon had not sustained too much damage; one repaired wheel and it was as good as new, and the horses were without serious injury. He paid the man for the repairs and left town that very afternoon, retracing the route he had taken with his Maggie. It was a sad but hurried journey and not remotely as enjoyable as his last; without her eyes he saw no wonder in the Exmoor countryside; without her hand pulling at his arm in excitement, he felt no awe in the simple things like the stream in the woods where the wild cranberries grew. He passed through Lynmouth, unable to bring himself to stop at a place that now had so many beautiful memories and when it became dark, simply pulled over and slept in the wagon alongside the road. It was a very lonely trip back to Barnstable.

Mother Hanfield was distraught and took to her bed as soon as she heard the news, refusing to have further discussion with poor Tom.

His father-in-law looked on sadly as Tom packed all of their belongings to take back to the ship. He wasn't sure how long Maggie's recovery would take; nevertheless, they had already decided to take the cottage in Porlock.

"I will miss you, Son," said Father Hanfield. "It's been good having you here with us. Please come by when you are in port and let us know how Margaret is doing. As soon as her mother feels up to it, we will come for a visit."

Knowing that possibility was highly unlikely Tom shook his hand and walked down the street toward the docks with a sea bag on each shoulder, eager to get back to Maggie. As soon as he gained sight of the *Dove* his spirit lifted. The crew, who had been anxiously awaiting his return, greeted him warmly as he came on deck.

"We're glad to have you back, Captain!" said Wallace.

"It's good to be back, Lads," said Tom. "We'll be shoving off this morning."

"We'll be running empty, Captain?"

Tom explained to his crew the circumstances and promised they would pick up cargo as soon as they dropped anchor up north. "I just have to get back as quickly as I can," he said.

The crew understood and immediately prepared the *Dove* for sailing to their new home port of *Porlock.*

Chapter Eighteen "Gifts Great and Small"

When he returned to the Snow house, he found Maggie propped up in bed playing a card game with Amy Anne. When she saw Tom, she broke into a smile and tears at seeing him again.

"How is my wife doing today?" he asked.

"She is almost ready to start taking short walks the doctor says," said Amy Anne. "She is coming along most handsomely!"

She stood up and excused herself. "We can finish our card game later, Maggie. You can have her all to yourself, Tom. I must get supper started. You *will* be staying to eat with us, won't you?"

"Yes, thank you, Amy. I would like that."

When Amy Anne left the room, Tom put his arms around Maggie and kissed her gently. "I've missed you, Sweetheart. I got back as quickly as I could. The crew is loading cargo now for Bristol, so I will have to go after supper."

"I know that Tom. I am used to having an absent husband. It must be like being married to a knight who goes off to war. I am so glad you aren't gone for months at a time!"

Her face turned serious. "Tell me, how did my mother take the news of our staying in Porlock?"

Tom shook his head and looked down at the floor.

"That bad?" asked Maggie. "Was she *that* upset?"

"I'm not sure. She went into her room and refused to speak to me after that."

Maggie rolled her eyes. "I don't know why she gets like that. Poor Father! All alone to deal with Mother's mood swings!"

"Your father said they would visit as soon as your mother is feeling up to it."

"That may be awhile," said Maggie. "Did you have a chance to speak to Lady Harrington about the house?"

"Rest assured, Wife. She gave me her word she would not rent it to anyone else until she heard from us."

He sat down on the bed trying not to scatter the cards and wooden pegs that were lying across the blankets. "What *are* you two playing?"

"Oh, it's ever so much fun Tom! Amy is teaching me a game called Crown of Roses. We play against each other to decide who will be crowned King of England."

"Much like real life I see," said Tom. "And who are you?"

"I am playing King Henry and Amy is Edward. The red wooden pegs are the armies of Lancaster and the white ones of York. She is winning though. She is far cleverer than I!"

Tom laughed. Maggie had the excitement of a little girl playing a new game. Amy Anne was good for Maggie. "If only political wars could be settled so simply!" he said.

When supper was ready and John and Little John came in from the fields, Maggie appeared in the doorway, walking ever so slowly across the room toward the kitchen table.

"Well, look at our patient! Up and walking on her own!" said John.

Tom helped his wife get seated. "I can't thank you all enough for the care you have given to Maggie. Especially you, Amy. I am in your debt."

"It has been so much fun having her here! We have become like sisters!"

Maggie smiled up at Amy Anne. "You have nursed me so well. I will have to repay the favor when your baby arrives."

After supper Tom bade his farewells to the Snow family and Maggie, promising to be gone no more than a few days. Amy Anne put Maggie to bed and retired to her own bedchamber for the first time since the accident.

Little John was ecstatic. "Welcome home, Wife! The bed will be much warmer tonight!"

Amy Anne laughed and then she gasped, her mouth falling open. "Oh, John!" she said, running to the chest of drawers in the corner of the room. "Can you *ever* forgive me? I completely forgot to give you your name-day gift!"

Little John laughed as she pulled out a small package from the drawer wrapped in thin paper and tied with string. She sat down and handed it to him.

"With all the excitement and nursing Maggie I did not remember until just now!"

Little John kissed his wife on the nose and began to unwrap the small package. Out of the paper he pulled a small parchment tract, hardly wider than his hand, held together with knotted yarn with handwritten words and a picture of a large awkward-looking ship drawn on its cover.

"It is the story of Noah from the Book of Genesis," said Amy Anne. "I translated it from one of my Latin lessons."

Little John recalled the day they had sat together on the rock wall of Porlock Bridge talking about rainbows and the memory was as fresh as if it had been yesterday. Because of Amy Anne he could now read most of the words on the pages. "Did you do the pictures too?" he asked referring to the little animal figures that were drawn in the margins of every page.

"Yes. Alas, I am not much of an artist. My *lions* look a bit like *goats*."

"It is beautiful, Amy. It is a very thoughtful gift and I have never had such a happy name-day!"

Amy Anne reclined on the bed with her hands on her abdomen. "For your next name-day I will give you a son," she said simply.

"Or a daughter! A miniature Amy Anne!" Little John laughed and put his arms around her.

"Which would you prefer?" asked Amy Anne.

Little John shrugged. "It matters not, Amy. Boy or girl. I will be happy with whatever you give me."

The candle on the dresser was burning low, its flame flickering and drowning in a tiny puddle of liquid wax, and the house was quiet and still. For now, in the darkness of their little room, Amy Anne's love surpassed any gift she could ever bestow upon him.

Chapter Nineteen "A Harrington Welcome"

When Tom returned from his voyage to Bristol, he was pleasantly surprised to find Maggie sitting outside in the sun. Her face had taken on a rosy glow, and she was sitting with a basket on her lap, shucking peas from their pods as Amy Anne picked them from her garden. He tied up his rented horse and joined them in the yard.

"You are just in time, Tom!" exclaimed Amy Anne. "Maggie is preparing supper tonight. She says I cannot set foot in the kitchen! I haven't any idea what she has in the pot!"

"She must be feeling better if she is taking over your kitchen!" Tom said as he bent and kissed his wife. "How good you look, Maggie! I do believe the country air is speeding your recovery!"

"The doctor says she is almost as good as new," said Amy Anne.

"Good enough for a visit to Lady Harrington tomorrow I hope!"

Maggie smiled wide. "Oh, Tom I would love to meet her *and her horses*!"

"Horses, horses, horses," said Amy Anne. "That is all your wife talks about, Tom. I fear she is obsessed!"

When they retired to the house joined by John and Little John from the fields Tom announced he had taken another hiatus from his work and would be moving Maggie into town as soon as they squared things away with Lady Harrington.

Amy Anne pursed her lips into a playful pout. "I will have to teach you to ride, Maggie. Then we can visit each other often."

When everyone was seated at the table, Maggie came in from the kitchen with a warm loaf of rosemary bread and a bowl of butter. When she removed the lid from the pot that had been simmering on the fire all day, the aroma of sweet carrots and hearty beef filled the room, and the men were holding out their bowls eagerly. Amy Anne sat there smiling while the men were served, overjoyed in the sight of her new friend's recovery. Then she too held out her bowl touching Maggie's hand ever so slightly. "I will miss having you here with me," she whispered.

"Little John, I think our wives will forevermore be inseparable," Tom said.

"Aye," said Little John. "Heaven help us if they ever conspire against us; we had best be on our good behavior!"

John sat mute at the head of the table listening to the conversations. He was thinking about his inheritance again and how he could not have picked young people more deserving of Lady Harrington's trust. No longer did he fear that such a bounty would go to their heads; he had raised Little John to be thrifty and wise. Amy Anne, he thought, was what he imagined Lady Harrington to have been as a young woman; vibrant and quick witted. Their alliance with Captain Tom and Maggie was just an added blessing. One day soon, he told himself, he would reveal Lady Harrington's plans.

The next morning John hitched the horses to the wagon for Tom and Maggie's trip to the Harrington manor. "You can just leave the wagon at the livery when you get back to town."

"John, I don't know how I can ever repay you for all that your family has done. I will forever be in your debt."

Tom helped Maggie into the wagon and boarded himself. Reaching down he shook John's hand warmly.

"The Lord truly does work in mysterious ways, Tom, when He can take a tragic accident and turn it into a lifelong friendship."

"I shall return your horses forthwith, Sir!" Tom said as he slapped the reins.

"There are no sharp turns between here and Lady Harrington's house, Tom. Try to keep the wagon upright this time!" John chided the captain.

"Ha!" said Tom. "I will handle it like the *Dove* with both hands on the wheel!"

Laughing, they made their way up the road with Maggie taking in all the details of the countryside. When they arrived at the manor her eyes passed quickly over the Harrington house; her immediate attention was turned toward the stable. "Tom, the stable is as almost as big as the house! How many horses do you suppose she has?"

"You will have to ask her. I am sure she will be most happy to give you a tour."

They climbed down from the wagon and started up the pathway to the house when a familiar voice rang out from an upstairs window. "Captain Tom! Welcome!"

Lady Harrington must have flown down the stairs, for she opened the door before they could knock.

"How good to see you! And this must be your wife!" she gushed.

"Yes, M'Lady. This is Maggie."

Maggie was startled when Lady Harrington gave her a warm hug; such intimacy at an introduction was unheard of in her family. Still, she thought about how quickly she had become friends with Amy Anne. The people of Porlock were very different than the people in Barnstable.

"What a pretty thing you are!" she said. "I heard all about your terrible accident and I am so pleased to see that you are up and about!"

"Yes, she even prepared the supper at the Snow house last night all by herself. The doctor says she has recovered fully from the bump on her head."

"John tells me that you are a lover of horses too! We shall get along famously!!"

"Yes, I love them, M'Lady. I have never ridden one, as my mother would not allow it when I was a child, but I have always been drawn to them."

"Well, come then. I shall introduce you to my babies. We shall have plenty of time to talk of real estate matters later."

Lady Harrington led them back down the rock path and into the barn.

The first stall that had belonged to Majesty was empty. Maggie noticed the letters carved in the stall gate. "Who is Majesty?" she asked.

"Majesty was my stallion. He died a few years back. Did you get a chance to see his son, Morning Star, before he died? They were almost identical in confirmation."

Maggie remembered the striking black horse from the night before the accident. "Yes, I saw him. I was so sorry about his death. Majesty must have been beautiful!"

"Yes," answered Lady Harrington. "There will never be another like him."

She went on to introduce by name every horse in the stable until Maggie had stroked every head, while Tom followed behind.

"Perhaps Amy Anne will bring you out sometime and you can learn to ride. She and Little John both learned their horsemanship skills right here in my arena."

"Yes, M'Lady. I would love that."

"Only if you promise you won't fall on your head again!" Tom said laughing.

They returned to the house to talk about the cottage.

"I took the liberty of having the cottage cleaned so it is all ready for you to move in. I think we can exchange shipping fees for rent Tom if that is acceptable to you. That way neither of us gets taxed on the income."

Tom agreed. "I like the way you think, M'Lady. It will be a beneficial arrangement for us both!"

"Then *off* with you two so you will not be travelling Porlock Hill in the dark again! You come visit soon, Maggie!"

Tom was a little surprised at Lady Harrington's manner; usually she wanted to extend their visits. Perhaps she wasn't feeling well; she *was* getting on in years. Perhaps she had other matters to attend to. Had he offended her in some way? He wasn't sure why he felt she was hurrying them to leave.

After passing the Snow farm, they continued on to Porlock and pulled up in front of the cottage. Maggie jumped down and Tom secured the team. "I will have to get to town to speak to the carpenter about building us some furniture. I am sure I can secure a mattress to sleep on tonight and you will want to pick out what you need for your kitchen."

"I am sorry I did not bring you a handsome dowry, Tom," said Maggie.

"Dowries are for rich noblemen, Maggie. Beside which, I have seen what some of those rich women look like...... their fathers *had* to pay to get them wed! You, my dear, are worth far more to me. I have put away a bit of money over the years. I am sure we can purchase all that we need."

Maggie opened the door and stared into the main room of the cottage. Tom had turned momentarily toward the harbor affirming that he could see the masts of the *Dove*.

"You may not have to do that, Tom," Maggie said quietly as she entered the room.

Tom followed her and was equally in awe of what he saw. The main room was fully furnished with chairs and tables and oil lamps. Throughout the house on the windows were freshly starched curtains and rugs woven from rushes were covering the floors. In the kitchen the cupboards were filled with an array of bowls and plates and mugs, and the drawers were stocked with eating utensils and large wooden spoons. The bedchamber had a plump new mattress covered with several woolen blankets and feather pillows, sitting beside an oak chest of drawers and a lovely rocking chair.

Maggie was the first to speak, "Who would have done this? Do you suppose it was Amy Anne?"

Her husband shook his head. There was no doubt in Tom's mind who had bestowed upon them such a generous gift. "'Twas Lady Harrington! I am sure of it!"

Chapter Twenty "A Knight in Nappies"

The baby that was due in the fall decided to make his appearance early. The first pain hit when Amy Anne was collecting the eggs that morning. It took her by surprise, and she dropped two eggs on the ground that were immediately pecked to pieces by the chickens at her feet. She didn't want to panic; it was only *one* pain after all. Maybe, she surmised, it was just gas. She'd had a lot of that lately especially with the abundant crop of fava beans from the garden they had been enjoying of late. Little John and his father were down in the barley fields in the vale that day and she was all alone on the farm going through the ritual of her morning chores. She took what was left of the eggs to the larder and drew herself a mug of milk. If it was just gas, hopefully the milk would calm it.

Returning to the house she sat down at the kitchen table and drank her milk, waiting for another pain. When there was none, she went out to her garden to harvest some vegetables for supper. She bent over the lettuce patch to pick some fresh greens when the second pain doubled her over and she fell to her knees in the dirt.

Oh my! That was a good one! she thought, picking herself up and brushing the dirt from her skirt. Amy Anne thought herself quite prepared for the birth of her child;

she had studied all she could and had asked questions of her mother and Little John's Aunt Mary until she could think of nothing else to ask. She knew there would be pain. She was ready for that. Now that it was upon her, she went over in her mind all the advice she had been given. *Relax and breathe,* she thought. She could do that.

She returned to the house where she raised the pot on the fire a few inches higher to keep it at a slow simmer in case she couldn't get back to it right away and found the thick wool pads she had stitched together for just this purpose spreading them across the bed to absorb the fluids. She fetched her sewing scissors, a spool of twine and her monthly "women's rags" from the chest of drawers laying them at the foot of the bed. Having removed her skirt and covering herself with a blanket she stretched out her legs and felt for movement in her belly. In her hand she held a small hourglass to time the contractions which she balanced over her swollen navel and began to count.

In the space of an hour, she only felt one more pain. Just as she was becoming convinced it was only gas after all, and she pulled herself up into a seated position on the bed, she felt a gush of water between her legs and the stickiness that followed. *No,* thought Amy Anne. *This is the real thing.* Suddenly she wanted Little John; not because he would know what to do but just to know he was near. Then, as was Amy Anne's nature, she thought how funny it would be if she delivered the child all by herself and had him bathed and swaddled before the men returned from the fields to find their supper on the table! Another pain interrupted her thoughts; half an hour had passed since the last. They were coming quicker. She took a deep breath and closed her eyes. Maybe she would just daydream in between contractions.

There had been much discussion on what name their son would have; they both were sure it would be a boy. They had rejected the idea of calling him John feeling there were already enough Johns in the house. Peter, Henry, and Thomas too had been considered. Finally, they had agreed on the one they both liked the best: Richard, after King Richard the Lion Heart. They had not even considered a girl's name they were both so sure of the baby's gender.

Amy Anne put the palms of her hands on her swollen abdomen. "Hello Richard," she said aloud in the silent room. "This is your mother speaking." *I wonder if he can hear me,* she thought; *I wonder if he will know my voice since I have held so many conversations with him.* "You will like it here, little one. Your daddy will be so proud of you!" she said to him. "Oh…….my……!" she shrieked, caught unaware by the next pain. "We will have to talk later, my little knight. Mother is going to be a little busy for a while."

Soon the hourglass was of no use; the pains were coming too rapidly. *I shall start counting*, she thought, *just to keep my mind busy. I must not panic. This is a natural thing and babies are born all the time.* "One, two, three, four, five" she began. When she reached fifty her body contracted again. "Fifty Sssssix, fifty sssseven, fifty-eight, fifty-nine," she continued and kept counting.

Soon the contractions felt different, more like pressure than pain, much stronger and lower on her body. She realized the baby was moving downward. She felt more fluid escape and she reached down between her legs. *The baby's head! I can feel it! Now is the time to push!* The word *unbearable* came to her mind but she refused to listen. "Eighty-one…. eighty-two…" she was almost out of breath and found it difficult to keep her mind on her counting. "Eighty-three…. eighty-four…."

"Push!" she yelled into the silence of the empty house and push she did with all her strength pulling her knees up to her chest. *The baby is almost here*! said her inner voice. Her hands were shaking; her forehead was dripping with sweat. She waited with eyes closed and breathing as much air into her lungs as she had the energy to do. *You can do this Amy Anne!* she repeated over and over in her mind.

The last pain was intense; she pushed as hard as she could. Suddenly the extreme pressure was relieved, replaced by mild cramps in comparison. She heard a raspy cry and looked down to see the babe, streaked with blood and wiggling like a pollywog between her knees. Exhausted and limp she could not sit up immediately; she could feel the baby's body touching her inner legs and she cradled him between them. She raised her head for a moment and could see that it was a boy. He continued to cry and cough and squirm against the cool air to which he was not accustomed. Just when she thought it was over another sharp pain came as the afterbirth was expelled from her body.

Amy Anne pulled herself up into a halfway sitting position and reached for the baby pulling him close to her breast. She covered them both with the woolen blanket and leaned back to rest for several minutes against the pillow. She could feel his tiny fingers scratching against her blouse and she pressed her nose against his tiny head that was covered in black hair just like his father. His smell lingered in her nostrils. She held his tiny hand in hers and with her other hand felt the curve in his little back and the roundness of his pink bottom.

 Determined but feeling weak she rolled the baby off her stomach onto the bed and tried to stand. She reached for her women's rags and secured them between her legs tying them in a knot around her waist. With hands trembling she picked up her scissors and tied off the baby's umbilical cord with the twine. When she was sure the twine was tight enough to cut off the blood flow, she snipped it off close to his little navel, wrapping the afterbirth in a larger rag to dispose of it.

She had been standing on her feet too long and dizziness caused her to collapse against the straw mattress. She sat down and gripped the bed frame to steady herself. The baby seemed to be looking up at her although his eyes seemed glazed and unfocused. *How handsome you are, my little knight!* she thought. *So much like your father!*

Amy Anne was determined to stand up again and she put her feet on the floor. With a deep breath she gathered up the soiled pads and fetched a basin of water with which to wash the baby. She swaddled him tightly placing him in a large basket she had saved for the occasion. Once more dizziness swept over her, and she was forced to sit down beside the basket on the bed and let her body rest again. "We did it!" she said weakly to the baby. Proudly, she thought a*nd all by ourselves!*

When John and Little John came in shortly after from the fields, they were tired and hungry. Little John lifted the lid and peeked in the pot on the fire, tasting the broth with his fingers. "We are starving, Wife! Why is there no supper on the table?" he called playfully.

"I'll be there in a minute, Little John," Amy Anne replied from the bedchamber. "Did you both wash your hands?"

Father and son glanced at each other and obediently went into the kitchen to the wash basin. Amy had her rules and they obeyed them if they wanted to eat.

When Amy Anne appeared standing in the doorway her husband stared at her for a moment. "Are you feeling all right Amy? You look peculiar," remarked Little John.

Something *was* different about his wife. He couldn't quite put his finger on it. She looked……. *thinner!*

"Amy Anne!" he exclaimed, nearly shouting. Fear came over him until he saw her smile; that girlish smile she always had when she had a surprise for him.

He ran to the bedchamber and saw the basket on the bed. "But how? When?" he blubbered. "And *what are you doing out of bed*?"

Amy sat down next to the basket and watched as Little John peeked over the edge of the blanket. The baby was sleeping soundly.

"A boy?" he whispered.

Amy Anne nodded.

"He's *beautiful*," said Little John, taking Amy Anne into his arms and he began to cry. "You are a most amazing, Wife!"

Amy Anne beamed with pride to hide her exhaustion. "Little John, women have been having babies for thousands of years. It's *hardly* a miracle," she boasted.

Her father-in-law came to the bedroom door. "I will fetch Little John's aunts. They will come and help you, Amy."

John seemed reluctant to enter the room.

"Do you not want to see your grandson, John?" asked Amy Anne and John timidly approached the bed. He stood there not saying a word, marveling at the baby in the basket that looked very much like his son, his joy tempered by bitter memories. "I will go fetch the ladies straightaway," he said.

Amy Anne looked up at her father-in-law. "It can wait until morning. I will be all right tonight, John. But, when you go, can you fetch Maggie too? I know Tom is at sea. I would like to have my best friend with me as well."

"Of course, Amy."

"You both go eat your supper now before it scorches."

"And you must get back into bed where you belong," said Little John.

The next morning John hitched the horses to the wagon and was off to spread the good news, stopping first at Mary's house and then proceeding on to Porlock. Within an hour the Snow house was full of happy well-wishers; Mary, Agnes, and Sarah were scurrying around Amy Anne's bed taking laundry out to be done and bringing her breakfast and the men were feeding the livestock when John returned from town with Maggie.

Maggie went quickly to Amy Anne's bedside and bent to kiss her friend on the forehead. The babe was sleeping soundly beside his mother, cradled in the crook of her left arm.

"I am happy for you, Amy Anne," said Maggie. "I wish I could have been here for you."

Amy Anne smiled up at her. "It matters not, Maggie, for you are here now."

Maggie was in awe of the infant. "He is just beautiful, Amy. And what have you decided to name him?"

"We have decided on Richard after the good king Richard the Lionheart," replied Amy Anne. "I just know my little knight in nappies will be a *real* knight someday!"

Maggie sat on the edge of the bed and spoke in a low whisper, out of earshot of the other women. "Tom does not know it yet, but *I am expecting too.*"

Amy Anne's eyes danced. "Oh Maggie, that is the best news ever! We will be able to raise our babies together. Maybe you will have a girl and they can grow up and marry one day! Would that not be wonderful?"

Maggie nodded. "Please do not tell anyone until I have had a chance to tell Tom the news."

"It will be our secret, but I am ever so glad you told me!"

Mary and the other family members returned home that afternoon, but Maggie stayed on to care for Amy Anne and take care of the household duties. Little John, who up until then had been afraid to hold the baby, finally carried him to the kitchen table where he held him with one arm while he ate his supper with the other and his father marveled at how quickly Amy Anne was up and around. He was beginning to see what a truly remarkable girl his son had married and with each passing day the old memories that haunted his mind began to come less often.

Chapter Twenty-One "Double Trouble"

Unbeknownst to Maggie, Tom had returned from the sea that very morning. The sun was already approaching the center of the cloudless blue sky when they tied up at the dock in Porlock having delivered a load of contraband goods outside Bristol the night before. Tom disembarked and went directly to the cottage to see his wife. When he called out for Maggie and there was no reply, he was sorely disappointed. The house was empty, but the embers of a morning fire were still glowing hot in the fireplace. He suspected she was probably with Amy Anne. He stowed his sea bag inside and walked into town to the livery.

"Good morn to you, Captain!" said the stable hand seeing Tom's now familiar face. "Will you be needing a horse again?"

"Aye," said Tom. "But I think it is time I *purchased* a wagon and a *team* of horses. I can see that my trips up the road will be frequent from now on. Perhaps you can suggest where I may enter into such an arrangement?"

"Indeed, I can, Sir. Mister Potter, the wainwright, just down the way, always has at least one wagon for sale and I have two mares I can sell you."

"How much for the horses?" asked Tom.

"For you, Captain, eight quid should cover it," replied the stable hand, "And for that price I will throw in the harness as well."

"And can you give me a lesson in harnessing too?"

The stable hand laughed. "There is nothing to it, Captain. You will learn in no time at all!"

And learn he did. He spent an hour in the stable learning the art of getting the bit into the horse's mouth and how to run the long reins through the metal rings on the yoke. When he felt he had mastered that he was off to the wainwright's shop.

Mister Potter came to the shop door. "Are you becoming a landsman, Captain?" he asked, a bit startled at Tom's request.

"No, but my wife has made friends in the hill country, and I must have a way to escort her back and forth."

"Oh, I see," said Potter. "You'll need a double yoke and two horses then if you will be travelling Porlock Hill. It's far too steep for one horse to handle a wagon alone."

"I expected as much," laughed Tom, "and I am prepared to pay you a decent price. Without a wagon I fear I will never see my wife again!"

By the end of the afternoon Tom had become the owner of a team of horses and a wagon and had arranged to board the horses at the livery until such time he could build a corral for them behind the cottage. "I will come for them in the morning. I will never again travel Porlock Hill in the dark!"

He stopped at the inn for some supper before he returned home and sat down at his usual table near the door; the inn was empty except for two strangers sitting at a table near the kitchen. When the innkeeper brought him his food, Tom asked quietly, "Who are those men?"

The innkeeper, in a voice barely above a whisper, answered, "Tis the new tax men. I hear tell the king fired those lazy ones."

The men were watching Tom, casting glances over their shoulders at him with suspicious eyes. Finally, one of them stood up and approached Tom's table. He was dressed in a tight tunic and a leather vest and sported a sword on his hip. He spoke in an arrogant manner. "You are Captain Hatherly of the *Dove*?" he asked.

"Yes, I am," replied Tom. "I don't believe I know you, Sir."

"Well, I expect we will be seeing quite a lot of each other in the future. My partner and I have been assigned to the Porlock docks. It appears there has been a bit of mischief going on here abouts and we're here to correct that."

Tom kept his voice calm. "I am sure I don't know of any mischief. Porlock is a very quiet port."

The second man got up from his table and joined them. "Not as quiet as you would like the king to think," he said. This one was taller and older with graying hair and pock marked cheeks above his beard. "But we will uncover the rascals wherever they may be hiding. You can wager on that! And the *gallows* will be their end!"

With that they left abruptly. The innkeeper came and sat down in the chair across from Tom. "They'll be trouble, those two," he said.

Tom nodded. "I'm afraid you are right."

Tom needed to return to his ship and warn his crew. He finished his supper and rose to leave.

"Be careful, Tom," said the innkeeper.

When Tom arrived at the docks, he immediately looked around for the king's men but they were nowhere to be seen. Just as he took his first step up the gangway Wallace was there to greet him.

"Have you encountered the new tax men" Tom asked.

"Aye," replied Wallace. "They were here earlier, asking a lot of questions."

"What kind of questions?"

"They wanted to know the name of our captain, which ports we had been to recently and who our main shippers of goods were."

Tom's voice was edgy. "What exactly did you tell them?"

"No more than I had to, Sir, I swear. They asked to see our manifest and I didn't see any harm in that."

"Whose names did you give them?"

"Only Master Hartley and Lady Harrington."

Tom looked again down the dock wondering where the men had gone and what it was they were up to. The ship was empty with nothing to hide but he knew he had to get to Lady Harrington to warn her of their presence as quickly as possible.

"Go warn Hartley. I will ride out to Lady Harrington's."

He dared not take the wagon in the dark; he would just have to bring Maggie home later. For now, he returned to the stable and saddled up one of his newly purchased horses and started up the road. The further away from town he got the blacker the darkness became. By the time he reached the foot of Porlock Hill he had to strain his eyes to even make out the road. "I think I shall call you Beacon, for you are truly my light in the dark," he said to the horse. *Now I am talking to horses!* he thought. *Madness is sure to follow!*

"Beacon", while not the handsomest of horses, was a sure-footed animal and knew the hill well enough to stay close to the inside of the road and avoid the cliff's edge. Tom's hands gripped the reins tightly, anxious to be on level ground again. "Where is the bloody moon tonight?" he said aloud.

Just as he felt the horse's stride change from labored climbing to an even walk, he saw ahead a light from the Snow house, a single lamp flickering in the window. As much as he wanted to stop and see his wife again, he dared not waste any time getting to Lady Harrington's, so he pushed on. Again, the road took a turn upward, though not nearly as steep as the hill. As soon as they scaled the last rise, he could see the lights of the manor house; beyond it he could see brilliant orange flames shooting into the night air. Without thinking he urged the horse on into a canter, holding on to the saddle for dear life.

The manor house was in no danger, being made of stone and brick; but they had unfortunately built the stable from wood. It was burning along with the fencing surrounding it as well as the framework and drying trays of her hops field; anything that had been constructed with wood was in flames. The grooms had led all the horses out and secured them in a lower pasture away from the fire. Lady Harrington herself sat on the front lawn with the house servants who could only sit idly by and witness the destruction. He went to her side and knelt beside her. "M'Lady, are you hurt?"

Lady Harrington turned her head slowly, looking at Tom with a somber expression. "Tom? What are you doing here?" she asked.

"I was coming to see you when I saw the flames."

"All of John's hard work on the hops field! My barn and all my fencing! We tried to save it, but buckets of water did no good."

"Do you know who did this?"

Lady Harrington nodded. "Indeed, I do. They left their calling card in the tar they used to kindle the fire."

Tom shook his head. "They had no right."

"Why did they have to burn my *barn,* Tom? Now my babies will have to stand in the snow until I can build a new one."

She stood up and turned toward Tom. "I will be going to town at first light, "she said defiantly. "I want to look into the eyes of the knaves that did this."

"Do you think that is a good idea, M'Lady? For your own safety, I urge you to reconsider."

"They would never have gotten away with this when Lord Harrington was alive. I am sure my husband is turning over in his grave this very moment."

The last of the barn roof collapsed with a loud crash and the flames soon dwindled down to heaps of smoldering ash. Lady Harrington retreated to the house. "You are welcome to rest here until morning, Tom, although my couch is not the most comfortable for sleeping. My cook will prepare something for you to eat if you are famished."

"M'Lady, will you allow me to accompany you into Porlock? I fear of you going alone."

She smiled and shook her head. "No, Tom. This is something *I* must do. I do not wish to bring you and your family into it. I am not afraid of those men. Only cowards tiptoe around in the dark burning barns."

"Will you at least allow me to ride along with you as far as the Snow farm then?" Tom was hoping John could talk some sense into her and convince her not to go on this dangerous mission.

"That would be fine, Tom," she said as she began to ascend the stairs. "Goodnight."

Tom reclined on the lady's couch resting his head on a tiny round cushion, but sleep was elusive. He was still awake by the time the sun hit the stained-glass windows to the east streaming through in vivid blues and intense reds. For the first time he noticed the pictures depicted in the windows; each had the Harrington family crest against a blue sky. In the sunlight they cast rays of rainbow- like colors on the walls of the great room. He had no sooner sat up from the uncomfortable couch to stretch when Lady Harrington came briskly down the stairs, dressed impeccably in a bright blue gown, her hair hidden under an elegant headdress that arched high over her head and framed her face with a crust of pearls. She noticed his expression of wonderment at her appearance. "You look surprised, Tom. I have to dress accordingly to have an audience with the *king* do I not?"

Tom was dumbfounded. "M'Lady, I thought you were just going into Porlock to confront the perpetrators of the crimes against you!"

"I am, Tom, I am. First, I will get their confessions and then I am going to see the king himself. My husband would not have done less under the circumstances!"

"M'Lady, I must strongly caution you against doing this!" Tom pleaded.

She would hear nothing of his warnings, and she marched out of the house toward what was left of the barn. "Were you able to save all the saddles?" she inquired of her lead groom.

"Yes, M'Lady. I have stored them in your carriage for now," he replied.

"Well go and fetch me that wretched old side-saddle and put it on my black mare. I am going to London!"

"But M'Lady, that is a very long distance!" said the groom. "Would you not prefer to ride in your carriage?"

"No," she said. "I hate riding in that bumpy old thing. I would prefer to ride astride but that would never do in the city. Hurry now I must be on my way!"

The horses were saddled, and the grooms looked on as the pair rode off together. "These old saddles feel so clumsy to me now," she said, "I do wish that before I die it will become fashionable for women to ride as men do. It makes ever so much sense."

Tom smiled. He was still trying to figure out a way to talk her out of her dangerous plan. *Maybe John will have more luck*, he thought to himself. He was wrong. When they arrived at the Snow farm, Amy Anne and Maggie came running out of the house at the sight of them and the men came in from the field. Tom dismounted and embraced his wife.

"When did you get home?" Maggie asked happily.

While Lady Harrington rode her horse down to meet John Tom explained about the fire to the women.

John was aghast when he found out what Lady Harrington was planning to do. "You *mustn't,* M'Lady!" he said emphatically. "At least not *alone*! Let us ride with you! The roads to London are riddled with thieves and worse."

She had always trusted John's opinion and, while she was not the least bit in fear of the rascals who had set the fire, she had not considered what evil might lie on the long road to London. She thought about it for a few moments as they walked alongside her horse back to the house. "All right, John. I will allow you to come if you think it is wise."

"I will ride with you as well!" said Tom.

"And I as well!" chimed in Little John.

"Goodness," said Lady Harrington, "am I to take *all the men in Porlock*? Who will stay behind and tend to business?" She looked at Amy Anne and Maggie. "I do not want to put your men in danger. I will respect your concerns."

Amy Anne spoke first. "Lady Harrington, we all owe allegiance to you. For myself, I am proud that my husband seeks to protect you!"

"And what about you, Maggie? How do you feel about the matter?"

Maggie came forward and bowed her head. "My gracious lady, you have done so much for us that we can never repay you. I would consider it an honor that my husband rides with you."

She reached down and squeezed Maggie's hand affectionately. "Well, that settles it then!" said Lady Harrington. "Saddle your horses, John. The king's men should be on the docks by now."

The lady and her loyal protectors rode off down Porlock Hill waving to Amy Anne and Maggie who were still standing in the road and soon arrived at the rock bridge outside of town.

"Have you a weapon, Tom?" asked John.

"Aye. I have a knife in my belt."

Lady Harrington looked at Tom. "They would not *dare* challenge me," she said. "Keep your knives tucked away and let me handle this."

Their arrival did not go unnoticed. There were several men on the docks, but it was not difficult to pick out the king's men; in their nappy woolen tunics and weathered leather vests they had the look of hired thugs.

"Lady Harrington!" one of them said, bowing as she rode her mare right up and stopped within a few feet of them. "What brings you to the docks?"

Lady Harrington starred coldly into their eyes until both men fidgeted under her direct gaze. "You are King Henry's men?" she asked.

"Yes, M'Lady. What can we do for you?"

"My barn was burned down last night" she said. "I want to arrest those responsible."

The two men looked at each other; in their eyes was a mixture of surprise and fear.

"Alas, M'Lady, we were assigned only to supervise the *docks*. The king did not grant us any authority to settle *local disputes*."

Lady Harrington was seething underneath her calm demeanor. "But what am I to do? I am but an unfortunate widow. I have no husband to protect me from such vandals! Surely the king's gentlemen would come to the aid of a lady in distress!" Referring to them as gentlemen was galling her so much that she could hardly restrain herself.

"Well then how can we assist you, M'Lady?"

"Can you at least *investigate* the matter?" she pleaded.

"How did they gain access your property? Do you not have *walls* around your estate to guard against such assaults?"

"I have never had the need for walls around my estate until now," she replied. "And, even if there *were* walls, the serpents that did this cowardly thing would just slither under them!"

The men looked at each other again. "What do you wish us to do, then, if you leave yourself so vulnerable?"

"Promise me you will seek out these culprits and punish them severely!"

"Yes, M'Lady. We will do our very best." The men were growing impatient and were willing to promise her *anything* to be rid of her.

Lady Harrington reached down from her horse and extended her hand to the man. "Do I have your *word* on that, Sir?" she asked demurely.

The king's man reached out and took her hand, bowing his head with feigned respect. Lady Harrington looked down and held his fingers tightly in hers. There was the proof she was looking for: *the undeniable stain of black tar in the creases of his knuckles and under his nails.* Tar was not an easy thing to wash away quickly! "It is as I expected!" snapped Lady Harrington. "*You* are the snakes that burned my barn!" Before the men could react, she turned toward the captain. "Have you any rope on board, Tom?"

Any physical prowess the king's men may have possessed was far outweighed by their lack of mental abilities. They immediately froze, their eyes bulging in fear, thinking she intended to hang them on the spot. Anticipating trouble, both Tom and John dismounted quickly from their horses. One of the men reached down to draw his sword but Little John quickly overpowered him and held him down on the dock while John managed to restrain the other.

"Yes, M'Lady, I believe I do," Tom replied and went on board to fetch the rope.

"Tie them up then. Put them in the hold and padlock the hatch. I don't want them to go *anywhere* until I have spoken to the king."

As soon as the king's men were safely imprisoned on the *Dove,* she urged her mare on and the four rode out of Porlock.

Chapter Twenty-Two "The Lady and the King"

By the year 1437, when Henry VI had reached his legal majority, his kingdom was rapidly crumbling around him. Although he was still young, he seemed to have absolutely no interest in government or warfare for that matter. He might have been more successful as a monk for he was piously religious and abhorred the thought of bloodshed. To make matters worse, he surrounded himself with a circle of advisors who had no scruples about taking advantage of his naiveté. In his youth, and continuing throughout his life, he wore the round toed shoes of a farmer and sported a long gown with a rolled hood like a commoner. He had no desire to look or act like a king and when, on formal occasions he was required to wear his crown, he wore a hair shirt under his royal robes to atone for it.

In 1446 he married Margaret of Anjou to help improve relations with France. Instead of insuring peace however it quickly led to war. By 1453 most of French lands under English control had been forfeited, in some part due to the advice of the Queen. It was said the king would *promise her anything.* It was a terrible mismatch, however. She dominated the weak Henry although he rarely came near her. Henry began to have periodic fits of insanity. When, eight years into the marriage Margaret finally conceived a child, Henry was sure it was by *divine intervention*.

By 1460, when Lady Harrington and her escorts arrived in London, the queen had allied herself with the Duke of Suffolk, whom she considered a father-like figure, and the Duke of Somerset with whom she was accused of having a love affair and was off waging war in the north against Richard of York while her husband the king was sitting idle at home.

Although it had been many years since Lady Harrington had been to London, it was much less attractive than she remembered it. *Perhaps*, she thought to herself, *I only had eyes and ears for my husband and failed to notice the coarseness of the city.* For Tom, John, and Little John, who had never been east of the Cotswolds, it was a revelation. They arrived early, just as the city gates were being opened for business after spending the last night of their journey at the home of one of Lady Harrington's dear friends. It gave her time to refresh her outfit, which was dusty and wrinkled from the long ride, and she tried to get a good night's sleep. Sleep however eluded her that night; Lady Harrington was too busy rehearsing the words she planned to say to the king.

They rode down a narrow street toward the east end of the city; it was one of only two that had been paved with cobblestones, the rest of the streets were mere dirt pathways, muddy and strewn with litter and smelling of waste, both animal and human. Flocks of grey-winged kites circled in the skies above the city like vultures waiting for death, to feed off the garbage that lay rotting in the streets. As they passed the steps of St. Paul's church hordes of beggars and pickpockets encircled them, pulling at the lady's skirt and the men's trousers.

"Alms for the poor, M'Lady?" they cried in a continual drone. Suddenly surrounded by a sea of dirty uplifted palms she dared not give to one thereby causing a riot among the rest. She reached into her pouch and threw a handful of gold coins far across the street to temporarily divert their attention and keep them from pulling her off her horse. Quickly they rode off before the horde returned. *My God how I miss Porlock*! thought Lady Harrington.

The north bank of the River Thames came into view, and they finally reached the outer gatehouse of the king's castle. John, Little John, and Tom stared up at the intimidating rock walls on the other side of a wide moat while an armed guard approached Lady Harrington's horse.

"I wish to have an audience with the king," she said confidently. "I have an important matter I would like to discuss with him."

"Your name, M'Lady?" asked the guard most politely.

"Lady Harrington of Somerset," she replied. "Wife of the late Lord Harrington of the king's army."

"And these are your men?" he asked, pointing at the others behind her.

"Yes. Master John Snow and his son John and Captain Tom Hatherly of Porlock. They have been kind enough to escort me on my journey."

The guard turned from Lady Harrington and sent a young messenger to announce them to the king. "If you will be so kind as to wait a moment, M'Lady, we shall inquire whether the king is entertaining visitors at this time."

Lady Harrington said nothing to betray her feelings. *He is probably still sitting on his privy*, she thought smugly. She had never met this new king; she had only heard rumors of his unseemly behavior. She hoped she had come on a good day when the king was in his right mind, not on a bad day when he would be ranting and talking to ghosts.

The messenger returned and whispered to the guard, and they were granted entrance to the inner courtyard. As the messenger walked ahead, they rode their horses over a wooden drawbridge that spanned the putrid moat, the vile fumes of which impregnated the air around them. Lady Harrington covered her nose with her scarf to avoid the overwhelming stench. Inside the second gate that was set in the castle wall was another city within a city, busy with blacksmiths, weavers, coopers, and other craftsmen who were conducting the daily business of the royal household. Chickens and goats ran about freely, and several women were scrubbing laundry in large basins and hanging it out to dry. The lady and her entourage were directed to the stable where the king's horses were housed.

John came forward and assisted Lady Harrington down from her horse.

"I am so sore from this miserable saddle," she whispered. "I hope I never have to make this trip again!"

"Shall we remain here, M'Lady?" he asked.

"Yes," she replied. "I will see the king in private. See that they water our horses and rest awhile. I shouldn't be long."

She followed the young messenger into an inner chamber of the royal residence and up a flight of stairs that led to a long hallway lined on either side with high straight-backed chairs.

"Please be seated, M'Lady. The king will be with you shortly," the messenger said and disappeared back down the stairwell.

When the king entered the hall her first impression of him was that he did not look like his father at all. He had a long horse-face and unkempt hair and was most unattractive. He approached her with his head bowed, in an almost subservient manner and she rose and curtsied properly.

"Welcome to London, Lady Harrington," he said in a low voice barely above a whisper. The vast difference between the king and his father was apparent in every aspect of his mannerisms. She could still remember the commanding voice of Henry V.

"Thank you, Your Majesty, for seeing me on such short notice. I would not have imposed upon your privacy had it not been a matter of utmost importance."

She followed the king into a room which must have sufficed as his office. There was a large desk in the middle strewn with papers and half-eaten food and a portrait of the king himself on the wall behind it. The room was dark except for a single oil lamp burning on a side table and the air smelled of musty linens. *Probably the king's unwashed undergarments,* she thought to herself in disgust for the king's appearance was most appalling. Indeed, all of London smelled badly, including the king!

The same messenger who had escorted her into the castle returned with a large book which he handed to the king and then disappeared again.

"What matter is it you wish to discuss with me?" asked the king, sitting behind the desk.

"Your Majesty, my property has been destroyed by two of your men. I am here to seek their punishment and their removal from Porlock."

She wasn't at all sure the king was listening. He seemed to be staring into the air between them. Slowly he opened the book given to him by the messenger and after reading for a moment looked up at her. "I see that your wool production has diminished considerably in the past few years Lady Harrington. Have you an explanation for that?"

"Yes, Your Majesty I do. My husband died a year after he served your father at Agincourt. Since that time, without the help of a husband, I have been forced to downsize my operations. I am no longer a young woman, and I can barely keep up with the flocks I have now."

"It has also been reported that you have been growing hops for a while now and we have yet to see a profit!"

"There is an explanation for that as well, Your Majesty. The hops venture was an experimental one, unlike any I have ever attempted before. It is a *perennial* crop and it produced very little the first two years. Last season, it barely supplied the needs of our local ale makers. Not only that but---"

The king did not let her finish her sentence. "It appears you have a lot of wasted land, Lady Harrington. Perhaps you should consider signing it over to someone who will make better use of it."

She was furious. Her foot was tapping and her knuckles on her clenched fists were white with anger. He meant turn it over to *him* no doubt! "With all due respect, Your

Majesty, I made a promise to my late husband to keep his estate intact. And now, your men have completely destroyed my hops operation and my barn by burning them to the ground without any provocation! I shall have to re-build, and it will be another two years before the plants are producing again! That is the matter I came to discuss!"

There was an extended silence.

"Do you have proof that it was *my* men who committed these crimes?"

"Yes. I would not have accused them otherwise. I caught them with the very evidence on their own hands!"

"Where are these men now?"

"I have secured them in the hold of a ship. Is it not my right as the landowner to detain them? Shall they be allowed to freely terrorize me and the people of Porlock and get away with it?"

She knew she was winning the argument. The king's shoulders slumped, and he rarely raised his head that was hidden by his hooded garment. It appeared he could not come up with anything else to say. At that moment, she was actually glad he was henpecked by the queen. Perhaps this time being a woman would prove to be an *advantage*!

"I will send for them and have them brought back here for punishment," said the king.

"Will you be replacing them with others?"

"M'Lady, there is rampant smuggling going on in every port in England. I cannot run a country without being able to tax goods bought and sold. There were rumors that…"

This time it was Lady Harrington who interrupted. She was no longer afraid of this pitiful excuse for a ruler. "They were just that, Your Majesty, *rumors*! Porlock has long been a law- abiding town. We have had no trouble until your men came brandishing their swords and accusing us of the sins of others!"

The king was silent for a long moment before he uttered a response. "Very well then. I will hold you to your word. See to it that I do not have reason in the future to change my mind!"

Lady Harrington rose and bowed again to the king. "Thank you, Your Majesty," she said.

Triumphantly she picked up her skirts and marched out of the room. As soon as she had left a curtain in the corner of the room moved and a tall grey-haired man appeared and crossed the room toward the king, having listened to the entire conversation in secret. "Do you actually *believe* her, Your Grace? When we know she is hiding bushels of hops and importing them in secret to all the ports on the west coast?"

The king's advisor was aghast that the king had given in to her so readily.

"My dear Mr. Percy," replied the king. "I may be sometimes insane, but I am far from stupid. The lady owns a good deal of prime land in Somerset and Devon. She is now an aging widow with no children to inherit her wealth. Her holdings will be back in our hands in a very short time. You must learn *patience* my friend. *Any buzzard can tell you it is a virtue that is most valuable.*"

Chapter Twenty-Three "The Long Road Home"

The return trip from London was, for the most part, uneventful except for a rainstorm they encountered several miles outside the small town of Swindon and were forced to take shelter in a farmer's barn. The sky was black and ominous, and it looked as if the rain would not stop soon so they decided to settle in for the night; the men took the straw on the main floor and allowed Lady Harrington the privacy of the hay loft above. She found climbing the ladder a bit awkward in her long dress, but her straw bed was quite comfortable.

"I'll wager this is the first time you have slept on the hay, M'Lady!" called Tom.

"Oh no, Tom," she replied. "I have spent many nights in the barn with my babies."

She recalled the night Majesty died in her arms and she began to recount the life of her beloved stallion. "When Majesty was first born, I knew he was destined to be a warhorse," she began. "He was stronger and braver than any colt we ever raised, afraid of nothing he was! Part of a colt's early training is to get them accustomed to things like the sounds of steel against steel, flags flapping in the wind and walking through water. We exposed them to just about everything we could think of, so they would not spook on the battlefield and throw their riders. It was a test to winnow out the weaker ones."

She paused to catch her breath and went on. "When other foals would run behind their mothers, Majesty stuck his little nose into just about everything he could. Lord Harrington used to say if there was trouble to find he would find it! But that only meant he was intelligent and eager to learn. Nothing seemed to frighten him, and he was so smart! I'll never forget the day he escaped the paddock behind the barn by slipping under the bottom rail. It was an accident really; he was lying too close to the fence, and he decided to take a roll and his legs went right under the rail. When he found himself half-way in and half-way out, he thrashed around a bit and finally ended up on the outside."

Lady Harrington laughed out loud at the fond memory. "Well, his mother was going quite crazy, calling to him and running up and down the fence ready to jump over to get to her baby, when Majesty went back up to the fence, put his little nose down and shimmied on his belly like a dog until he got himself back in. I thought he would surely break his back or a leg from the position he was in, but their little bodies are more flexible than ours I suppose. I've never seen a colt do that since."

There was another pause. The barn was still except for the showers on the roof; the raindrops were seeping in through a crack at the ridge and running in rivulets down the supporting beams to form several large puddles on the barn's earthen floor. Fortunately, there were no leaks over the loft and the beds of the barn's unlikely guests stayed dry.

"Are you boys still awake?" Lady Harrington asked in a loud whisper. *This must be what it feels like to read bedtime stories to your children,* she thought, smiling in the dark.

There was no sound from below, just the soft snoring of her protectors. She looked up at the rafters, thinking about her barn and fences that lay in a pile of charred rubble at home. She thought of starting all over to rebuild her hops field. She had so much to do and yet she felt so blessed by the loyalty of these three men. It was with grateful prayers on her lips that she too fell asleep in the straw.

By morning the rainclouds had moved north, and the four tired travelers started out on the puddled road toward home, all anxious to get back to Porlock. The farmer's wife offered them some slices of bread and a bag of fresh red apples to eat on their journey. Lady Harrington pocketed her bread to nibble on later and gave the apple to her mare. By now, her dress was disheveled and her face pink and blistered from so many days in the sun, but she didn't seem to care. She had removed her withered headdress the night before and stowed it in a bag she carried behind her saddle. The men's clothing too needed laundering and their boots were caked with mud. They were a motley group to look at by the time they crested the hill above the Harrington manor. Even the horses sensed their closeness to home; their gait became lively and animated. Lady Harrington was the first to break into a canter and John followed while Little John and Tom trotted along behind with their sore buttocks bouncing uncomfortably in their saddles.

When they arrived at the manor Lady Harrington's attention was immediately drawn to a large group of men gathered in the clearing where the barn had been. She expected there was trouble coming until she recognized the faces of Peter and his brothers, Mr. Hartley, Doctor Philby, Mr. Potter and most of the men from town. When Tom pulled his horse up behind her he noticed that Wallace and his crew were there also. Lady Harrington dismounted and walked up to the men. The pile of rubble that had been left behind by the fire was gone; raked up and hauled away. In its place were timbers laid across sawhorses beside a wagonload of uncut wood. They had replaced most of the burnt fencing and the framework of a new barn wall was laid out on the ground ready to be raised. She broke into tears; full of emotion and exhausted from the long journey she collapsed on the ground. John ran to her side and helped her to her feet.

When her tears had dissipated enough so that she could speak she smiled at the men. The diminutive lady in her soiled dress, with her hair awry and her cheeks streaked with tears went along the line of men, taking the hands of each in hers. Despite her appearance, no queen could have been queenlier. "I don't know quite what to say," she began. "There are not adequate words to express what I feel. I......" she paused choking back more tears and then continued, "I fell asleep in a barn last night when we were caught in the rain, and I thought about *my* barn and *my* horses and how much work there was to be done to repair the damage. Now, here you all are, the answer to my prayers."

John, who was standing at her side and who was usually a man of few words, spoke directly to her. "It is *you*, M'Lady, who is the answer to *our* prayers. There is not one among us you have not blessed in some way." He looked at the group of men. "Our lady rode all the way to London and spoke to the king himself *on our behalf*. Because of that there are to be no more tax men in Porlock. The two that are being held on Captain Tom's ship will go back to London and face their punishment."

That brought a rousing cheer from the men.

"Thank you all," said Lady Harrington and John escorted Porlock's beloved benefactress up the steps to the manor house.

Chapter Twenty-Four "Captain Tom and the Sea of Tears"

Everyday life resumed in Porlock. Within the month Lady Harrington's barn was raised and her hops fields replanted. The perpetrators of the crime were returned to London to face their punishment. It was a time of new beginning and new life. Little John was finally getting acquainted with his son and Tom was preparing to be a father for the first time. *Babies* seemed to be the topic of most of the discussions in both the Snow and the Hatherly households for the next several months. Commerce experienced a sudden boom without the restraints of the king's men; the port became much busier in the following year than it had ever been before and rarely did a ship leave Porlock harbor without a full cargo aboard. The king should have been pleased as well; when the merchants were not being spied on and constantly threatened, they began to trade more openly and that meant more taxes in the royal coffers.

Elizabeth Hatherly was born on the sixth day of May in the little cottage by the harbor while her father was at sea. Amy's mother had promised her daughter to check in on Maggie every day when the date of confinement drew near and was there to assist in the birth. She had gone calling that morning with a basket of bread and some freshly picked vegetables from her garden. "Miss Maggie?" she called from the front step. "Are you up and about? I brought you a little something for your supper tonight."

"Please come in, Mrs. Hartley!" Maggie called from the back of the cottage.

Mrs. Hartley found her lying on the bed wrapped in a blanket with a trail of tears streaming down her face. "Oh my, have the pains started, my dear?" the older woman asked.

Maggie nodded and wiped her face with one of her mother's handkerchiefs. "I didn't know the pains would be so bad," she said. "Amy made it sound as if it would be ever so easy!"

"My daughter thinks she could take on the king's army and return without a blemish!" said Mrs. Hartley. "Not everyone is as strong-willed as Amy Anne. Now, how far apart are the pains?"

Maggie's face was blank. "I have not been paying attention to the time," she said. "Is that important?"

"Did your mother not tell you anything about childbirth my child? The pains come more frequently and much harder when the baby is about to be born."

"You mean the pain will get worse than *this*?" Maggie asked in horror. "Oh, I need Tom here. I do not think I can stand to go through it without my husband!"

"Oh yes you will, Maggie. Come now, let's get you undressed and ready for that baby!"

Mrs. Hartley went about the house collecting the items necessary to facilitate the birth thinking to herself *poor little Maggie; she must really miss her mother.* For the rest of the afternoon, she sat at the bedside while Maggie clung to her hand through each contraction. In between pains she dried Maggie's tears and tried to cheer her. "When is Tom due to return?" she asked during a placid moment.

"I don't know. I never know really. I wish I had never come here! I wish I had stayed in Barnstable!"

Mrs. Hartley disregarded her ranting; she knew how the pain of childbirth could affect a woman's mind and that it would all be forgotten as soon as she delivered her baby. *It is no different than the ramblings of a drunkard* she thought; *they don't mean anything they say, and they can't remember it afterward!* She stayed and coached her through the delivery which was without complications.

A few more contractions and the birth was over.

"It's a girl!" she said.

Maggie collapsed onto her pillow in a state of exhaustion and closed her eyes while Mrs. Hartley tended to the baby and refreshed the bed linens. She helped Maggie into a clean nightgown and brought her the swaddled infant, securely wrapped in a warm woolen shawl.

Maggie had turned toward the wall and was weeping again uncontrollably.

"I want Tom!" she cried when Mrs. Hartley touched her on the shoulder.

"Here is your little girl, Maggie. Do you not want to hold her?"

Maggie turned her head and her puffy eyes softened as she stared at the tiny, wrinkled face peering from beneath the shawl. She reached out and took the baby from Mrs. Hartley's arms.

"I am sorry, Mrs. Hartley. I have not acted very ladylike today. I have not even thanked you for staying with me all day and helping me."

"There is no need, Child. When I bore Amy Anne, I did not know quite what to expect either. But it is all right now. You have a beautiful healthy child. Pain goes away. And look," said Mrs. Hartley peeling back the shawl, "is she not worth it?"

Maggie held her little girl and touched her little face. "Yes, Elizabeth, you are worth it. But I don't believe I will be having any more children!"

Mrs. Hartley made her some supper and put another log on the fire. "I will stay with you until Tom comes home," she assured her. "Don't you worry, Maggie. I won't leave you alone."

Mr. Hartley came to check on the women at nightfall just to be sure they were all right and his wife stayed over, waking several times during the night when she heard Maggie crying again. *Poor child*, she thought, *she is going to have a difficult time with Tom being gone so much of the time.*

An unsuspecting Tom arrived the following day, whistling cheerfully as he came up the path. He heard the baby cry as soon as he opened the door and dropped his bag to run to the bedchamber. Maggie was trying unsuccessfully to nurse the infant and both mother and daughter were frustrated with the whole affair. Mrs. Hartley was standing by trying to give encouragement.

"Sometimes it takes time for the milk to flow," Mrs. Hartley said.

"But it hurts!" complained Maggie. "I am *bleeding*!"

When she saw Tom in the doorway, she smiled through her tears at him.

"Welcome home, Tom," said Mrs. Hartley. "You have a beautiful child!"

Tom approached the bed staring down at the little creature who by now was screaming at the top of her little lungs.

"I am not doing very well at this nursing thing," said Maggie. "It is not as easy as Amy Anne makes it look!"

"It is sometimes difficult at first, but it will come in time," Mrs. Hartley assured both parents and left the room quietly to give them privacy. She was relieved Tom was home at last. She hoped his presence would cheer Maggie up a little.

"Maggie, Maggie," Tom said, giving his wife a kiss. "I am home now. Don't cry. I am sure all new mothers go through a learning process."

"I am trying Tom, really I am! I just didn't know what to expect. I thought nursing the baby would be the easy part but it's not."

She started to cry again, and Tom took the baby from her and walked into the other room. "Mrs. Hartley isn't there something else we can give the baby to eat?"

She shook her head. "I'm sorry Tom. The baby needs her mother's milk. Maggie will get past her soreness in time."

"Can't we give her goat or cow milk for now?"

"I would advise against it. Babies can get sick from the milk of animals. No, it is best for Maggie to just keep trying."

Tom was perplexed and he looked to Mrs. Hartley for answers.

"I have some clean rainwater at home that I collected. I can boil it and soak a rag for the baby to suckle on temporarily."

"Yes! Please get the water," pleaded Tom. *"Anything!"*

Mrs. Hartley left the house and Tom realized the baby had stopped crying and had fallen asleep in his arms. He stared down at the infant and smiled.

"I didn't get a chance to ask. Is it a boy or a girl?" he asked Maggie.

"A girl," said Maggie flatly.

Tom crossed the room and sat on the bed.

"I'm sorry, Tom. I'm just not very good at this."

"Maggie you mustn't be so hard on yourself," he tried to console her. "Look how peacefully she is sleeping now."

Tom knew Maggie was a fragile woman; his mother-in-law became bedridden with the slightest sniffle and Maggie took after her mother. He realized he had to convince his wife she was stronger than that. He was heartbroken to see her in so much misery at what should have been a time of joy. He laid the baby down gently on the bed and put his arms around his wife just as another spasm of tears began to flow. For once in his life Tom felt totally helpless.

Chapter Twenty-Five "Courage Comes in All Sizes"

Richard was destined to be a warrior; from the time he was but a toddler under the watchful eye of Amy Anne, he would always find a makeshift sword with which to do battle. Whether it was a crooked oak branch or a sliver of wood from a split fence rail he was always brandishing a weapon of some sort and practicing his knightly craft against anything that crossed his path.

The day he met his match was the day he squared off with the Snow family's old rooster *King George.* George was a tall fellow with deep red feathers and a bad attitude toward anyone coming near his flock of hens. As he aged and the razor-sharp spurs on the back of his feet grew, he became even more aggressive and collecting the eggs became a test of human against fowl. Richard had watched his mother arm herself with a broom handle every morning with which to protect herself from the bird's attacks and on more than one occasion saw her running to the larder with an apron full of eggs with the rooster squawking and flapping at her heels. It was all the little knight could take; he was determined to protect his mother from the wicked bird!

At the next opportunity he followed along several paces behind his mother on her morning excursion to the chicken coop. With his stick-sword in hand he tiptoed along with a watchful eye out for King George. As soon as Amy Anne neared the nesting boxes, the rooster came around the corner of the backyard woodpile and, flapping his wings, came running across the yard straight for little Richard.

Richard held out his stick-sword and yelled at the rooster to go away and they circled each other; each time the rooster would attempt to lunge at the youngster Richard would jab at him with his stick-sword and challenge the bird. Amy's maternal instinct at first was to interfere and chase the bird away, but when she saw that Richard was doing just fine on his own she allowed the battle to continue as she watched silently from the chicken coop.

The bird's feathers were ruffled, and he pecked at the stick-sword but Richard did not back away from the danger of the rooster's spurs. The battle went on for several minutes until the bird finally gave up and walked away never again to challenge the boy.

"You were very brave, my little knight," said Amy who repeated the story to his father and grandfather later that day.

Richard's fearlessness was also apparent at one of Lady Harrington's Christmas parties when one of the games on the children's day was a sheep riding contest. Several of Lady Harrington's sheep had been gathered in the arena and the contest was to see which child could ride from one end of the arena to the other without falling off. The first several children were not able to hang on for the entire ride. When it was Richard's turn, Little John lifted his son up on the sheep. "Now whatever you do son, don't let go!" he told him.

Richard sunk his fingers deep down in the thick wool and squeezed his little knees firmly around the fat middle section of the old ewe. When they turned the sheep loose, Richard held on tightly but halfway down the arena he felt his balance shifting with the sheep's bouncing gait and he was soon listing to one side. Remembering his father's words to *not let go,* further and further he leaned until he was literally riding upside down, holding on tightly to the sheep's belly wool, and was being dragged along in the dirt. He passed the finish line without ever relinquishing his grip on the animal.

Richard stood up and brushed himself off; even though *technically* he had not stayed upright on the sheep he had not given up and let go of the wool. Upside down or not his courage earned him a roar of applause from the crowd.

When he returned to his mother who was waiting at the arena gate, she could see the scratches on his face from the rough ride on the sheep's belly and she whispered in his ear so as not to embarrass her little knight. "My son, are you hurt?"

"Of course, I'm not hurt, Mother!" he replied. "I just had to eat a little dirt, that's all!"

A few weeks later, Lady Harrington presented Richard with a gift; a small steel sword with an inscription on it that read: *Courage Comes in All Sizes.*

As he grew, Richard took lessons in horseback riding from his father in Lady Harrington's arena and his talent with the lance and the sword was ever improving. By the time he was ten he could chuck his lance through a six-inch ring while by galloping past on his horse.

"He is destined to become a knight," Lady Harrington said on many occasions.

Elizabeth, who was two years Richard's junior, was maturing in a very different way. She was no tomboy as Amy Anne had been, and she took after Maggie in all her habits and mannerisms. When the families would gather at social events, Elizabeth would sit quietly doing needlework as far away from animals and soil as she could get.

"Our children are as different as night and day," Amy Anne told Maggie one afternoon as they sat on the Hatherly porch while their children played in the yard. Richard was practicing his skill with a bow using a target John had made for him while Elizabeth sat on the grass braiding flowers into chains.

"Watch this!" Richard told Elizabeth switching from his right arm to his left and still hitting the bull's eye with his arrow.

Elizabeth watched in a quiet, ladylike way and smiled as her gallant knight performed feats of his ability to impress her. She reciprocated by sharing her cake with him. As their mothers watched them together on the lawn it was obvious that as different as the two were they still seemed right for each other.

Elizabeth was learning to cook and sew, and Maggie was schooling her in reading and simple mathematics and the girl was turning out to be a very well-rounded young lady. She always stayed close to her mother's side showing the same quiet reserve as her mother exhibited except when her father returned home from the sea. Then she became lively and silly; she simply *adored* the captain! She would watch for the sails of the *Dove* on the horizon beyond Porlock harbor and would gather up her skirt and run for the docks to greet him.

Maggie disciplined the girl and kept her behavior lady-like and proper, but Tom spoiled his daughter and encouraged her childish ways. It became the seed of many a disagreement between her parents; Maggie wanting to raise her properly and Tom wanting the child to be happy. It seemed as if Mother Hanfield was reaching out all the way from Barnstable to have her way with the child. Had it not been for the affection she felt for Amy Anne and the obvious infatuation Elizabeth had for her father, Maggie would have returned to Barnstable.

Chapter Twenty-Six "Just Call Me Master John"

"Can I ride along with you, Grandfather?" young Richard begged.

Little John interrupted and shook his head. "No, Richard. You have to help me in the fields." He waved to his father who was on his way to the Harrington Manor. "You go ahead, Paa. My son and I will take care of things here."

John left riding a new mare he had purchased to replace Pockets who had died earlier that spring. It had saddened him to lose his mare almost as much as losing Morning Star. He decided with this horse he was not going to get attached so he told himself he would not give her a name. He couldn't help but be fond of her though; she was an adaptable animal, compliant and easy going under the bit or the yoke. Nameless or not, John loved his horses.

He was enjoying a break from work in the fields; Little John and Richard were taking on more and more responsibility around the farm and John was able to spend more time with Lady Harrington's horses. Little John encouraged it. He knew farming had never been his father's first love; he was a born horseman and was most at home in a stable. Besides it was hard work, and his father was getting on in age. The trouble was young Richard showed no interest at all in farming; he would rather be riding horses or fighting in mock battles in Lady Harrington's arena. Little John knew that one day he would lose his son to the call of the sword.

John tied his horse up in the barn and greeted the grooms busy mucking stalls. "Is Lady Harrington up and about this morning?" he asked of them.

"No, Master John. We have not seen her today."

That is odd, John thought to himself. *Lady Harrington was usually up with the chickens and busy in the barn long before the noonday sun.* He went up to the door and knocked twice. One of her servants came to the door.

"Is Lady Harrington here?" John asked. "I would just like a minute to speak to her."

The servant shook his head. "The lady is not feeling well, Master John. She has not risen from her bed yet."

John was concerned and entered the great room. "Has anyone checked on her? Has anyone called Doctor Philby?"

"No, Sir. She said she did not want a doctor."

John sought out the lady's chambermaid. It would never do for him to enter the lady's bed chamber unannounced. "Can you go up and check on Lady Harrington?" he asked.

She complied and went up the stairs. Within a minute she appeared at the top of the banister. "Master John, come quickly! Something is very wrong!"

John ran up the stairs as fast as his old knees would allow and entered the lady's room. There propped up against a mound of pillows was Lady Harrington looking very tiny in the huge bed she had once shared with Lord Harrington. Her eyes were half closed and she coughed a little covering her mouth with a lace handkerchief. "John," she said weakly. "How good of you to come. I was just thinking of sending for you."

She dismissed her chambermaid.

"Lady Harrington! Do you wish me to call the doctor?" asked John.

"No, John. Please, come and sit with me."

She coughed again and spit phlegm into the handkerchief. "I must look a fright," she said. "But probably not any worse than I looked after our trip to London, aye?"

It was always there, that Harrington sense of humor. John sat down and took her hand. "Are you *very* ill, M'Lady?"

"No, John," she smiled. "Just very *old*."

"Aye," he said. "It is a fate we all have to face eventually."

"I believe it is finally my time, John."

The words came so naturally to her; both life and death were a certainty, there was nothing *extraordinary* about either.

John was searching for a response. The memory of his wife came back. *How does one say goodbye to someone you love?* he was thinking at that moment when she spoke again. "It is your time to take over, John. You and Little John will have everything that is mine very soon."

"M'Lady, it will never be the same without you."

"Just promise me something, John. Promise me you will not let the king take over Porlock." She had a coughing spell that lasted several minutes. When it was over, she closed her eyes and rested. Then suddenly she spoke again. "Do you remember the old stories about the wild boars of Pool Wood?"

It had been many years since John had thought about the old legend surrounding the wooded area on the outskirts of town. It was a tale the mothers of Porlock always told their children to keep them from wandering too far astray. "Yes, M'Lady. I believe the story was that there were wild boars that would eat you up, *bones and all*, if you ventured into the woods," replied John. "It never worked on me until I went there once and was actually chased by one of those hairy creatures with tusks the size of elephants! I ran all the way home and never went there again."

Lady Harrington laughed a hoarse and broken laugh. Her eyes seemed to be failing her and even though she still had his hand in her grasp she leaned forward squinting as if to see if John was still at her bedside. "Most of the men growing up in Porlock have had the same experience I am sure," she replied. "That is why I must ask you to go there again, just once more, for me."

John was befuddled. *Why would Lady Harrington want him to venture into Pool Wood now that he was a grown man and had long since stopped being afraid of boars? It made no sense; perhaps it was just the delusional ranting of a dying woman.*

"You will find it between two oak trees under a large white rock. You will have to dig down a few inches under the rock."

"M'Lady, what I am I digging for?" John was convinced she had really lost her sanity and he was just humoring her last words.

"It will be there. It was the safest place to put it……."

She sighed deeply and closed her eyes again. Her breathing had become labored and shallow. Her small, wrinkled hands trembled in his. Then she became very still. John closed his own eyes and began to weep. *Porlock had lost its great lady.*

John covered her face gently with the bed covering and sat a few moments longer in silence. He looked around him and remembered the many times he had visited Lord Harrington in this very room. The memory was vivid and fresh in his mind even though it had been so many years ago. He remembered Lady Harrington as a young woman, so energetic, so beautiful and so fascinating in a young boy's eyes. They shared many loves throughout their lives; their mutual admiration and respect for Lord Harrington; their passion for horses; their pride in Porlock. He remembered the excitement in her eyes when the lord would return from the battlefield and the obvious affection they had for each other.

The room seemed to darken and grow suddenly cold despite the sun shining brightly outside the bed chamber windows. John's mind awoke from his memories suddenly and then began spinning in confusion and disbelief. *She was gone*! The stark reality of the situation grew in his mind until he wanted to scream. *What am I to do now?* The will! He had stored his copy of the will in a drawer at home. *The servants!* He had to tell the *servants!* He was frozen with apprehension over what he should do first and the best way to handle spreading the news of the lady's death. He again delved into his memories and revived his feelings from the day Lady Harrington had promoted him from a stable hand to a landowner and he was plunged into the world of farming. He had been overwhelmed then but his determination not to let the lady down overcame his feelings of incompetence. The same feelings came over him now. He would not let her down!

He rose and left the room, closing the door softly behind him as if to keep from waking her from her slumber. When he got downstairs, he summoned the house servants and sent for the stable grooms to all gather in the great hall. When they were all there, they stared at him with sad eyes and broken hearts that already knew the dreadful truth he was about to speak.

"As you all have probably guessed by now, Lady Harrington has passed away."

The female servants began to sob while John continued his speech. "Nothing will change straightaway," he assured them. "Lady Harrington has left me in charge, and everything will remain just as it is. I will have to go over the manor accounts and complete the necessary legal process. You all know me. We are all a family. We all loved her, and her wishes will be carried out. That is my oath to you."

"What shall we call you, Master John? Will it be *Lord* John now?" one of the stable hands asked.

John laughed. "No. That will not be the case. I have no ambitions to be anything more than a servant of Lady Harrington, just as you are. I will have to make decisions in her stead, that much is true. First, I must go into town and secure a proper coffin for her and arrange for her funeral. After that we will take things one day at a time."

The servants gathered around John and sought out his hand in friendship and support after which John mounted his horse and rode away. John's plate that had been half-full was suddenly brimming with an enormous serving of responsibility. Before his trip to town where the news would spread quickly, John first had to stop to speak to Little John and Amy Anne about the changes that were about to occur in the Snow household. They both were sitting at the table listening to Richard recite his daily language lesson when John entered the room.

Amy Anne at first smiled up at him, then her expression turned inquisitive. "Is everything all right John? You look like you've just seen a ghost," she said.

Little John looked up at his father as well. "Aye, Paa, you do look a bit *peculiar*. Is everything all right at the Harrington Manor?"

John shook his head and sat down. "Lady Harrington is dead."

There was a shocked silence that fell over the room. Amy Anne's usually sparkling blue eyes welled with tears and Little John wore a look of disbelief. "It can't be so, Paa! Never have I seen anyone with so much life in them! Why, just last week she was helping Richard with his archery lessons!"

"Aye," said John sadly. "She was full of life until the very end."

"She was not ill then?" Amy asked.

"No. But you have to remember she was eighty-four years old, and one can't live forever."

"I just can't believe she is gone," said Amy Anne.

"And neither will the town of Porlock. I am not looking forward to being the messenger of this news. Indeed, I have to ride in to see the carpenter about a coffin and see the priest about the funeral arrangements but first I needed to speak to you both about a different matter."

By now he held their rapt attention. *What more could there be*? they wondered.

"Lady Harrington has willed her estate to me. I will have to take on all her responsibilities," John continued. "And I will need you both to help me. You both are still young and have more energy than I do."

Both Little John and Amy Anne's eyes bulged in surprise. "*You* Paa?" asked Little John.

"It makes perfect sense," Amy interjected once she had pondered the news a minute. "She had no children and she always loved you like a son. She trusted you like no other."

"Does that mean all her horses will be *ours* now?" Richard asked excitedly.

John looked at Richard. "Aye, but I am an old man. When I am gone, the responsibility will pass to your father and then to you. So, we must all be prepared."

With that he stood and walked toward the door. "I must get to town now. Think about what I have said. When I return, we will make a plan."

When he arrived in town John took a side trip to the Hatherly house; he wanted to have Tom aware of what was happening just in case there was trouble. He was invited in to stay to supper, but he declined, apologizing for his untimely visit. He quickly explained what had happened. "Tom, I might need to call on you for assistance in the matter. I am not sure how this will be received by everyone. I expect there may be legal problems."

"Aye, Lady Harrington was aware of that. That is why she had me witness the will, John. But don't worry my friend. I promised Lady Harrington and I swear to you now that I will be there to support you in any way I can."

"There is something you must know, Tom," said John. "I have not read the will. I am afraid I have never been taught to read."

Tom nodded. "Lady Harrington knew that John. But, as she put it to me, *trust* was far more important to her than *education*. I am sure you will find that the people of Porlock will stand behind you too."

Maggie had theretofore not uttered a word. She sat at the table beside Elizabeth. "You have an educated daughter-in-law and a strong, loyal son," she said quietly.

John nodded in agreement. "Yes, that is true, Maggie. I have a good family. It is my *own* inadequacies that I fear the most."

He started for the door and Tom followed. "I will be in port for a few days, John. You call on me for *anything* my friend."

Chapter Twenty-Seven "The White Snake of Sorrow"

John went to speak to Father Clary first. When he entered the church, he automatically turned to the east side and went through the archway to kneel at the foot of the stone box that held the remains of his beloved Lord Harrington. Silently he spoke,

My Lord I hope your lady is with you now, sitting at the foot of Jesus. I only pray that I can carry out your wishes. I will do my very best. I loved you both as much as my own parents and Porlock will sorely miss you. I will always be your humble servant.

He stood then and backed away from the crypt just as Father Clary came up beside him. "Good day, Master John. What brings you to the Lord's house this afternoon?"

John started to speak, but suddenly stopped. *Am I in a dream? Is this real?* he thought; the pain in his eyes did not escape Father Clary's notice.

"It is Lady Harrington is it not?" he asked gently.

"How did you know, Father?"

"The lady and I have spoken several times in recent weeks. She knew her time was coming, and she wanted to take care of as many of the details as she could before she went to meet our Lord. She spoke very highly of you, John. She loved you every bit as much as if you were her own son."

"Forgive me, Father," John replied. "I am feeling a little overwhelmed at the moment. There are so many things to do, and I am not sure quite where to start."

Father Clary took John by the shoulders and led him into the side room which served as a rectory and his private office. John sat down across from a simple wooden desk and waited for the priest to speak.

"Lady Harrington took care of a lot of the details ahead of time so that should ease your mind somewhat."

"I look to you, Father, for guidance," said John. "Please tell me what needs to be done forthwith?"

"First of all, Lady Harrington had the foresight to arrange for her coffin; to be sure it would fit within the crypt next to his lordship. It has been here in storage for many years now, ever since his death. An effigy to match her husband's has been ordered. She gave me a copy of her will as well, since, as you know, she left provisions for the maintenance of the church and the almshouse."

John was relieved but ashamed that he had not read the will himself and after burying his wife he dreaded the thought of ordering another coffin.

Father Clary continued, "I will send messages to the other parishes right away. A noblewoman of Lady Harrington's stature had friends all over England who undoubtedly will want to pay their respects."

"What should I do now?" asked John.

"Have her chambermaids dress and prepare her body. Have you a wagon to take the coffin to the Harrington estate?"

"I did not drive the wagon today, Father. I did not know quite what to do *first*."

"Then I will send a wagon to the manor at first light. We will have an evening prayer service tomorrow night and the funeral the following day. Why don't you go on home and get some rest? Shall we set the time for eleven in the morn for the service? As the administrator of the estate the rest of the decisions shall be yours to make."

Administrator of the estate? How did I, a simple stable boy with no education earn this title? John reflected on the question all the way home. When he arrived and unsaddled his horse, he noticed that the livestock had all been fed and the cows milked. *Little John is a good son. I could not have asked for better*, he thought upon entering the house where he found his supper on the table. Amy served him and gave him a kiss on his cheek.

"I paid a visit to Harrington Manor after you left, John. I hope you don't mind. I knew her ladies would be wanting to know how to dress her for the funeral, so I helped them in the selection of a gown and headdress. I thought the gold one she always wears at Christmas time would be appropriate," she said matter-of-factly. His daughter in law was an amazing woman; she could just take charge and handle things.

"You are very much like her, you know," John said.

"Me? Like Lady Harrington?" Amy asked with a look of surprise.

"Yes," replied John. "Very much like her in spirit."

Little John agreed. "I see that too. That must be why I fell in love with you."

Amy laughed. John laughed thinking *here it is again; Life goes on. Babies are born and the old die off. My grandson is growing bigger every day and Lady Harrington has lived a long full life and is at peace with her husband now.*

John went to his room and retrieved the copy of the will which he handed to Amy Anne while he sat down to eat his supper. "Why don't you just read it aloud to us, Amy?"

Amy moved closer to the oil lamp and began to read Lady Harrington's will while John and Little John listened intently. John lowered his head shyly when she read: *"All my earthly possessions and properties do I hereby bequeath to John Anthony Snow, my friend and advisor in matters of farming and animal husbandry, who has given his lifelong service to myself and my late husband Lord Harrington, who was considered by both my husband and I as dear as if he had been a natural son born to us."*

In the will she had made provisions for all her servants and stable hands as well as the church in Porlock and the almshouse so that they would never again be in need of anything. Her final wish was to be placed in the crypt next to her husband's body so that she would thereafter be at peace with God and England.

"The will is certainly clear as to Lady Harrington's intentions. Do you think the king will challenge it, John?" Amy Anne asked.

"I'm not sure. I know that when Lord Harrington died, she had a visit from the king's court; they wanted her to relinquish some of her land pretending they were concerned with her welfare. She would have none of it and told them so."

"What did she say to you of her wishes, Paa?" Little John asked.

"Only to promise not to let the king take over Porlock."

Amy Anne agreed. "The will appears legal to me. You should wait and let the king make the first move."

John could not find words to express how he felt. He stood up and walked outside to make his nightly trip to Margaret's grave stopping to pick some roses from the little rose bush. When he knelt to pick the roses, he noticed that there were no longer any white blooms but pale pink ones! In all his years farming he had never known a plant to produce flowers of a different color from one year to the next; it was very strange. At the top of the hill, he spent a great deal of time there reflecting on all the unusual events of the day before he returned to the house. As he opened the door, he turned to the east toward Harrington Manor and made a silent oath: *I will not let you down, M'Lady.*

The following day was a blur of rushed activity in preparation for the funeral and the road between Porlock and the Harrington Manor was worn flat from so many wagon wheels and horses' hooves. The wagon arrived with the empty coffin and John followed it up the hill. The hearse that had been used for Lord Harrington's funeral procession was stored in the back of the barn under a tarp and the stable hands helped John bring it out and clean it thoroughly, applying a bit of grease to the spoked wheels, polishing, and touching it up with white paint until the metal glistened.

They carried the coffin inside and upstairs to the bedchamber where John went forward and lifted Lady Harrington's lifeless body and placed it gently against the satin lining inside the box. The chambermaids rearranged her hair and smoothed the creases of her gown tucking bunches of sweet, scented flowers all around her; her appearance was one of sleep and peace. The men carried her back down the stairs and placed the coffin in the great hall to await the funeral.

The evening prayer service was crowded; it appeared that every citizen of Porlock was there, and some from nearby towns who had received the news first, some standing in the back of the church for lack of a seat and some outside straining their ears toward the open door to hear, even if the priest spoke in Latin which very few understood. Most went home in a melancholy mood to get a good night's sleep before the morning pilgrimage.

John arrived at the Manor at daybreak and was surprised to see many strange faces already coming in and out of the barn and lingering on the manor lawn. As the morning went on more visitors arrived on the grounds to join what was apparently going to be a very *long* procession; some riding on horses or in carriages and those without means to walk along behind the coffin to the church.

The stable hands rolled the hearse to the west end of the driveway nearest the house to hitch up the horses. They had groomed the lady's two finest mares until their coats were lustrous and smooth trimming their manes and tails before braiding them with white ribbons. The other guests began to line up and take their places behind the hearse and soon the funeral march began. Not even at the annual Christmas celebration had John seen such a crowd; they even outnumbered those attending Lord Harrington's funeral. The explanation, John thought, was because Lord Harrington was away much of the time fighting and he was not as dear to the people as Lady Harrington who was always there; she was the mother who took care of Porlock in his absence.

The lead groom drove the hearse, dressed in a white coat. The coffin was draped in a woven shawl embroidered with the Harrington Crest and above four tall candles burned at the corners of the cart. John rode immediately behind the coffin, representing the family while Little John, Richard, and Amy Anne rode behind him.

Next in the procession were knights on leave from the wars sporting full armor from as far away as Cornwall, Devon and Dorset followed on foot by their squires. Dukes and earls in their carriages came next followed by all the citizens of Porlock, indeed most of Somerset County. While a few rode horse-back, most were walking. The men who did not have anything white to wear sported white arm bands and the women wore white scarves on their heads in honor of the renowned lady. The parade took a somber tone looking like a long white snake as it wound its way slowly down Porlock Hill.

The parish church in Porlock had been built by St. Dubricious, a sixth century archbishop. It had been completely rebuilt after the original structure had been burned to the ground in the year 1052 when Porlock was sacked by Harold of Wessex in retaliation for an attack on the king's Norman supporters. Dubricious was every bit a real person but was also known in folklore as a friend and advisor of the legendary King Arthur and was said to have officiated at the marriage of Arthur and Lady Guinevere. Although there were other nobles immortalized within the church walls, the Harrington monument was the most spectacular; the image of Lord Harrington was carved from alabaster, in his plate armor with his head resting on his tilted helmet and bearing the Harrington crest of a lion's head. His helmet was surrounded by a garland of roses and leaves and behind his head were angels, which was considered very unusual in the case of a knight. Lord Harrington obviously meant more to the people of Porlock than a mere protector of the crown; the angels alluded to the softer, more humanitarian side of the man himself. His feet were resting appropriately on a figure of a lion. It was under this stone canopy next to her husband that Lady Harrington was to rest.

When the procession reached the church, the guests filed in and took their seats while the squires and grooms outside scrambled to control the multitude of horses. Father Clary began with a prayer for Lady Harrington which he spoke in English for the benefit of the crowd. A Eucharist was performed celebrating the death and resurrection of Jesus Christ followed by a eulogy in which he made specific mention of John Snow's relationship to the Harringtons calling him *"the closest thing to a son they would ever have"*. More prayers were spoken, and the lady's favorite hymns were sung then her coffin was lifted and placed in the crypt. When it was over a single dry eye was not to be found in all of Porlock.

Chapter Twenty-Eight "A Very Short Visit"

By 1471, when Lady Harrington died, England had a new king; a Yorkist named Edward IV. Although his predecessor, Henry VI, had been an ineffective king for the most part, bending to the will of a demanding French wife and other unscrupulous advisors, he was still a *Lancastrian* king from the line of Henry V who had been admired by Lord Harrington. Even though Edward was popular among many Englishmen the house of York had long been enemies of the Lancastrian dynasty and when Edward took the throne it provided him an opportunity to seek revenge on all their supporters. The valuable Harrington lands in Devon and Somerset were of keen interest to the king and his court.

News of the lady's death reached London within weeks of the funeral and the king immediately sent out his representative to protect the crown's interest. The *master of the rolls* was, in effect, a temporary judge who travelled around the country to hear petitions and administer estates in the name of the king. He arrived in Porlock on a summer afternoon; a serious and somewhat sour looking little fellow who rode into town and tied his horse out in front of the inn.

When he jumped down from his horse, his unusual physical appearance amused those passing by as they watched him shake out his cramped legs; the man was barely five feet tall with a rotund mid-section and a head as bald and red as a newborn baby's bottom. He had the look of a dwarf or an elf; even the toes of his shoes, which were obviously too large for his feet, curled up at the ends making him appear even more comical. Once he entered the inn, he was the topic of conversation for the rest of the afternoon.

"Who in this town may I speak to regarding the Harrington estate?" he asked the innkeeper.

"That would most likely be John Snow," was the reply. "You will find him either on his farm or out at the Harrington manor. He only comes to town about once a week. Take this road out over the bridge up Porlock Hill and you can't miss the Snow farm on the left."

The dwarf-man had a hurried mug of ale and thanked the innkeeper for the information. He returned to his horse, leading the animal down to a nearby rock that he used to boost himself back up into the saddle and he was gone.

"Shall we warn Master John that there is a leprechaun stalking him?" joked the innkeeper after the little man had left.

"Aye," said one of the patrons. "Tell him to shield his knees!"

Indeed, the little man's appearance was laughable, but his mission was not. The king expected him to return to

London with a valid claim on the Harrington property and the little man was determined not to disappoint the crown. Little John was the first to notice the unusual visitor coming up the road; his father had gone up to the manor to tend to his newly assigned responsibilities. At first, he thought it was a child in the saddle until he came nearer, and he saw it was a grown albeit *very short* man.

"Is this the Snow farm?" the man inquired.

"Yes, Sir, it is," answered Little John. "I am John Snow."

"You are handling the estate of the late Lady Harrington?"

"No, you must want my father. He is at the manor now. Is there something I can help you with?"

"No, I will need to speak to your father. I have legal papers that require his signature," the little man said, appearing to grow impatient. "How much further up the road do I need to go?"

"Only about a mile, straight ahead," Little John answered. He noticed Amy Anne had come out of the house and was standing on the porch listening to the conversation.

When the man rode away, she approached her husband. "Is the king already starting trouble?" she asked. "I think I should ride up there to be sure your father doesn't sign anything he shouldn't."

"Perhaps you are right, Amy. I didn't think of that. You had better go."

He saddled her a horse.

"Where is Richard?" Amy asked.

"He has taken one of the horses to town to be shod."

"If I have not returned, be sure he comes in and studies his lessons before supper," said Amy Anne.

After tucking the copy of Lady Harrington's will into her pouch, Amy Anne galloped up the road to the manor and found the little man talking to John on the front lawn of the estate. When they made eye contact, she could see John was relieved to see her.

"This is my daughter in law. Amy Anne, this gentleman is from the king's court."

Amy went forward and stood beside John, peeking over his shoulder at the papers the little man had in his hand.

"Are you telling me, Sir, that *you* are Lady Harrington's rightful heir? How can that be when the Harringtons had no children?" the man continued, disregarding Amy Anne's presence completely. His manner was most rude.

John took the papers and immediately handed them to Amy who began to read them word for word. The man glared at her and continued speaking. "Sir, the Harrington estate has debts that need to be paid before any legacy can be valid. Are you aware how much she owes the crown in delinquent taxes?"

"I don't believe that Sir. She would have informed us if that was the case," said Amy Anne, tired of being ignored. "This paper relinquishes any claim to what my father-in-law inherited legally, and he will not sign such a document. This is a copy of the will and I assure you, Sir, it is legal!"

The little man looked over the will and handed it back to Amy Anne. He looked up and addressed John directly. "If you refuse to sign this document you will have to present your case to the Court of Chancery in London. The Lord Chancellor will ultimately decide. In order to have the land turned over to you the debts attached to the land must be paid, the amount of which is quite considerable, and you will not be allowed to liquidate any portion of the property to do so. Are you solvent enough to pay the taxes?"

John's mind was spinning. The land was *his,* but he had to pay the debt first and he could not sell any of Lady Harrington's property to raise the money? It didn't make any sense. It was an impossible situation.

Amy Anne took charge. "You may tell the court that we are prepared to have our case heard."

The man's face turned even redder than the top of his sunburned head and he stomped off to his horse, standing on a fence rail to reach his stirrups.

"Just remember, I warned you. I am much easier to deal with than the Lord Chancellor!"
With that he rode off in a huff.

John was mute. Amy was agitated. "Let's go home, John, and discuss this. Are you almost finished with your work here? I have supper waiting for you."

"Yes, I will ride with you, Amy."

She waited for him to retrieve his horse from the barn, and they rode home together.

"I never realized what an advantage *literacy* would be. I never needed it when I was farming. Thank you for coming to my rescue," he said.

"You would not have signed that paper. You are smarter than that," Amy said. "And you needn't worry, John. Little John reads quite well now except for the big words. And we won't let you go through this alone."

"Thank you, Amy Anne. You are truly a blessing to me."

"You are my family now," Amy replied.

After dinner the Snow family sat at the kitchen table and went over the will and the document left by the little man.

"How can we prove we do not owe any taxes if the king insists that we do?" Little John asked.

Amy was making a list on a small piece of note paper. "You get receipts for every shipment at the dock, don't you?" she asked. "We will just have to collect all those receipts. Captain Tom will have copies of any we are missing. That should be simple to do. That will show that we paid taxes on all the goods we shipped." In her mind she was forming a plan. "John, did you go through all of Lady Harrington's papers yet? She must have kept records! We will need those too. You must go to the manor tomorrow and collect everything. Go through all the drawers. And you mustn't be shy, John; she might have hidden them in with her undergarments! Little John, you must get a message to Tom. When we have everything, we will be ready for court!"

John had not said a word and was sitting there with a most peculiar expression on his face.

"What is it, Paa?" Little John asked.

"It was just something Lady Harrington said the day that she died."

Both Amy Anne and Little John looked at him inquisitively. "What did she say?"

"I thought she was just talking crazy because it made no sense at all. I thought it was because she was dying and her mind was not right," said John almost apologetically.

"For goodness sake, *what* did she say John?"

"She told me I had to go to Pool Wood one more time for her. She said there was something hidden there."

Amy's eyes widened. Little John agreed with his father. "Aye, that sounds a little crazy to me too, Paa."

"Lady Harrington was *anything* but crazy! Of that, I am sure!" Amy said and quickly added *Trip to Pool Wood* to her list.

Chapter Twenty-Nine "Pool Wood"

When John had returned from the manor the following morning, bringing Amy Anne all the papers he could find in Lady Harrington's belongings, Little John had saddled his horse and was ready to accompany him on their mystery mission to Pool Wood. "I always wanted to go there just to see if the boars are as terrible as in the story," he said.

John shook his head. "I fear we are going out on a wild *goose* chase rather than a wild *boar* chase. But I will honor Lady Harrington's wishes. Did you bring a shovel with which to dig up the buried treasure?"

"I have one here," said Little John, pointing to the spade he had tied to his saddle.

"Can't I go along, Father?" pleaded Richard.

"No," replied Little John. "You must stay here and help your mother with chores."

Richard walked off with a pout. Amy watched them as they rode off down the hill.

The wood was to the west of town, out an old rarely used road to the old pottery yard which had been destroyed before John was born and never rebuilt. It was situated down in the gully, at the end of a very steep path, so steep that the horses literally sat on their tails and slid all the way down.

"If we find something there, I hope it is not very large," remarked Little John. "How would we ever get it back up this hill?"

"I believe there is another path on the other side of the wood that is not nearly as steep," John said. "But I seriously doubt we will find anything."

At the bottom of the hill, where the ground leveled out, there was a rapidly running stream emerging from the thicket of oak trees and they stopped to give their horses a drink. When they proceeded into the trees, it became very dark with only the slightest slivers of sunlight breaking through the branches above. It took a few moments for their eyes to adjust to the darkness. Though overgrown and seldom used over the years the old path along the banks of the stream was still visible amongst fields of ferns that appeared to be thriving in the shade of the oak trees.

"She said there would be two oak trees and a white rock in between," said John, doubting they would be able to find such a rock. They strayed from the path walking their horses between every pair of trees that were close together but found nothing. The stream soon widened and emptied into a pool at the foot of a waterfall. There, drinking from the pool in the sunlight, they got their first glimpse of the dreaded boar; a family with one sow and two piglets splashing in the shallows. The sow had a large wide snout and a bristled coat of charcoal grey while the piglets' coats were striped and the color of a newborn deer. The sow snorted when she smelled the horses and pushed her babies along up the shoreline away from danger. As soon as they ran off a huge boar appeared out of the brush. He was twice the size of the sow and had long yellowing tusks protruding from under his jawbone. He gave a terrifying grunt as a warning and pawed the ground with his sharp hooves staring at the men on their horses.

"Do not move," whispered John. "Boars are not afraid of anything. They can slice our horses' legs to ribbons."

The boar waited a moment to see if he would be challenged then satisfied he was not he snorted again and walked slowly away up the bank of the stream.

"They sure are *ugly* beasts," said Little John.

"That they are, Son," John answered, "And I am ever so glad we came on horseback or else he would have attacked us for sure."

They continued up the trail to where the wood ended in a clearing carpeted with a thick layer of fallen leaves. Wild moss grew all around the clearing, climbing up the trunks of the trees and hanging down like thick green cobwebs from the branches so that they had to brush them away to ride through. John was almost ready to give up the search when he saw two very gnarled old trees standing about ten feet apart at the outward edge of the clearing. His horse suddenly jumped sideways as something startled him; there through the grass and ferns it was, a flat white rock just like Lady Harrington said there would be.

"Well, I will be damned," said John. "She wasn't rambling after all."

He got down from his horse and Little John followed him. The rock was wedged tightly from many years in the dirt, and it took both father and son's strength to move it. Little John went back for the spade, and he began to dig in the bare spot that had been hidden by the rock unearthing nothing but some fat brown worms and a multitude of crawly bugs from their homes. When he had dug down a few inches he hit something with the spade that sounded like wood. He scraped the loose dirt away and saw that it was indeed a box of some kind. As he dug away around the edges of the box the outline became visible, and he stopped abruptly.

"Paa!"

John was standing right behind him and saw what his son had seen. The object hidden under the rock was a coffin!

Little John dropped his spade. "Shall I cover it back up?" he asked, visibly shaken at the discovery.

John tried to remember Lady Harrington's *exact* words. What had she said? *It was the safest place to put it.* He looked at his son and smiled. "Remember that story Tom told us about the brandy in the coffin?" he asked.

Little John nodded. "You don't think…."

"Indeed, I do. It's the *one* place the king's men wouldn't snoop. Let's lift it out and see what mischief Lady Harrington was up to."

After Little John had dug a trench around the coffin wide enough for their fingers to grip the edges, they tried to pull it up onto the ground.

"It is too heavy, Son," said John. "Maybe we can get it open if we make the trench a little deeper."

Little John dug down and then watched his father try to lift the lid. When he had finally loosened it enough to pry it open both father and son sank to the ground in laughter.

The coffin was filled to the brim with gold sovereigns!

"She must have anticipated that the king would try to tax us and take the land when we couldn't pay. She must have been saving this for years! I am sure there is enough here to pay the king's ransom and more!"

Little John was astonished. "She was always one step ahead of them."

"Yes, Son," said John. "She never failed to amaze me."

John filled his pockets with as many coins as he could carry, and they buried the coffin again under the rock.

"Do you think that will be enough to pay the taxes?" asked Little John.

"If not, we will come back for more."

Little John laughed. "Imagine! A treasure guarded by the wild boars of Pool Wood! It's just like one of Amy's bedtime stories."

"But we must keep this a secret from *everyone*," said John. "It could be dangerous even for Amy to know of it."

"I will try, Paa. But I have never been able to keep anything from my wife. She has an uncanny knack for figuring out the truth. She knew we were smuggling long before I ever told her so."

"If she doesn't have any knowledge of this, she can't be forced to tell the king's men anything."

When they returned to the house Amy Anne was at the door with questions. "Well, did you find anything?" she asked.

"Not a thing," replied John. "I guess Lady Harrington was just talking nonsense."

"Well, no matter," said Amy Anne. "I think we will be ready for the king's chancellor. At least we know we have the *truth* on our side."

"Yes," said Little John. "There isn't much else we can do."

Amy stared at her husband for a moment and then she fixed her gaze on her father-in-law. They all sat down to have their supper and afterward gathered around the fire.

"Tell us a story!" said Richard. Even as the lad got older, he never bored with his mother's stories.

"Yes, Amy. Tell us one of your stories," said John who enjoyed them too.

Amy Anne sat down on the stool near the hearth and rubbed her hands together over the fire. She thought for a moment. "Well, did I ever tell you the one about the devil and St. Dubricious?"

"No," said Richard, "Tell us *that* one, Mother!"

"Well, let's see," she began, "it was a long, long time ago when St. Dubricious came to Porlock to build our church. He had come all the way across the channel floating on his cloak. When he got here, they say the devil met him on the shore and challenged him to a contest. "If you can out-throw *me*," said the devil, "then I will let you pass. If I can out-throw *you*, however, you must return to Wales from whence you came and never return to England."

She paused to catch her breath and recollect the story she had heard her mother tell so many years before. She looked at the faces of her audience; Richard was lying on the floor at her feet, Little John was leaning his back against the hearth and John was sitting in his chair; all were waiting anxiously for her to go on.

"Well," she continued, "they were down on the beach, you know the one that is covered with white rocks? St. Dubricious accepted the devil's challenge and he picked up what looked like a good chucking rock and tried to throw it, but his hand got caught in his cloak and the rock dropped into the water at his feet. The devil laughed heartily at poor Dubricious and picked up an even *bigger* stone. He took a deep breath and hurled it with all his might, and it landed two miles away on the top of Porlock Hill! St. Dubricious was not going to let the devil beat him and keep him from doing the Lord's work. He took off his cloak and rolled up his shirt sleeves and looked around for an even *larger* rock. He found a great big white one lying on the ground that was *twice* the size of the devil's rock and was very heavy. "Get thee out of my way devil!" he said, and he spun round and round three times and hurled the white stone clear to the edge of the woods and *twice* as far as the devil. So, the devil went away with his forked tail between his legs and our dear patron saint came to Porlock and built our church."

After a moment she added: "By the way the rocks are still there today. The one he dropped in the water can still be seen off Hurlstone Point when the tide is low. The devil's white rock is still at the top of Porlock Hill, where it scares the horses as they round the bend in the road."

"That part is true! There *is* indeed a white rock on the hill. Even the horses that have passed it a million times get spooky when they go by it!" exclaimed Richard.

"All legends have *some* truth in them, Son," Amy answered.

"But what happened to the *last* white rock, Mother?"

"Well, no one knows," said Amy Anne. "Some say that it landed *somewhere over in Pool Wood.*"

"That was a good story, Mother!" said Richard.

John and Little John just looked at each other trying not to roll their eyes.

"*I'm* going to bed," said Little John.

Chapter Thirty "Porlock Guild"

John received a message from Father Clary the next day regarding Lady Harrington's effigy. It had arrived at the church from the stone mason, and he wanted John to approve of it before it was installed atop the crypt. John had hurried to town, anxious to see how the statue had turned out; it had taken far too long and the plain stone lid over her coffin looked so barren beside the beautiful image of her husband. He entered the church in the early morning when the sun through the stained-glass windows was casting a rosy glow on the interior walls and giving a semblance of life to the gray stone memorial. He bowed and paid his respects and then followed Father Clary down the stairs to the basement of the church.

It was laid there on the basement floor; the carved image of Lady Harrington in a long gown; the lower part of her dress was delicately shaped in rounded folds and on her head was an elegant, mitered headdress all created from a single block of alabaster cut out of the Somerset quarries. Her head was resting on two cushions with small wrought tassels on each corner.

John walked around the statue, taking in every detail of the work and he stopped suddenly at the foot of the effigy.

"I know *that* is a little *unusual*, Master John," Father Clary explained. "I *do* hope that it is not offensive to you.

Most effigies of noblewomen are sculpted with their feet resting on a dog. But we had no choice but to follow her final wishes."

John stood there for a moment and then his face broke into a smile. "No, Father," he replied. "I think it is just *perfect.*"

The feet of Lady Harrington, instead of resting on a dog like noblewomen before her, were resting on the back of a *wild boar.*

At home that night, after they had eaten their supper and were resting by the fire, John told the family about Lady Harrington's statue.

"It has something to do with Pool Wood, doesn't it?" Amy Anne asked. "The old story about the wild boars that ate children, *bones and all,* if they ventured into the wood?"

"I don't know what it meant," said John. "Like I told you, she wasn't in her right mind right before she died."

"I'll never believe that John. Lady Harrington's mind was as sharp as a sword."

There was a lull in the conversation and Little John took the opportunity to change the subject with a question.

"What was your impression of London, Paa?"

John shook his head. "It's a terrible place, Son. I don't know why anyone would want to live there."

Little John agreed.

"Just from your description of the place I know *I* never want to go there," said Amy Anne.

"I was just thinking about it; comparing London to Porlock, you know," said Little John.

"*There is no comparison to Porlock*," John remarked.

"Aye, there is no comparison *now*," said Little John. "But what of the future? Do we not throw our garbage and empty our chamber pots into the street just as they do in London? Do we not let the dung from our livestock run down and foul the river water and the bay?"

"It *does* get a bit ripe in the summer when we haven't had a good rain in a while," answered John. "But we don't live in town now do we?"

"That's my point exactly. We don't care much if we don't have it offending our own nostrils! If we think that way, we are no better than the king himself sitting up in his castle."

"What *is* your point, John?" Amy Anne's interest had now peaked.

"I was just thinking, maybe the town should have someone in charge of sweeping the streets and disposing of the waste and burning the garbage."

"Who has the time, with all the other work we have to do?" asked John.

"Well, if we all worked together…."

John shook his head. "Amy, I know your parents always keep the front of their shop clean. Most of the merchants take care of their own area. That's the way it's always been."

"Yes, John. But some don't clean it every day and if a good rain comes before they sweep, my poor father has to clean up what runs downhill."

"That's exactly what I mean, Paa. Porlock is growing. Tom and others have moved their families here. I would just hate to see Porlock end up like London."

John was not convinced. *Change* was not something that came naturally to him.

"I don't know if you've noticed it since you have been spending a lot of time out at the Harrington manor, but I have dug trenches around all of all our fields and I've got the runoff flowing from one field to another instead of down the hill into the river. Uncle Peter has done the same on his land. It saves the water because we reuse it and none of the horse manure we use to fertilize the crops goes downhill into the river. They call it *irrigation*, Paa."

"That sounds like a practical idea, Son," said John. "But what has that to do with the garbage in town?"

"It is doing *our* part for the *good* of the town," Little John answered. "If all the farms did the same our river would run clean from the melting snow and not smell so foul. Maybe someday we would be able to drink the water again as it comes down from Exmoor."

John had no argument with that.

"Porlock needs to govern itself now that the Harringtons are gone. If we continue to grow as we have been, who knows what lawlessness and corruption will find its way in? We should form a guild to discuss important matters."

"Well, *I* think it is a *wonderful* idea, John," said Amy Anne.

"Do you suppose it would be all right to have a meeting and see what everyone thinks of the idea?"

"Where would you have such a meeting?" his father asked.

"I thought maybe we could have it at Harrington Manor. That great hall is just sitting there not being used."

John rubbed his chin and appeared to be in deep thought. "I suppose that would be all right, Son," he said. "I think Lady Harrington would approve of anything that was in the interests of Porlock."

Amy Anne rode to town the next day to visit with Maggie and the two of them went out together and knocked on every door in Porlock with an invitation to the meeting at the manor after church on the Sabbath. Little John and Richard paid visits to every farm in Somerset doing the same. Little John was excited but nervous at the same time.

"I hope they won't run me out and string me up," he said to Amy Anne as they were getting ready for bed the night before the meeting.

"I think you have very good ideas, John. I am very proud of you, and I am sure Lady Harrington would be as well."

When Sabbath finally arrived, there was a long line of wagons stretching all the way up Porlock Hill. Not since Lady Harrington's funeral had they seen such a procession on the road to the Harrington Manor. They hadn't enough chairs for everyone so most of the townsfolk just sat on the wood floor of the great hall. When they all had assembled Little John walked to the front of the room and began to speak.

"Lady Harrington is no longer with us to look out for the best interests of Porlock," he began. "And it is neither my father's nor my ambition to take her place. We are working folk just as you all are. The decisions we have had to make in her stead we believe would be decisions she would have made herself. Above all she loved the town of Porlock and all of you. My father swore to her that he would protect Porlock from outside threats and takeovers."

He paused. He was not accustomed to public speaking and his hands were shaking. He looked down and saw his wife and his father sitting in the front row smiling at him. She gave him a little wink of encouragement and he went on.

"When my father and I travelled to London with Lady Harrington several years ago I was shocked at the disgusting conditions in the king's city. You cannot drink the water or breathe the air. The streets are not safe, and they must lock the city gates at night to protect themselves. Beggars are starving in the streets and attacking anyone passing by who might have a shilling in their pocket. I do not wish to ever see Porlock look like that."

"I agree, Little John," shouted Mr. Potter. "But tell us what exactly you had in mind?"

"My idea is that we form a guild to help each other now that we do not have a lord or lady to go to with our needs. We must unite and stay strong so that no tyrants move in on us and take over our lands. I was thinking about working together to clean up the streets and dispose of the wastes, to dig drainage ditches around our crops and clean up our river and harbor. If we pool our resources, I believe it could be done."

"How will that keep a new lord from coming in and staking his claim?" shouted someone in the back of the room.

"The Harrington lands now belong to my father. They will eventually be mine. I would be willing to establish Harrington Manor as property of the guild, to be used for the good of all Porlock; for growing additional crops to store for hard winters, for producing wool for blankets and clothing necessary to us all. This could be our meeting hall. I think Lady Harrington would like that. And no one could ever take away our Christmas celebrations and other community events. I believe it is what Lady Harrington would have wanted. Harrington Manor will continue to be the center of Porlock. If we can show the king that we can govern and police ourselves perhaps he won't see the need to interfere with our lives as in the past."

"As long as we pay our taxes!" said a man in the front and everyone laughed.

"What it means is that we would govern ourselves in place of having an overseer; the guild which would be made up of all of us would make decisions for Porlock. We could improve our little town and be united in a common interest."

"I would like to see a school established for our children," said Mrs. Hartley.

"I would like to see a fund set up for our widows and orphans," said Father Clary.

"Those are all good ideas. First, we must agree to *form* the guild. Then we can get on to the business of running our town."

When the vote was taken it was unanimous in favor of Little John's proposal and Little John was named Master of the Guild. As they left Harrington Manor, John congratulated his son on his victory. "Lady Harrington would be proud of you. *I am proud of you, Son*," he said simply. "I know I am leaving Porlock in good hands."

Two weeks later John was dead.

Chapter Thirty-One "The Court of Chancery"

John's death came quietly in his sleep; his weary body worn out by over sixty years of hard labor in the fields. As it was with his wife, Margaret, the family gathered and laid him to rest next to her on the hill without fanfare. They dried their tears and then they did what John would have wanted them to do: *they got on with the business of Porlock.*

It now fell upon Little John and Amy Anne to travel to London to present their case to the king's court. In their possession they had receipts from every one of Lady Harrington's shipments of goods showing taxes paid, their copy of the lady's last will and testament and a letter of petition to the court. In their absence they left Richard in charge of the farm. Captain Tom took leave from his ship to accompany them just in case his signature as a witness was questioned. The three rode side by side, following the same route as they had with Lady Harrington and entered the gates of London to find a city in worse condition than Little John and Tom remembered from their first trip. Aided by a brisk wind, the stench of London hit them all in the face with a nauseating punch as soon as they set foot in the city. Amy Anne had to stop her horse for a few moments until the urge to vomit left her.

"I'm sorry, my love. I should have warned you. It is ever so much worse than before," Little John said riding up beside her.

"It's best to cover your nose with something," said Tom.

Not to be deterred from their mission, Amy Anne buried her face in a handkerchief and urged her horse on. Now she was seeing firsthand the horrible conditions her husband was determined would not spread to Porlock. Her pride in her husband gave her new strength. They arrived at the court and were immediately escorted to the Lord Chancellor's office.

The chancellor was an older man, much older than the king himself, but as elegantly dressed as any monarch in a long bright coat with brass buttons and silk stockings. He looked quite prosperous and well-fed. He was sitting at a long table flanked on either side by young clerks; one who refilled the chancellor's goblet each time his lord took a sip and the other who held the edge of the scrolled paper so that the chancellor could read without lifting a finger. It was a busy place with lawyers scurrying in and out with papers in their hands.

"Please sit down," he invited them in a most cordial tone.

"You are John Snow of Porlock?" he asked looking at Tom.

"No, Lord Chancellor, I am Captain Tom Hatherly," Tom corrected him. *"This* is John Snow and his wife."

The chancellor looked at Little John. "I expected a much older man," he said.

"You must be thinking of my father," Little John replied. "He passed away earlier this year. I am here in his stead representing Lady Harrington."

"There is a matter of a will I am told," said the chancellor. "Have you brought it with you?"

Amy Anne stepped forward and handed the will to him.

They all waited until he had finished reading it and handed it back to Amy Anne.

"The issue here is not the validity of the will. I see that the document appears proper and that you have brought your witness with you. The issue is the *debt* owed by Lady Harrington which must be paid before any title can be transferred."

"M'Lord, can you explain what she owed?" asked Little John. "We have searched all her records and have not found any evidence of any debt."

The chancellor reached in a drawer and pulled out some papers which he studied for a moment before he answered.

"First of all, there must be an error in the number of sheep she claims to own. It has dropped very low when compared to the number of bales of wool she has reported over the last several years."

Little John remembered how Lady Harrington had been enraged at the double tax on her sheep. He knew that at least a third of her herds were farmed out on the hills of the Devon countryside. He had to think quickly to respond.

"M'Lord, there was a sickness all over Somerset County last year. Lady Harrington lost a great number of ewes to influenza just before shearing season. Not wanting to disappoint the king she had us shear the wool off the *dead* carcasses as well. There were, however, fewer *live* sheep to report."

The chancellor raised his eyebrows. "There are other taxes as well. On the hops production, she still shows no profit at all after years of cultivation."

"If you check with the records, M'Lord, you will see that her hops operation sustained major damage at the hands of King Henry's men. She reported the assault to the king and the culprits were punished but she was forced to rebuild. The hops fields now produce only enough for our own local use in the brewing of our ale. It was never meant to be an export crop."

"And you are testifying that she paid *all* her taxes on *all* her wool shipments?"

"Yes, M'Lord. I have all the receipts here. And Captain Hatherly can testify to each and every one. Lady Harrington trusted no other captain to handle her goods."

The chancellor looked down at the pile of receipts with a look of exasperation not expecting such an organized and well-planned case to be presented by what he was told were common peasants. His only hope was to challenge the son's right to the inheritance. "Have you any siblings, Sir?" he asked Little John.

"No, M'Lord. I am an only child. My mother died at my birth."

The chancellor searched desperately for one last card to play. "There is, of course, a substantial *fee* for the court's time spent on this matter."

"And how much do we owe for that, M'Lord?" asked Little John.

"Forty sovereigns," said the clerk.

Little John reached into his pocket and produced the forty gold coins while Amy Anne and Tom watched in surprise. The Lord Chancellor sighed in defeat. There were no other objections he could offer. He had no choice but to grant the inheritance of the Harrington estate to Little John, as sole heir of his father. He signed the petition and stamped it with his seal.

As soon as they got back to their horses and mounted for the long ride back to Porlock, Amy Anne looked at her husband with the inevitable question. "Where did you get that money?"

Tom was curious too and he was anxious to hear Little John's answer.

"Lady Harrington left some money for Paa. She expected there would be a tax to pay."

"*Forty sovereigns*? Where was your father keeping that much money? *In his socks?*" Amy Anne asked.

"I don't know, Amy. What does it matter? We won! We're going home!"

Little John cantered ahead, and the subject was not brought up again. The ever-vigilant Amy Anne was not convinced however and decided to wait for a better opportunity to interrogate her husband.

Chapter Thirty-Two "Bullies and Bows"

Two weeks after their return from London, Richard had an important name-day. Turning fifteen was considered a milestone in the eyes of English society; old enough to make his own decisions and live on his own if he so chose. He approached his parents after supper with a request.

"Father," he said. "I want to go to Bossington and become a squire for Sir Reynolds."

This was the first Little John and Amy Anne had heard of this opportunity and, although they were both aware of their son's proclivity for the talents of swordsmanship and archery, there were no knights locally from whom he could receive professional instruction. There had not been a knight living in Porlock since the death of Lord Harrington.

"How is it that Sir Reynolds contacted you to make you such an offer, Son?" asked Little John. He knew peasant boys were rarely bestowed such an honorable position, only the sons of nobles and knights themselves.

"It was at Lady Harrington's funeral. I was admiring his sword. I asked him if he would have openings for squires and told him of my inclinations. He told me then that whenever I was ready, I would be welcome to come to his house and train with him."

"And did you *also* mention that you had trained in Lord Harrington's arena?"

"Yes, Father. I thought that would impress him."

"And apparently it did. You are very fortunate to be connected to the Harrington name."

"I know that Father," said Richard humbly.

"And it was only because your grandfather was the Harrington heir that you were favored in this way. Do not ever forget that Son."

Richard shook his head.

"And why have you never told us of this plan?" Amy Anne asked. "Do you think you might have warned your poor mother that she would be losing her only son?"

"I wanted to practice and get as good at my craft as possible before I told you both. I was not sure I was ready," said Richard. "Now, I am sure."

"Your talent with swords and lances is exceptional son," said Little John. "But do you think you are truly prepared for battle? For *killing*? "

"Father, if I am not ready, Sir Reynolds' schooling will prove it to me."

Amy Anne didn't want Richard to see her cry and she turned her head away.

"Mother?" said Richard. "Please don't be upset. You are not losing me. I promise I will make you proud. I am just not cut out to be a farmer or a ship's captain."

"I know that Son," replied Amy Anne. "Ever since that day when you fought the feathers off King George in my honor, I knew it would be your destiny. I shall just be sad to see you go."

It was decided then that Richard was to leave for Bossington forthwith. He only had one last thing to do before he left. The very next morning he saddled his horse and rode into Porlock and knocked on the Hatherly door.

"Good morning, Mistress Maggie. Please forgive me for coming unannounced. I am leaving Porlock tomorrow and I wanted to say goodbye to Elizabeth. May I speak to her?"

Maggie called for her daughter.

"And where is it you are going, Richard?" she asked.

"I am going to Bossington to be a squire for Sir Reynolds." Just as he spoke Elizabeth stepped forward from behind her mother.

"You will make a fine knight someday, Richard," said Maggie and went back to the kitchen.

Elizabeth put on her shawl and stepped out on the front step. She was not surprised at Richard's news; he had confided in her many times of his ambition.

"When are you leaving?" she asked.

"Tomorrow at first light," said Richard. "I wanted to see you before I left."

"I knew you would leave someday. I just wasn't expecting it quite so soon," said Elizabeth.

Richard took her hand and led her away from the house and out of sight before he turned to her and kissed her quickly on the lips.

"Elizabeth, I want to marry you someday! After I am a knight, I will need a lady by my side. Will you wait for me?"

Elizabeth was still tasting his kiss that lingered on her mouth and fighting tears of happiness mixed with tears of sadness. It was an overwhelming mix of emotions. Surely, he knew there was no other that she held in her heart so dearly; none of the young men in Porlock could even compare to Richard! "Yes, Richard, "she answered, "I will wait for you. *No matter how long it takes.*"

The next morning it seemed as if the sun would never rise to the young man lying fully clothed in his bed with his bag packed beside him. When he heard rain falling outside, he jumped up thinking the rain clouds had hidden the dawn from him.

Amy Anne was already in the kitchen, packing food for Richard to eat on his journey. As he sat by the fire to put his boots on, she brought him a cloth bag containing the food and kissed the top of his head. "I will miss you, my son," she said softly. "Your father will miss you too."

Richard hugged his mother; now that he was grown, she seemed as tiny as a doll in his arms. "Is Father up yet?" he asked.

"He was up before you were. I think he is out saddling your horse."

Richard went out into the rain and found Little John standing there holding the reins of a large black gelding that he immediately recognized as one that had belonged to Lady Harrington.

"He is all ready to go, Son. Take it slow for the roads may be slippery. No sense breaking your neck before you get to Bossington."

Richard looked at his father with a quizzical expression.

"What?" said Little John smiling. "Am I not allowed to share my inheritance with my only son? I can't send you off to Bossington on a *plough* horse, can I?"

Richard tied his bow and quiver to the saddle and secured the tiny sword that Lady Harrington had given him in his belt. Now that he had grown it looked like a very long knife, but Richard believed it would bring him luck. He pulled his hooded cloak up over his head. "Goodbye, Father," he said. "Thank you for everything. I will take good care of the horse and I will write to you and Mother as soon as I have settled in."

He rode off up the wet road at a slow trot, passing the Harrington manor and into the woods beyond the hops fields. Once in the wooded area the thick canopy that the trees provided temporarily sheltered him from the rain and he urged his horse into a canter over the well-worn path. When he emerged again from the woods the road sloped down through a low- lying field, much like the marshlands of Porlock; the rain had turned to sleet. He could see the town of Bossington in the distance at the foot of Bossington Hill surrounded by bare apple trees and brown hills that were dusted with a thin layer of snow. He knew he was close to his destination.

Sir Reynolds' manor was rumored to be twice the size of Lady Harrington's but seemed somehow smaller due to the thick granite walls and iron gates that surrounded it. A man at the gate greeted him and allowed him entrance. "The stables are to your right," said the man. "The squires' and pages' quarters are in the upstairs loft."

As Richard approached the barn, he suddenly felt a twinge of uncertainty; most of the squires here would most likely have started their schooling as pages at the age of six or seven. Even though he had listened to Lady

Harrington's instruction and had practiced whenever he was not needed in the fields, he was aware he might be at a disadvantage. He looked down at the horse he was riding which gave him a small bit of courage; at least no one could find fault with his horse!

As he was dismounting a young page came up to him. "I'm Peter," said the boy, "I'm assigned to show the new students around."

"Glad to know you, Peter. I am Richard Snow of Porlock."

The boy led Richard into the barn where there was an empty stall in which to put his horse. Then he showed him the stairs in the back of the barn that led up to the loft where all the students slept. "You can stow your belongings here under your bed and I will show you the rest of the place."

Instead of one arena there were four, each one set up for specific instruction. The first one they passed had bales of straw all along one side, with targets in the shape of armored knights. At one end, several young squires were being instructed in the art of arrow-making and the carving of bows. In the next arena the students were practicing their swordsmanship, sparring with each other while the teacher corrected their footwork. Several others sat nearby learning how to clean and sharpen their weapons. They all seemed totally oblivious to the light snow falling around them. As Richard was soon to understand *war had no season*; it appeared it had no effect on a squire's training either.

The third arena was set up for horsemanship classes; the students were learning the art of maneuvering in bulky armor as well as how to throw the lance accurately at a target while galloping past at a high rate of speed.

In the fourth arena the students were gathered around their instructor in a tight circle, sitting around him on straw bales.

"What is that class for?" Richard asked Peter.

"That is the last part of the training. They are learning the code of chivalry preparing them to take their final vows," Peter replied.

He then took Richard on a tour of the rest of the school, where to bathe his horse, where to dispose of his horse's manure, where to store his gear, and the "chow-house" where they would eat their meals. It was all highly organized, and Richard noticed that everything was immaculate, from the floor of the barn to the way the beds were made in the loft. Sloppiness or laziness was obviously not allowed. "You will start in the first arena and work your way up to the last. Everything here is based on skill," he said. "You will stay in Level One until your instructor believes you are ready for the next level."

"When do we actually work with Sir Reynolds?" Richard wanted to know.

"*After* you have reached the fourth level," said Peter. "You have a good way to go."

After Richard had stowed all his gear under his bed, he retrieved his bow and quiver and went directly to the first arena where he was greeted by a young pimply faced squire named William. "Where are you from?" William asked as Richard took his place next to him.

"Porlock," answered Richard.

"You are a Harrington then?"

"No, not exactly. My grandfather was the Harrington heir. I trained in Lady Harrington's arena," Richard replied.

"Is that a Harrington horse you were riding?" asked young William. "I noticed him when you came in. Good looking animal he is!"

"Aye. The Harrington horses are truly remarkable."

The instructor came up quietly behind them and interrupted the boys' conversation. "Are you lads so perfect in your skills that you feel you do not need to practice?" he shouted." Let's get busy and stop cackling like old hens."

The other boys laughed as Richard sheepishly stepped up to the line, pulling an arrow over his shoulder he aimed at the first target. His hands were a bit shaky; he was not used to having other boys watching him. He released his arrow and missed the target completely. There was more laughter.

One squire, a lanky boy with long blond hair, had been listening to the conversation between William and Richard. "Is that how they teach you to shoot an arrow in Porlock? No wonder the town was sacked and burned!"

The boy moved around behind Richard and stood so close Richard could feel his breath on the back of his neck. He drew another arrow and aimed again. This time he hit the target in the stomach.

"You're *improving*, little Porlock boy."

Richard aimed a third time and hit the target square on the helmet.

"Bravo!" cheered William. "You are much better than I."

Richard stepped back to give William a turn at the target. The blond boy circled around Richard eyeing the little sword in his belt. "And what weapon is this you carry, Porlock Boy?" he taunted, reaching in and pulling the sword away. Tauntingly he read the inscription aloud.

"*Courage comes in all sizes,* does it? It's a little *small* for a sword, wouldn't you say?"

Richard took hold of the boy's arm and grabbed his little sword away from him.

The instructor walked up behind them with an arrow in his hand and swung at them both cracking the wood across their shoulders. "You two! Fighting amongst ourselves is not a way to win wars! Back to the barn for you both. You will be shoveling dung together until you can get along!"

Richard was mortified; to be thrown out of the class on his first day! The other boy didn't seem to care. They returned to the barn and began their punishment; side by side they mucked stalls.

"I've done this before," said the blond boy. "The master won't let us go back to class until we act like we are friends."

The *last* thing Richard wanted was to be friends with this bully! He kept working but remained mute. He just wanted the boy to leave him alone.

"I'm Geoffrey of Devon. My father was killed in the war."

Richard finally turned and looked directly at the boy. "I don't care *who* your father was. I am here to become a squire and I won't let *you* or *anyone else* stand in my way!"

Geoffrey realized he was not intimidating the new boy at all, and it was no longer entertaining. He decided to try another tack. "Aw, I was just fooling with you, *Richard,* is it? I didn't mean anything by it."

Richard still did not trust the boy, but he wanted desperately to get back to class. "You know, Geoffrey, I didn't ride all the way from Porlock to shovel horse manure! What do you say we shake hands and go back to class?"

"Sounds good to me!" Geoffrey replied with a wily grin.

The boys returned to the arena and Richard apologized to the instructor who replied, "If you interrupt class again you will both be going home."

Chapter Thirty-Three "So Much to Learn"

Richard was determined to do well in his classes and earn the acceptance of his young peers once he could prove that his abilities overshadowed the lowliness of his background. Even the troublesome Geoffrey could not fault his Harrington-bred horse, but his blond locked nemesis continued to tease Richard at every opportunity; he had an especially keen eye for the little sword Richard carried in his belt.

In Level One, the archery class, Richard was confident that he would move quickly to the head of the class for his accuracy with a bow and arrow was quite good. He soon found out he had much to learn, however. In the afternoon the entire class took an excursion into the nearby woods; their mission was to find the perfect specimens of wood with which to make bows and arrows. As they wandered amongst the trees, the instructor was lecturing them on what to look for. "Find wood that is dry and dead," he said to the boys, "but not gray and cracking. For your bows you need a piece about five feet long without knots, twists, or limbs. For the arrows look for a piece half as long as your bow and very straight."

The students spread out in the wood, hunting for just the right pieces. When they had collected enough wood, they went back to the arena where the instructor showed them everything from how to determine the natural curve of the bow wood to the correct way to cut the notches for the string. They learned how to whittle their arrows and straighten them by holding them over hot coals. One of the pages was sent to the manor chicken pens to collect feathers with which to make the fletchings.

"You should always have at least three or four bows," said the instructor. "The more you use your bow the more likely it will snap. If you have several bows and you alternate them every few months, they will last much longer."

Richard soon realized that becoming a squire was not something that he was going to accomplish overnight. When the boys gathered in the chow house for their supper that night, their talk was of war and the latest battles across England. When they retired to their beds above the stable, however, the talk died down; some boys sat on their beds working on their bows and arrows while others wrote letters to their parents or sweethearts. Richard borrowed two sheets of paper from William and wrote quick notes to Elizabeth and his mother putting them in a box on the wall for the next messenger. He leaned back and stared out the window above his bed watching the snow fall. The loft was drafty, and the cold outside wind was finding its way upstairs from the stable below. Soon all the boys were under their blankets and asleep.

The next few weeks Richard remained with the Level One group; as precise as his aim was with the bow, he was having a great deal of difficulty keeping his handmade bows from breaking. Several times he returned to the woods to find better specimens, but it became more difficult as winter progressed.

"You may have to use green wood now that the snow is on the ground," his instructor told him. "It is a last resort, and it will not give you the same power as dry wood."

Richard made the trek back to the woods again and broke several branches from the trees. Surprisingly the new bows he made did not break and he finally succeeded in passing his first class.

At supper on the night Richard and William had graduated to Level Two the annoying Geoffrey came to sit next to them; having worn out his welcome at all the other tables.

"So, you two finally passed archery," he said sarcastically.

"Yes," answered Richard, paying more attention to his food than the conversation; learning to become a squire was exhausting, starting in the mornings with strengthening exercises and classes that lasted until suppertime. By the end of the day, he was ravenous for food.

"I think I will just stay at Level One," continued Geoffrey. "It is far easier than the other classes I am told."

"Are you planning to stay in school forever?" asked William. "Don't you want to be out in the battlefields?"

"And die with an arrow or a lance through my gut?" Geoffrey retorted. "Not hardly! My father wanted me to attend this school, it wasn't *my* idea."

Richard was shocked; here was a boy with all the right social connections to become a knight and he was wasting them!

"Don't you want to carry on the honor of your father's name?" Richard asked.

"I don't see much honor in getting yourself killed."

"Well," said Richard, "I didn't inherit a noble name, but I intend to become the best squire I can be. I am not afraid."

"I never said I was *afraid*," answered Geoffrey, "I just value my head a little more than you do."

"I am with *you,* Richard," said William. "My father is fighting somewhere on the border of Scotland right now and I will be standing beside him as soon as I can.

One thing became apparent to Richard when he started his Level Two class the following day; the classes were designed to become increasingly harder and more challenging. In this level they began by issuing each student a wooden sword called a *waster*. They had to practice fighting against a pole called a *pell* that simulated a human target. From this he was to learn the proper footwork and how to correctly handle his weapon. At the end of each class each student had to apply linseed oil to their wasters to prevent splintering of the wood and store them away for the next day's practice. Much to his disappointment it would be many weeks before he would be allowed to handle a *steel* sword.

When that much anticipated day arrived, a wooden box appeared in the Level Two arena. In it were the short, lightweight steel swords that would facilitate the next step in their training. With these swords they would at last learn to spar with *human opponents*. They each were issued padded chest protectors and they paired up with partners. Richard and William spent the days fighting mock battles; it was the most enjoyable part of their training so far! They returned to the loft every night in a state of satisfied exhaustion. Richard felt the muscles in his arms and legs, though aching by the end of each day, were becoming harder and stronger and just when he and William thought they were on the top of their game, the instructor introduced them to the long swords, much heavier and thicker weapons that required two hands to wield and Level Three suddenly seemed far away again. Tired and weary all the boys began to quarrel among themselves. A few dropped out and went home.

Becoming a squire, they were both learning, *was not for the weak of heart!*

Chapter Thirty-Four "Amy Anne's Patient"

When Elizabeth received Richard's message back in Porlock it was delivered by a young horseman with a fancy letter "R" embroidered on his horse's blanket. She immediately showed it to Maggie hoping to boost her mother's sagging spirits. Tom had been gone almost two weeks on a trip across the English Channel to pick up cargo in France and Maggie had been sinking deeper and deeper into a melancholy state. After Maggie had read Richard's letter, she shook her head. "It seems that we have both pinned our happiness to faraway stars, Daughter," she said.

"Father will be home soon, Mother. He said he could not turn down such a lucrative trip. He is only looking after our welfare."

Maggie sighed and went back to her needlework. It had been a week since she had seen Amy Anne who could usually cheer her up, but as of late even her best friend had a difficult time drawing Maggie out of her pit of despair. She rarely left the house, leaving the errands to her daughter and she hadn't eaten more than a few bites in days. Try as she might Elizabeth could not coax her to eat. Taking the wagon up Porlock Hill to visit Amy Anne was out of the question now that the snows had come, and her mother was no longer interested in learning to ride. Elizabeth decided to go into town to ask Mrs. Hartley for advice; she bundled herself up in her heavy wool shawl and told her mother she was going for a visit with Amy Anne's parents with whom they had become good friends.

Mrs. Hartley opened the door and welcomed Elizabeth in from the cold and led her to a chair near the fire where she could warm herself. "How is your mother?" she asked.

Elizabeth pulled off her mittens and stretched her hands out toward the fire. She shook her head. "Mother is not doing well, Mrs. Hartley. I have come to you for advice."

"I am hardly an expert, Elizabeth, but I will help if I can," said Mrs. Hartley.

"Mother won't eat. She cries all the time and I know she doesn't sleep...I can hear her up at all hours of the night walking the floor. Mrs. Hartley, I don't know what to do!"

"Have you mentioned this to Amy Anne?"

Elizabeth shook her head. "With the snow and ice on Porlock Hill we haven't dared to travel. Mother *does* seem to cheer up when Amy Anne is with her."

"I will ask my husband to ride out to the Snow farm and fetch her. I am worried about your mother as well."

Amy Anne was concerned when she got the news; she immediately rode back to town with her father and after much debate convinced Maggie to come and stay with her on the Snow farm, at least until Tom returned from the sea. "Remember how much fun we had when you stayed with me before?" she chirped happily. "You and Elizabeth can take John's old room."

As was usually the case Amy Anne prevailed. Taking the wagon was not an option in the snow, so with Maggie sitting on the back of her horse and a terrified Elizabeth holding on to Mr. Hartley they left Porlock. By that evening Maggie and Elizabeth were sitting at the Snow supper table where Maggie sat silently pushing the food around on her plate without ever taking a bite.

"You must *eat* something, Maggie," said Amy Anne. "Hunger is why you feel so weak."

Little John sat quietly as his wife fussed over Maggie. When it was time for everyone to retire for the night Amy Anne sat on the bed brushing Maggie's hair. *How childlike she is* thought Elizabeth, marveling at how artfully Amy Anne handled her mother's melancholy.

"Maggie, now that my Richard has gone off to school, I need you here to keep me company," she said, tucking her into bed as a mother would.

Maggie began to cry, and Amy Anne wiped the tears from her cheeks.

"Tom will be home soon. In the meantime, we can teach Elizabeth to play Crown of Roses and we will have ever so much fun!"

Maggie rolled away and buried her face in the pillow as Elizabeth climbed into the bed beside her.

"Tomorrow will be better. You'll see," said Amy Anne as she extinguished the candle and closed the door to the bedchamber.

Little John was sitting in his father's chair, staring into the fire. He was not looking forward to his house being turned into a hospital again; he was beginning to feel slightly resentful toward Maggie for being so immature and dependent on his wife.

"I am very worried about Maggie," Amy Anne said sitting down with her husband by the fire. "It is almost like she has lost the will to live!"

"Maybe she should be under a doctor's care, Amy."

"I don't think herbs and potions will cure her John," replied Amy Anne. "I think she is seriously ill."

"You mean ill in her *brain*?" asked Little John.

"Yes," she said, "but she is not crazy. It just seems like her *spirit* has departed from her."

John shook his head. "I just hope you are not taking on more than you should, Amy. If she is as sick as you say she may need more help than you can give her."

Chapter Thirty-Five "The Battle of Bosworth"

While Richard was away at school much was happening across England. The bloody civil war between the Yorks and the Lancasters wore on under the Yorkist King Edward IV. When the king died suddenly in 1483, his twelve-year-old son Edward V was next in line for the throne, with his uncle Richard III acting as his protector. There was some question as to young Edward's true parentage and he was declared illegitimate; the prince and his younger brother then disappeared under mysterious circumstances. For the next two years Richard ruled in his position of protector until he was challenged by Henry Tudor, a Lancastrian knight from Wales which would soon bring the War of the Roses to an end.

Richard and William had finally mastered the long sword and had moved on to Level Three in their training where they attended their classes on horseback. The class had gotten smaller, as the weaker students were winnowed out and it was down to only a handful of the most determined young men. Richard rode into the arena proudly on his Harrington gelding and took his place among the others; he couldn't help but notice that his horse towered over the other horses, and he remembered his father's last words when he had left home: *I can't send you to Bossington on a plough horse can I?* As he looked around at the other horses, he realized how truly fortunate he was.

Level Three proved to be the easiest of all the classes for Richard. Chucking the lance through a hoop was one of the exercises he had practiced often in Lady Harrington's arena, so it came natural to him. His instructor was impressed with his agility and accuracy and Richard noticed Sir Reynolds himself observing them as they practiced one day.

"Well done, Richard!" Sir Reynolds called to him.

Richard was beside himself with pride to receive such a compliment. The next day he was promoted to Level Four, and his friend William joined him a week later. Within the month they were both kneeling at Sir Reynolds' feet in a dubbing ceremony each having earned the rank of squire.

As spring wore on and the snow on the ground was finally melting Richard had not seen his parents or Elizabeth for a very long time. He was hoping to be given leave to go home for a short visit. He was pleased that Elizabeth and her mother were now living with his parents; he had worried about the two women living alone now that Tom was making long trips to France.

Now that he was officially Sir Reynolds' squire, he was getting to know his mentor. Although Sir Reynolds had many squires, some to take care of his horses, some to keep his armor in good shape and others to serve in other ways on the estate, Richard soon became his favorite. Sir Reynolds confided in Richard in matters of politics; the most important thing he learned was that Sir Reynolds' allegiance was not to the Yorkist king, Richard; he was a *Lancastrian* knight as had been Lord Harrington and was waiting for the tide to turn.

"There will be an uprising soon," he told Richard one day, "and you will ride with me."

Richard was thrilled and by summertime any plans to visit Porlock were quickly forgotten; he dared not leave and not be present when he was needed.

He didn't have to wait long. In August of 1485 Henry Tudor landed on the southwest shore of his native Wales after a fourteen-year absence spent in Brittany. With two thousand troops he marched north from Mill Bay, captured Dale Castle, and crossed the border into England. Gathering support as he went his army soon numbered five thousand.

 Late one afternoon as Richard and the other squires were crossing the grounds toward the chow house a trio of riders appeared at the gates of the Reynolds manor. They watched with interest as the men rode in and were greeted by Sir Reynolds in the courtyard. The apparent leader of the group, a tall, dark-haired man dressed in battle chainmail and a tunic embroidered with a red dragon dismounted and hugged Sir Reynolds affectionately. They spoke a few hushed words, embraced each other again and the three men rode out of the gates leaving the squires much fodder for gossip about over their supper. That evening Richard and William were called to the manor house.

"This is it," Sir Reynolds told them. "Tomorrow we ride to join Henry. Prepare for a long journey for I do not know how long we will be gone."

Richard and William did not sleep at all and were up before the dawn packing weapons and supplies on their pack horse and saddling the other horses. They left Reynolds Manor to the cheering and fare thee wells of all their comrades as they rode out of the manor gates. Richard was assigned the care of all the weapons and Sir Reynolds' armor and William was in charge of the horses. Richard's adrenaline was high; never before had he witnessed a real battle. He knew when Henry finally clashed with Richard it would be nothing like the mock enactments in the training arena. He had written notes to both the women in his life the night before saying simply *"We are off to join Sir Henry."*

Sir Reynolds wore his battle armor, flanked by his two best squires, Richard and William, wearing matching tunics with the Reynolds' black and gold emblem over their protective chest guards. They rode north in the morning sun to join Sir Henry at Shrewsbury. All three wore red arm bands to show their fealty to Henry. As they rode, they were joined by others; every able-bodied man on Reynolds' lands dropped their work in the fields and unharnessed their plough horses to accompany them in support of their lord. Soon they were one hundred strong.

The road was long, and the sun was hot; Sir Reynolds soon removed his helmet, carrying it under his arm and peeled back his chainmail hood, wiping sweat from the back of his neck. Richard rode forward and offered to hold his helmet.

"Thank you, Richard," he said and added, "Are you boys nervous?"

"Well, Sir, a little," Richard said honestly. William nodded in agreement.

"That is normal. I feel shaky before a battle too."

"*You,* M'Lord?" asked William incredulously.

"Yes, William *even I*. It goes away, of course, when the fighting starts; when you are fighting you can only think of *surviving*."

"Do you think we will win, M'Lord?" Richard asked.

"I pray that we do. England has too long been under the rule of the Yorks. It is time the throne was back in Lancastrian hands."

"My grandfather told me stories of Sir Harrington coming home from the battles in France with Henry V."

"Ah, yes, that must have been Agincourt you speak of. I have heard those stories too, from *my* father. We had providence on our side in that one. But those French territories were lost. The crown has been too long in the hands of incompetent pretenders. We are fighting now to keep England from falling apart and that can only be accomplished under a strong king. I believe Henry Tudor is the man to do just that. It will be a victory of *good over evil*."

Sir Reynolds suddenly broke into a canter and for a while there was no conversation, only the sounds of a hundred horses' hooves on the road to Shrewsbury, leaving both Richard and William to their own thoughts. While Richard had admitted his nervousness to Sir Reynolds, he did not elaborate about the nightmares he had been having. He did not want to speak of dreaming he was on the battlefield with a lance coming at him and waking from his sleep in a cold sweat. He could not show weakness or fear; even though his heart fluttered, and his body tingled with anticipation, he would keep *that* to himself.

They rode until the roofs of Shrewsbury were visible in the distance and drew their horses in at the top of a hill overlooking the town. Richard and William looked out over the fields below in awe of what they saw; a gray blanket of smoke and steel blades for as far as they could see. They rode into the camp toward a tent embroidered with the red dragon. Henry himself walked up to greet them.

"I am glad you are here Arthur," said Henry. His accent was quite peculiar; something in between the Welsh brogue of his origin and the melodious language of France where he had spent half of his life. "We are ready to ride east. There is word that the king is heading north from London toward Leicester and hopefully we will cross paths with him there."

"I have brought with me nearly one hundred. Every one of my tenants who had a horse is here," said Sir Reynolds. "These are my two best pupils, Richard and William."

The two men embraced each other quickly with a firm hug and a slap on the back. "We will ride at first light," said Henry.

Sir Reynolds and his men found a place to camp for the night and Richard and William pitched his tent and bedded down just outside the canvas walls where neither could sleep from the excitement of it all. In the morning Henry gave the command to press on and the thunder of thousands of horses leaving Shrewsbury was something Richard would never forget in years to come. The dust cloud encompassed the little town completely obliterating it from view as they rode eastward. Richard and William were suddenly lost in the rush of horses, and they lost sight of Sir Reynolds who rode ahead with Henry and his field leaders.

"If you and I can stay together we will have to find Sir Reynolds when we get there," said William and Richard nodded.

"I don't think we shall get lost as long as we follow the crowd."

Although London was Henry's ultimate destination, he had not yet gathered enough troops to challenge the king. As they rode through the county of Staffordshire, their pace was slow due to the recruitment of more men. The Stanleys of Cheshire, a group whose support Henry wooed with great effort, were on the fence on the subject of their loyalty; they had followed Henry's group but set up a separate camp on the slopes north of the town of Dadlington while Henry and his troops made camp nearby at White Moors both facing the king who had moved his army to nearby Ambion Hill. It would have appeared to bystanders to be gearing up to be a three-way battle with three separate armies; the conniving Stanleys, however, were simply waiting to see who was to be the most likely victor before they joined in the fight.

Richard and William finally caught up with Sir Reynolds and were told to remain in camp keeping spare weapons handy and horses saddled to await further instructions. They watched as the archers lined up with the mounted lancers behind. Still far outnumbered, Henry's army, consisting of English, Scots, French and Welsh troops was only five thousand strong matched against King Richard's ten thousand troops. When Henry gave the call the first group marched down into the valley trudging through a boggy marshland toward the Ambion Hill. Henry had again sent messengers to the evasive Stanleys who stood quietly by watching the events, fervently hoping to gain their support; King Richard wooed them also; sending his messengers threatening to execute the son of Sir Stanley whom they had taken as a hostage if they did not support their king. Not knowing which direction the Stanley wind would blow, Henry had no choice but to attack the king's forces on his own.

The king was armed with cannons which he fired across the battlefield, exploding in a deafening barrage all around the camp where Richard and William waited. Amidst a steady hail of arrows Henry's men emerged from the marsh, but they managed to hold their own during the first ground scrimmage. Henry rode out with his lancers, splashing through the marsh. Even as the king released his mounted lancers Stanley's troops continued to sit by and watch as horses and knights clashed below them in a frenzy of steel and blood. Henry finally broke ranks and rode toward the Stanley camp knowing without their support there was no way he could defeat the king's forces. When King Richard saw Henry moving away from the protection of his guards he followed him with a group of his knights with the express intent of killing Henry himself and thereby eliminating any further claim on the throne. His men mowed down several of Henry's men in his path and the king closed in. Henry's guards, including Sir Reynolds, saw the danger and galloped quickly to Henry's side to form a protective circle around him. It was then that a Yorkist lance wounded Sir Reynolds in the chest and toppled him from his horse. The frightened animal bolted and ran back to the safety of the camp.

Richard and William saw Sir Reynolds' rider-less horse come galloping in and Richard went forward to collect him.

"What shall we do?" asked William.

Richard had no time to think about it.

"Fetch me another sword," he said as he pulled himself up into Sir Reynolds' saddle.

William was aghast. "Richard, you have no protection, save your padded chest guard! Please do not do this!" he begged.

Richard took the sword and looked down at his friend.

"I have to," he said, "Pray for me, William!"

Richard galloped down the hill and threw himself into the battle just as the indecisive Stanleys decided at last to join in the fight and they were all quickly fighting at Henry's side. Without thought as to his vulnerable condition, Richard urged his horse on wielding his sword right and left at the king's men wounding several foot soldiers in his path. One particularly burly knight with a white Yorkist rose on his tunic took notice of Richard, seeing him as an easy unprotected target. Richard watched him ride forward and he readied himself. When the knight came within striking distance, they clashed swords violently for several seconds. Richard almost dropped his weapon, slipping from his perspiring palms but he recouped just in time. He realized at that moment he had an advantage over his opponent; he was lighter and more agile than the knight and his horse was quicker without the extra weight of armor. Remembering his training Richard continued to fight looking for the knight's most vulnerable spot. When he found it, he dropped his reins and, with both hands, firmly on the hilt struck as hard as he could, delivering a single slicing blow to his opponent's neck; his sword piercing the thin layer of chainmail in the narrow gap where his helmet and his armor came together. The knight toppled from his horse spurting a fountain of blood from his severed neck and Richard pulled back his bloody sword with shaking hands. With his chest pounding he circled his horse holding his sword ready. All around him the Stanley troops had engaged the king's men and Richard could see many of them fleeing through the marshes back up Ambion Hill. Just at that moment he heard someone cry out from across the field:

"Richard is dead! Long live King Henry!"

The battle seemed to be over. The king's men were fleeing from the field of battle leaving behind their dead comrades. Richard turned his horse around and stepping through the bloody bodies on the ground looking for Sir Reynolds. When he found him, he jumped from his horse and knelt beside his mentor, pulling off his helmet and laying his head gently on the grass. Sir Reynolds was still alive but barely. Richard could see the ragged hole where a lance had pierced his armor. His voice was a raspy whisper, and he was choking up bloody bubbles from his throat.

"M'Lord, what can I do for you? Do you think you can ride?" he asked.

'No, Richard. I fear I won't make it. My wound is deep."

"I will fetch a litter for you then. We will get you back to camp!" said Richard standing up to look for help.

"*Get a litter for this soldier*!" someone suddenly called out behind him. Richard immediately recognized the distinctive voice of Sir Henry. "Which one are you; William or Richard?" he asked, looking down from his horse.

Richard knelt against his sword and bowed deeply. "I am Richard Snow of Porlock, M'Lord," he said.

Sir Reynolds smiled up at them both.

"You should have seen him fighting in the field today, Arthur, in nothing but a chest guard!" said Sir Henry.

"I expected as much of my best student," Sir Reynolds replied weakly. "He will be a true knight someday."

"Aye," said Sir Henry and dismounted from his horse. "And today is as good as any!"

He drew his sword from its scabbard.

"Kneel, Richard Snow of Porlock!" he commanded.

Richard knelt on one knee and Henry laid the heavy steel blade on his shoulder

"Do you, Richard Snow of Porlock, swear henceforth to always be loyal to your king, to be devoted to the church, to always defend ladies and the weak, and be always available to fight to defend England?"

"I do, M'Lord," said Richard.

"Then rise, *Sir* Richard Snow of Porlock! I am glad to have you among my knights!"

Henry removed a small circlet with the image of a rose with both red and white petals from around his neck and placed it over Richard's head.

"Thank you, M'Lord," Richard said with his head still bowed.

When he looked down at Sir Reynolds, his mentor's eyes had closed, and his breath had ceased.

"Take him home, Sir Richard Snow of Porlock," said Henry, "and bury him with the honor he deserves."

The tall Welshman with the peculiar accent was crowned King Henry VII that day on the battlefield of Bosworth. It began the Tudor dynasty which would rule England for another one hundred and eighteen years.

Chapter Thirty-Six "The Pierced Armor"

Richard and William returned to Bossington dragging the litter behind them that held Sir Reynolds' body which they had wrapped in their own blankets. His pierced armor and his scarred and scratched sword were secured on the back of the packhorse. The news had already reached the school and classes had been cancelled indefinitely but when they entered the gate almost all of the squires were still there waiting for their mentor's sad return. While the house servants took charge of the body in preparation for the burial, Richard and William mingled with the others, recounting the details of the battle that took their Sir Reynolds' life. It was William who told of Richard's bravery, of his fighting on the field at Bosworth and his knighting by Henry. Richard accepted the congratulations of those he still considered to be his peers with embarrassed modesty. He stayed on at Bossington only long enough to attend the funeral and then he bade goodbye to William and set out to return to Porlock.

Before he had passed through the manor gate, a house servant came outside and waved Richard down. "Lady Reynolds would like a word with you before you leave, Sir Richard," he said.

It sounded so very peculiar, being addressed as *Sir* and it took Richard by surprise. "*Me*? She wants to speak to *me*?"

Richard dismounted, and William came running up to hold his horse. Following the servant up to the manor house, he smoothed his hair and straightened his tunic. Looking down at his boots he realized they were still dusty from the barn but there was not ample time to remedy his appearance any further. He was escorted into the great room of the house which was much like the one on the Harrington estate, but there were not so many windows and the room seemed darker.

Lady Reynolds came forward, smiling at him and Richard bowed politely.

"You are my husband's faithful squire, Richard Snow of Porlock?" she inquired.

"Yes, M'Lady."

"Forgive me, you are *Sir* Richard now, knighted by King Henry! How proud my husband would have been of you!"

Richard found it easy to talk to the lady, almost as easy as with Lady Harrington.

"Sir Reynolds' was there when King Henry knighted me. He was still alive when…." Richard stopped in mid-sentence, fearing he had said too much.

Lady Reynolds, still smiling, said "I am pleased that he lived long enough to see that, Sir Richard. It is all right to speak of his death. I am not a woman prone to hysterics."

She noticed the circlet around Richard's neck and admired it, touching it with her delicate hands. "This was given to you by the king?" she asked.

"Yes, M'Lady."

"The Tudor rose," replied Lady Reynolds. "You must take very good care of it and never lose it. You should wear it inside your tunic and close to your heart where it will bring you luck."

Richard nodded.

"Tell me, Richard, did my husband die a quick death? What were his last words to you?"

Richard tried to think; the day of the battle had been such a turmoil he had not really pieced it all together yet in his mind. "When his horse came back to camp without him, I rode out to find him. He was lying on the ground," said Richard. "I remember he told King Henry that I would be a true knight someday. I tried to get him back to camp but it was too late to save him."

Lady Reynolds closed her eyes and paused before she spoke again. "I am glad you were there with him in the end. I am glad he did not die alone. To know King Henry was there too is a comfort."

She suddenly turned and motioned for Richard to follow her. In the next room sitting on the floor was a newly forged suit of armor. Next to it was Sir Reynolds' armor that had been punctured by the lance.

"My husband would have presented you with your armor if he had lived. He was so sure you would prove yourself worthy he ordered these before he left for Bosworth."

Richard looked down at the new armor then glanced over at the pierced armor beside it, still stained from Sir Reynolds' own blood. "M'Lady, what will you do with his damaged armor?"

"I am not sure, Sir Richard. I do not wish to keep it as a constant reminder of his death, but I had not decided quite what to do with it."

"Would you permit me to wear it, M'Lady? I feel it would bring me luck to always have Sir Reynolds close to me."

She did not look surprised. "If you think you can repair it you are most welcome to it. I am sure his spirit will be with you always *with or without* his armor. But you *must* take the sword for he had it made especially for you."

The sword was exquisite from the tip of the polished blade to the hilt engraved with a red rose. When Richard took it in his hands and pulled it from its scabbard he was overcome with emotion for his slain mentor.

"Thank you, M'Lady. I will never forget your kindness. Your husband was a great man and a wonderful teacher."

She walked him to the front steps and watched as William helped Richard on with the bulky armor which was easier worn than carried across his saddle. He tightened his belt and sword around his waist and mounted his horse.

"Goodbye, Sir Richard!" she said waving. "God be with you!"

"We'll see each other again," said William.

"Aye," said Richard, waving to them both as he exited the manor gate.

The news of the battle and of Henry's triumph had already reached Porlock. Amy Anne and Little John were anxiously awaiting news of their son and Elizabeth had been watching the road for messengers every day. Details of the lower ranking soldiers were rarely considered worthy of gossip; they knew that Sir Reynolds had been killed and could only wait for news of their son. The Snow house had been quiet and subdued as the time passed and there was no word since Richard's cryptic message that *"he was going to join Sir Henry"*.

As Richard rode along getting used to the feel of the bulky armor that surrounded him, he felt the sharpness of the pierced steel against his tunic and couldn't help but think about the excruciating pain Sir Reynolds must have endured and how brave he had been lying there knowing he was breathing his last. It would be a moment in time that was forever stamped on his memory. He touched the blood stains that ran across his chest and suddenly realized how his grandfather must have felt about Lord Harrington; the unspoken loyalty that was always there, the mutual pride in each other. He felt the same about Sir Reynolds. It was a kind of love, although not like the love a man had for a woman; in a strange way the bond was stronger yet so different. Richard ran his fingers over the etched surface of his new sword. Just to think that Sir Reynolds had that much confidence in a young inexperienced squire, confidence Richard hardly had for himself, was truly remarkable.

As he rode out of the Harrington woods and started down the road between the hops fields, he urged his horse into a canter clear to the top of the hill that looked down on the Snow farm. He could see his father in the fields and his mother at the fence; she turned and looked up the road just as he came over the crest of the hill.

"Richard is home!" cried Amy Anne, gathering up her skirt and running up the road to greet him. Little John dropped the reins of his plough and hurried in from the field. Elizabeth came out of the house at the sound of his name. All three watched as their knight in his armor, who had left home so many months before as a mere boy, rode in and dismounted from his horse.

Amy Anne, in her usual way, said immediately, "Son, take that thing off so that I can hug you properly!"

Little John took his horse to unsaddle him and give him food and water as Richard unfastened his chest piece.

"What is that hole in it? Were you injured?" Amy Anne asked.

"No, Mother. This was Sir Reynolds' armor. He was killed at Bosworth."

"We knew that Son," said Little John. "There was no news of *you,* however. Your mother and I were worried when we didn't hear from you after it was all over."

Richard looked toward the house and saw Elizabeth standing on the front step of the house.

Amy Anne smiled at her son. "Go on and kiss your betrothed. She has worried as much as I about you!"

Richard put his armor down on the grass and ran to Elizabeth, lifting her up in his arms and spinning her around.

"You look so different!" she exclaimed.

"For the better I hope!" said Richard.

"Yes, of course."

"He has grown taller by several inches, I am sure of it," said Amy Anne.

"And stronger I'll wager," added Little John.

"I am hungry, Mother. What are we having for supper?"

"Elizabeth does the cooking now. You will have to ask her," laughed Amy Anne and they all went in for supper. She put her arm around Elizabeth and said, "That is something you have to get used to, Elizabeth, when you marry. *Food always comes first with men!*"

All through their supper Richard told them all the stories of his schooling and riding with Henry's troops. Amy Anne listened to her son's voice that had changed from the squeakiness of an adolescent boy to the deep tones of a grown man, and she marveled at how big and strong he had become.

"How did the battle play out?" asked Little John, "Was it everything you expected it to be?"

Richard shook his head. "I learned that battles are not *exciting* if that is what you mean, Father. Killing is not what I would do naturally but sometimes it is necessary."

"And *did* you have to kill?" asked Amy Anne.

Richard paused, chewing his food. He reached out and took his mother's hand across the table. "Yes, Mother I had to kill. But it was only to avoid being killed myself. You can be assured I took no pleasure in it."

"And what of this new king?" Little John continued to question him. "Will he be a king of peace or a king of war?"

"He does not seem to be an evil man, Father. When he spoke to me on the battlefield, he was most sincere. He seemed to care deeply for Sir Reynolds and his men. And he was most kind to me. I will be proud to ride with him again."

There was a moaning sound from the bedchamber and Elizabeth rose and went to tend to her mother. Richard frowned and whispered to Amy Anne. "How long has Mistress Maggie been this way?"

Amy Anne shook her head. "Ever since you left. She has good days and bad days. If only Tom would come home. She always rebounds when she sees the captain!"

She began to clear the dishes from the table. "I worry for Elizabeth. I know she is exhausted from it all. She can barely sleep at night for all the tossing and turning Maggie does. I used to be able to cheer her, but nothing seems to work anymore."

Elizabeth rejoined them and spooned a bit of broth from the pot into a bowl to take to her mother.

"Are you getting her to eat tonight?" asked Amy Anne.

"I can only try," answered Elizabeth. "She knows Father should be home soon so that always piques her appetite."

Chapter Thirty-Seven "The Stowaway"

The *Dove* was riding low in the water, weighted down with her French cargo, as they sailed north up the Bristol Channel. Tom was anxious to get home to Maggie and Elizabeth; he had made a vow that he had made his last trip to France. He was worried about his wife's health; with each separation she seemed to sink further and further into a melancholy state that got progressively more serious. He had long before lost hope of ever having more children; Maggie had been determined not to ever get pregnant again after the difficult time she had experienced when Elizabeth was born. Every time he had to leave again, she would take to her bed, just like he had seen her mother do so many times. Amy Anne was worried too; even her best friend could not snap her out of it. And poor Elizabeth had to be her constant nurse; indeed, his daughter had spent most of her young life caring for her mother. He had put away a goodly amount of money and had made the decision to sell the *Dove* if necessary.

The sun had barely dipped below the mountains on Lundy Island highlighting them like a pink backdrop on a cameo brooch. The *Dove* was making good time as they neared the mouth of Barnstable Bay with the urging of a wayward wind. The current was rolling in smooth rhythmic humps like the slow flapping of a gull's wings in flight. Sunset was almost upon them coming quickly as if Lundy Island had swallowed the sun whole and suddenly darkness was surrounding them.

Tom was at ease at the helm, sipping on a mug of warm cider from the galley with one hand while the other hand held onto the wheel. The men were singing below deck, their scratchy voices rising from the crew's quarters in a strange slightly out of tune arrangement; some sang in English, some sang in their native French. The sea seemed at peace and so did the *Dove*.

Suddenly off the starboard side Tom caught the shadowy hint of white sails in his peripheral vision. He strained to see through the blackness, and it reappeared. The captain immediately blew the boatswain's pipe to summon the crew but before half of them could set foot on the deck lines were dropped from the other ship and the pirates began to swing across the water landing on board the *Dove*.

Swords were drawn, and Tom's crew put up a terrific fight; the sound of thrashing steel ripped through the silent night air. Tom secured the wheel with a long pole and drew his sword also as two of the intruders appeared on the quarter deck and he was forced to battle them both. He turned slightly to face one and was sliced across the back by the other; the pain was deep, hitting bone somewhere across his shoulder blades and he felt himself stumble.

Soon there were three coming at him; taking the captain was a mighty prize in the pirate world and he was considered a prime target. Another stinging blow took him in the chest, and he fell backward. Tom had no chance after that; a half-dozen men jumped in to finish him off. The crew was losing ground as well, all but two on the deck were dead but being far outnumbered were losing ground. *The Dove had been sacked.* The victors took control and the ship's wheel was turned back toward Lundy Island. As they went along the bodies were thrown overboard into the channel.

Deep inside the hold, unbeknownst to the pirates, a figure moved, well-hidden behind a roll of spare canvas. Bleeding from a great gash in his upper arm he had ripped his shirt into a makeshift tourniquet just above the elbow and had temporarily stopped the hemorrhage. Still weak and exhausted from the battle he rested, listening to the conversations on the deck, gleaning what he could of their plans. Assuming that the rest of his shipmates were dead and that he was the only survivor, he was now alone on a ship hijacked by the rascals who had no qualms about killing in order to steal.

He listened for what seemed to be the better part of an hour; he could tell that the ship was still moving forward by the sounds the water made against the hull. He suspected they were heading west to their lair on Lundy Island, and he wondered if he would ever get back to the mainland. *Would they use the Dove or scuttle it on the rocks after they had pillaged what they could from it?*

Very soon he heard the squeaking of the ship as it came to rest against a pier and the hurried footsteps of the pirates on the deck. Within minutes it seemed they had all disembarked and the ship was oddly silent. Wallace sat up from his hiding place behind the roll of canvas and decided to take the opportunity to ascertain his precarious situation. His arm ached terribly from the gash, and he discovered he had little use of it when he tried to grasp the rail of the companionway. With one arm hanging lifeless he used his good arm to pull himself up and found himself standing alone on the deck that was still sticky with the blood of his shipmates. He could see flickering rush lights on the shore from the portside and he walked quickly not knowing how soon the pirates would return to the ship. He went directly to the galley where he stuffed his pockets with food; finding an empty wine bottle and filling it from the galley cask and quickly found his way back down into the hold to search for a better hiding place. He found one in the aft of the ship under the backstays that supported the mast and he tucked himself down beneath them where he was sure the pirates would have no need to look. Knowing he could never swim across the strong currents in the channel he knew his only hope was to stowaway until they sailed back to the mainland where he might have a chance of swimming to shore with his one good arm. He ate a few bites and dozed off to sleep waiting for the pirates to return.

The next morning, he heard footsteps and laughter on the deck above as the pirates came back to ransack the *Dove*. Coiling himself up in his hiding place he listened and waited still trying to determine if they were going to scuttle it on the rocks of Lundy Island or turn it into a vessel of robbery and murder. One way or another he had to make it back to the mainland. Staying on Lundy Island was not an option! When a few of them came down the passageway and were rummaging through everything in the hold they came only feet away from where he was hiding. From bits and pieces of their conversation he expected them to take the Dove back out soon; that assumption was confirmed when he heard them bringing stores aboard.

As soon as the sun set, he heard the sails being unfurled above him and the calls of the pirate captain to shove off. They were soon under-way and Wallace hid in the darkness, waiting for his chance to escape. His arm ached terribly from his wound and even though he had bandaged it afresh it was oozing pus and he knew it had become infected. As he lay in the hold of the ship, he just kept opening the wound up again with his knife to let it drain. He knew he had a raging fever; his entire body was hot, but he could not sweat. He prayed to God silently and fervently and waited, his body becoming weaker and weaker.

The *Dove* with the pirate captain at the helm crossed the channel and before too long Wallace heard them drop their anchor. They had to be near the mouth of Barnstable Bay where they usually sat in wait for unsuspecting cargo ships. He could hear laughter from the deck. By now he was slipping in and out of consciousness while his body fought the infection and yet he waited. He had to wait until he heard them launch an attack on another ship. That, he thought would be his best opportunity to escape, while the pirates were otherwise occupied.

Hours seemed to pass slowly, and the *Dove* rocked back and forth on the current waiting for an unsuspecting ship. He had finished off the water in the wine bottle and the food he had ransacked from the galley as well. For the first time in his sea-going life he felt sick to his stomach. Indeed, the infection seemed to be ravishing his entire body.

Then, just as he closed his eyes trying not to retch in his tiny space under the mainstays, he heard rapid footsteps above him running across the deck and the sound of the anchor chains being pulled up into the ship. He could feel the *Dove* began to move and soon the familiar sound of the pirates yelling as they pulled alongside another ship in the dark. When he could hear screaming from the other ship he made his move, pulling himself up on his good arm and walking quickly toward the passageway. He looked up and could see no one on deck; it appeared all the crew were engrossed in their capture of the victim ship. He managed to make it to the deck and then to the gangway opening where he jumped into the black water.

It took a few moments for Wallace to recover from the shock of the cold water. He turned over on his back and kicked his feet. With his good arm he guided himself along the hull of the *Dove* until he was on the port side and out of sight of the crew. The pirates were now pulling the other ship alongside to pillage it. The cold seemed to sooth his feverish body and ease his pain although his arm tired quickly and he had to pause often to rest it. He could feel the direction of the currents around him and made a calculated guess at the direction he was going; the cross current had to be coming from the Celtic Sea to the southwest. He swam on in the darkness hoping to see lights on the shore to guide him. It seemed as if hours had passed, and his fever had left him as he floated in the water trembling with cold. Strangely enough the pain in his arm had numbed, the infection flushed out with the salt water, and he was able to move it again however slightly. When exhaustion was finally setting in and he was near the point of giving up, he heard a sound that renewed his spirit.

The sound he heard was the surf crashing against the rocks of Hartland Point.

Chapter Thirty-Eight "Wallace's Message"

It wasn't long before Richard received an urgent message from King Henry. Yorkist rebels backed by two thousand German mercenaries had landed in Lancaster shire and the king needed all his available knights. Amy Anne bravely packed him some food for his journey and Little John saddled his horse and assisted him with his armor. Elizabeth kissed him goodbye without tears; she had long since become accustomed to farewells being the daughter of a sea captain.

"Will you still wait for me?" Richard whispered in her ear.

"*For as long as it takes*," was again Elizabeth's reply.

As soon as he left Porlock and his family behind to fight with his king, sadness was again in the Snow house.

The day seemed melancholy too; the sky was cloudy with an occasional spritz of raindrops and a mist rising from the marshlands. The chickens were still in their nesting boxes at midday and Amy Anne went about collecting the eggs from under their warm feathers. Little John had ridden off to the Harrington Manor for a meeting of the guild. Elizabeth had gone outside to sit on the step to rest a moment while her mother had her nap. It was she who saw the man riding alone up from Porlock Hill.

She watched as the man grew closer and, suddenly, she felt as if she knew him. He looked disheveled and dirty, and he had one arm in a sling; she stared intently at him until she realized who it was. "Wallace!" she called and ran out into the yard to greet him.

He stopped his horse and removed his sailors cap. "Miss Elizabeth, it is good to see you again."

Elizabeth realized immediately that he had not come all the way from town for no reason. She knew it was bad news about her father. "What has happened to you, Wallace? And what of my father?" she asked desperately.

Wallace bowed his head. "I am truly sorry to bring you bad news Miss Elizabeth. We were sacked by pirates and your father was killed."

Elizabeth closed her eyes and collapsed on the ground and Wallace dismounted to assist her to her feet. Amy Anne came around the corner of the house and, seeing the exchange ran to them.

"My father is dead, Amy!" cried Elizabeth. "*Whatever* will I tell my mother?"

"Please come in, Mr. Wallace, and rest from your ride," Amy Anne said quietly. "Come, Elizabeth, let's get you inside too."

They sat by the fire as Wallace told them the story of the *Dove's* capture. Amy Anne put a blanket around

Elizabeth's shoulders and closed the bedchamber door so that Maggie would not hear their conversation.

"I came as soon as I could, Miss Elizabeth."

"You were very brave, Wallace," she replied. "You served my father well."

"And is your arm healing as it should?" asked Amy Anne. "Have you had a doctor look at it?"

"No, Mistress Amy. I believe the swim in the cold salt water helped immensely. It is healing quite nicely now."

"May I offer you some food, Mister Wallace?" Amy Anne asked. "You look weary from your long journey."

"No thank you, Mistress," he said. "I only came to bring the news to Mistress Maggie." He paused and looked around. "Is she well?"

Elizabeth shook her head. "No, Wallace. She hasn't been well for some time now. I think it will be best to wait until she is feeling better to tell her."

Wallace rose and Amy Anne showed him to the door where he replaced his cap. "I must be getting this horse back to the livery. Please tell your mother how very sorry I am, Miss Elizabeth."

He collected his horse and rode back down the hill. Amy Anne returned to Elizabeth who was staring blankly into the flames in the fireplace.

"How will I ever tell my mother?" she asked Amy Anne. "This will *kill* her!"

Just as Amy Anne was about to reply, Maggie appeared in the doorway.

"*Tell me what*?" she asked, standing there in her nightgown and bare feet.

Elizabeth stood up and went toward Maggie.

"Mother, you must get back into bed. I will bring you some broth."

"*What do you have to tell me, Elizabeth*?" Maggie asked again. Her eyes got larger and her breathing more rapid.

"Come, Mother," pleaded Elizabeth. "Let's get you back into bed and I will tell you all about it."

Maggie pulled away from her daughter and turned toward Amy Anne.

"*It's Tom, isn't it? My husband is dead is he not?*" she tried to scream but her voice came out in only a loud whisper.

She must be told thought Amy Anne. *We might as well get it over with.*

"Yes, Maggie. Tom's ship was sacked by pirates. Wallace was the only one to survive."

Hearing this Maggie collapsed on the floor. Amy Anne and Elizabeth carried her back to her bed and tucked her under the blanket. The memory of the accident so many years before flashed before Amy Anne's eyes. She sat down on the edge of the bed and felt for Maggie's pulse. "Just let her sleep Elizabeth," she said. "I'm sorry if I seemed harsh but she had to know sooner or later. There was no point in delaying the inevitable."

"You are right, Amy. Perhaps I coddle her too much."

"Hiding the truth from her will not make her well," replied Amy Anne. "She needs to *want* to get well."

They both went back to their chores and let Maggie sleep. When Little John returned, he had good news to share about the guild's progress.

"We can use a little good news today, John," said Amy Anne, "Tom has been killed by pirates."

Little John looked at his wife in disbelief. "How did you get the news?"

"Mr. Wallace came to tell us. Elizabeth will be fine, I think. Maggie fainted at the news and has been sleeping all afternoon."

Little John shook his head. "Poor Tom. Did Wallace bring back his body?"

"No" said Amy Anne. "He said the pirates dumped all the bodies in the channel."

Amy Anne prepared the supper that night and the atmosphere was a somber one. Little John and Amy Anne sat alone; Elizabeth was still behind the closed bedchamber door with her mother. They both could hear muffled conversation. Finally, the door opened, and Elizabeth walked out. There were tears in her eyes and Amy Anne went to her and took her hand.

"What is it, Elizabeth?" Amy Anne asked.

"Mother is awake," replied Elizabeth.

"Well, that's *good* isn't it?" asked Little John.

"John, would you be so kind as to take my mother home to Barnstable?"

Amy Anne shook her head. "Whatever will she do in Barnstable? She is not able to care for her aging mother! She can't even take care of herself! What foolishness is this?"

"My mother wants to go home, Amy."

"But why? There is no one to care for her in Barnstable!"

Elizabeth stared at Amy Anne; her eyes cast downward with defeat.

"She knows that Amy. *Mother wants to go home to die.*"

Chapter Thirty-Nine "Legacy of a Simple Man"

At dawn Little John fed the animals and went across the yard to fetch the wagon for the trip to Barnstable. Just as he did so, he looked up; the weather had soured, and he was worried about the dark clouds to the west. The open wagon could offer no shelter for Maggie on the long trip, but his passenger was determined to leave regardless of the weather. He informed Amy Anne he was going to fetch Lady Harrington's carriage so that, at the very least, Maggie would be protected from the rain.

When he returned from the manor in the carriage with two of Lady Harrington's horses hitched to it, he found Amy Anne and Elizabeth talking quietly together in the kitchen.

"Is she still insisting on leaving today?" asked Little John.

Elizabeth nodded sadly. "When my mother makes her mind up about something she rarely changes her mind."

"You will need to dress her very warmly. It looks like a storm brewing. I think it is far too early for snow, but it shall be very cold on the high moor, nonetheless," said Little John.

Amy Anne fetched her husband's heaviest tunic and cloak. "John, you will need to keep warm too."

Elizabeth had packed Maggie's belongings in one of Tom's old sea bags and Little John loaded it into the carriage. Maggie approached Amy Anne as she departed from the house and the two friends embraced. "I miss my mother," said Maggie.

Amy Anne understood somewhat; she missed her own mother too on occasion.

"It is all right, Maggie. I understand. I just pray you will get better once you are home in Barnstable."

Maggie then looked at her daughter and kissed her. Without a word she walked outside and let Little John assist her into the carriage.

"I have put a blanket inside in case you get cold," he said.

Little John slapped the horses with the reins and the carriage rolled down the road disappearing over Porlock Hill.

He had not travelled the coastal road west from Porlock since he had been just a boy on his father's horse. To eyes that were unfamiliar with the town and its surroundings the changes that had been made in Porlock might have gone unnoticed but Little John's eyes picked up on every detail. He was pleased with the work the guild had done to improve their little town. Several more families had moved in and there were several new cottages built along the main road. The barley fields had been expanded and there were now acres of new apple trees planted on the hillsides. Lady Harrington's sheep were grazing on the hillside above town; they had seen a good crop of lambs that spring and the flock was flourishing. As he steered the carriage over Porlock Bridge he could see that the water now appeared unclouded as it rushed over the river rocks on its way to the bay. While still not pure enough to drink the water had lost its nasty smell now that the farmers upstream had re-routed and recycled the runoff from their fields. Even the main street was free of debris; the guild had established a dumping site out near Pool Wood where trash was burned and were building a system of clay pipes leading out of town toward a pit to dispose of the sewage. They had expanded the dock on the bay long enough to moor several more ships bringing in more sea trade and added on a small schoolroom at the back of the almshouse where Amy Anne taught the younger children two days each week. They had accomplished much, and he was excited about the future. Little John was making careful use of the gold Lady Harrington had put away to make the improvements. *Porlock would never be like London!*

The rain started blowing in as soon as they had reached the high moor above the town of Lynmouth. Little John pulled the hood of his cloak over his head and put on his leather gloves to warm his hands. On the steep decline down toward the bridge that spanned the River Lyn the carriage began to slide in the mud; John had to keep the horses at a crawl until they had crossed over safely. By the time they reached the wooded area, his clothes were soaked, and he stopped the horses under a thick canopy of the trees. Climbing out to check on the welfare of his passenger, he saw that Maggie had reclined on the carriage seat, wrapped in the blanket with her head resting on Tom's sea bag. He changed into a dry set of clothes he had packed under the seat and stretched his wet clothes across the top of the carriage to dry if they ever found the sun again. As it turned out it rained all the way to Barnstable and as Maggie slept John urged the horses on trying to ignore his own discomfort.

When they finally arrived at the Hanfield house, Maggie was awake. John helped her climb down from the carriage and he gathered up her belongings. Slowly, leaning on his arm, they approached the door and her father greeted them with surprise. "Margaret! You've come home!" he said happily.

"Where is Mother?" Maggie asked.

"She is resting. Go on in. She would want you to wake her," said Mr. Hanfield. As Maggie disappeared into the bed chamber, he turned toward Little John. "Won't you come in out of the weather, John?"

"My horses are in need of rest and hay," Little John replied.

"The livery is just down the street. When you have taken care of your horses come and I will find you some dry clothes and some hot food."

When he returned Little John sat near the fire with Mr. Hanfield.

"Here are some of my clothes for you to change into. Take off your boots and put them here by the fire, John," said Mr. Hanfield. "You are welcome to stay with us tonight and get warm before your journey back to Porlock."

"Thank you, but I am sure I can find room at the inn."

"I won't hear of it!" insisted Mr. Hanfield. "You have come all this way to bring our daughter home. For that, we owe you a debt of gratitude."

Little John felt awkward in another man's clothes, but the warmth of the fire was very comforting, and he accepted Mr. Hanfield's invitation. The two men sat by the fire while Little John drank a mug of hot soup and talked until Little John put down his mug and began to nod off. Mr. Hanfield tiptoed to the bedchamber door and saw that Maggie had fallen asleep beside her mother.

"You may sleep in Margaret's room. She often falls asleep with her mother."

"Oh no, Sir. I will be quite comfortable here by the fire. You take the bed, please," replied Little John.

"At least, let me get you a blanket," said Mr. Hanfield before he retired to the bedchamber. "Thank you, John, for taking such good care of our daughter."

"She and my wife have become very good friends. And we were very sad to hear of Tom's death. It is a time that she needed her mother."

"Aye," answered Mr. Hanfield. "And her mother needs her daughter."

As tired as Little John was, he found it difficult to sleep on the hearth. Despite the warmth of the blanket, his body still ached from the cold and dampness. By morning he woke shivering next to the cold ashes, and he rose quietly so as not to wake the others who were still sleeping. He put on his clothes and boots which were still spongy on the inside and wandered out into the street toward town. There he retrieved the team from the livery and found a street vendor who had hot bread for sale. After stopping briefly by the Hanfield house on his way out of town to say goodbye he retraced his path home.

The rain had gone but the air was brutally cold and Little John's head and chest ached terribly. How he missed Amy Anne and their warm bed! His body was shivering yet his face felt hot. He gave the horses not a minute's rest until he could see Porlock in the distance.

When he pulled the carriage up in front of the house, Amy Anne came immediately out of the door. She took one look at her husband and insisted he go inside and get in his bed. "I will put the horses away, John," she said.

Once back inside she brought him hot broth and piled extra blankets over him.

"Did you have to sit in the rain all the way there?" she asked. "You have a very high fever, John. I think I should send for the doctor."

"No, Amy. I will be all right after a good night's rest in a warm bed," said Little John.

It was against her better judgment, but she gave in to her husband's wishes for once. There was a new doctor in town who had replaced the retiring Doctor Philby. She had heard rumors that he was very young, and she wasn't totally sure she trusted her husband's health to someone without much experience. Dr. Philby had been the town doctor for so long, she had faith in him. The house was quiet; Elizabeth had retired early; for once the poor girl would have a peaceful night's sleep without having to tend to her mother. Amy Anne undressed for bed and snuggled up next to Little John under the quilt; the warmth radiated from her body to his and within minutes Little John was sleeping soundly in the arms of the woman he loved.

By morning light, Little John's condition has worsened; his body felt like he had hot coals under his nightshirt and his breathing was labored and raspy. Amy Anne sponged his forehead and got him to drink some soup.

"I will go fetch the doctor," said Elizabeth. "It is *my* mother's fault he is so sick."

"The road is wet and slippery, and you do not ride that well, Elizabeth. If you will stay here with my husband, I can ride faster than you," Amy replied. "Try to keep him drinking the soup. And, whatever you do, do *not* let him get out of bed!"

Amy Anne saddled a horse and rode off.

She returned with the new doctor; a very handsome young man with ink black hair and piercing blue eyes. Little John's condition had worsened even more and the new doctor, whose name was Beaufort immediately made a poultice of ground mint leaves and hot water which he placed in a cloth bag to put on Little John's chest. He spread a bit of the healing concoction under Little John's nose to help him breathe while Amy Anne continued to sponge his forehead. Her husband opened his eyes and looked up at her but the fever had made him delusional and he mumbled something about Lady Harrington.

"Shhhhhh, John" whispered Amy Anne. "You just lie still."

He seemed to fall asleep yet all the while he was thrashing back and forth in the bed.

"It is pneumonia, I am sure. That is about all we can do for him until the fever breaks," Dr. Beaufort said shaking his head. "Keep him warm and get him to drink broth when he isn't delirious. I will be back in the morning to apply a new poultice."

At that moment Elizabeth came into the room. She stopped and stared at the doctor without thinking, then, embarrassed, she looked down at the floor with her cheeks turning scarlet.

"Hello!" he said. "I am Doctor Beaufort."

"I am very glad to meet you. I am Elizabeth Hatherly," she mumbled.

She quickly ran outside to feed the animals. She knew that the horses and cows ate hay although she wasn't quite sure how much. She knew where the eggs were stored in the larder. When it came time to milk the cows, she took the milk stool and the bucket and sat next to the first cow staring under her belly at the freckled pink udders before her with disgust. She sat there for such a long time the cow turned around chewing her hay and looked at her inquisitively. Elizabeth extended her hands and squeezed. Nothing happened. It all felt so *alien* to her; she did not share her mother's love of animals. They smelled *terrible* and she didn't like the flies that buzzed around them. She tried a different teat thinking perhaps the first one was empty. Still nothing happened. "All right, *cow*," she said in a frustrated tone. "A little cooperation from *you* would help right now."

The cow continued to chew and swish her tail in Elizabeth's face. Oh, how she hated these smelly beasts!

At that moment the young doctor came up to the fence. He watched poor Elizabeth's hopeless attempts at milking the cow and broke out in a laugh.

"No, Elizabeth, not like that! Here let me show you." He climbed over the fence and squatted down beside her. "You have to grip *here* and pull down like *this*," he demonstrated.

She tried again without success.

"Don't be afraid to *squeeze* Elizabeth. You won't get any milk that way!"

With the next attempt a small trickle of milk hit the bucket.

"Why don't you let me do it? It won't take me very long," said the doctor.

"No," insisted Elizabeth. "I wouldn't dream of taking up your time, Doctor. I will master this if it takes me all night!"

Doctor Beaufort just smiled. "Very well then," he said and climbed back over the fence. "Goodnight."

He mounted his horse and rode away. She finished the milking as best she could and took the milk to the larder. When she returned to the house Amy Anne was standing in the kitchen. "How is he?" she asked.

"Pray that the fever breaks tonight," replied Amy Anne and returned to the bedchamber.

Doctor Beaufort returned early the next morning. Elizabeth had braided her hair and scrubbed her fingernails even though she knew she would have to do it all again after her morning chores. She greeted him at the door with slightly more poise than the day before.

"Good morning, Doctor. Please come in."

Amy Anne led him into the bedchamber and Elizabeth went outside to attend to the morning chores.

"Have you a pan or a bowl I can use?" he asked as he rolled up Little John's sleeve in preparation for a bloodletting procedure. Amy Anne brought the bowl and watched as the doctor made a slight incision in Little John's forearm and cringed as her husband's blood began to drip into it. It went on for several minutes and then the doctor put a compress on his arm and stopped the bleeding. She took the bowl with her husband's blood and poured it out under the little rose bush in the back yard.

When she returned, Amy Anne stared at the doctor with hopeful eyes.

"Prepare more poultices just like I showed you. Change it as often as you can. Maybe the bloodletting will help. I will be back tomorrow."

"Thank you, Doctor Beaufort," Amy said.

She went back to the bedchamber and sat down on the bed. She reached out and stroked her husband's forehead with the cool cloth and noticed some new gray hair at his temples. *How long have I loved this man?* she thought. *Since that day at the seashore, so long ago.* He was such a good man; she could never have asked for a better husband, and she was so proud of the way he had organized the guild. Porlock could have easily fallen into the hands of the king or an unscrupulous overseer after Lady Harrington's death but for her husband. He had vision far beyond that of any educated man and Porlock would always be the better for it.

Little John began mumbling again, something about Pool Wood and white rocks this time.

"Shhhhhh," she said gently. "It's all right, John. Just sleep."

The doctor stopped again at the corral gate and watched Elizabeth milking the cows.

"I see that you are doing much better today!" he said. "Good day, Miss Elizabeth."

And he was gone. Elizabeth smiled. *What a handsome man he is!* she thought to herself and immediately felt guilty. *I should not be thinking such thoughts! I am betrothed!* She hurried back to the house trying to blot out the thoughts.

"I put the milk in the larder. How is Little John doing?" she asked.

"There has been no change, I'm afraid," answered Amy Anne from the bedchamber.

She spent the day lying next to him until she fell asleep herself. Elizabeth rekindled the fire and prepared supper which she ate alone. She wished Richard could be here when his father was so sick. She knew Amy Anne was terribly worried; she could see it in her eyes and hear it in her voice. When it seemed as if they were going to sleep right through supper, Elizabeth took the pot off the fire and went to bed herself. She awoke to the sound of weeping in the next room just before the dawn and went to find Amy Anne cradling her dead husband in her arms.

Chapter Forty "Love's Precious Value"

They laid Little John to rest next to his parents on the hill, which had by now become the family cemetery; they had buried Little John's Aunt Mary and Uncle Peter there several years prior and Amy Anne's parents who had passed away within a month of each other the previous summer were resting there too. The older generation seemed to be dying off making room for the new; now the only hope of continuing the Snow ancestral line seemed to reside with Richard and Elizabeth.

 Amy Anne and Elizabeth prepared food for his cousins who had helped dig the grave and his many friends from town who had come to pay their respects.

"We are on our own now, Elizabeth," Amy Anne commented after all the guests had gone home. "We must now be like Lady Harrington and take care of business as men would do!"

"I do hope Richard returns soon," said Elizabeth. "I know he will just be heartbroken that he was not here when his father died."

"I just pray that he is safe, wherever he is."

The two women settled in to spend the cold winter together. Amy Anne was sure they had sufficient food stored in the larder to get them through. They took turns going out in the snow to care for the animals and spent their evenings huddled by the fire where Amy Anne would write in her journal and Elizabeth would do needlework. Dr. Beaufort visited every week and chopped wood for them.

In the spring the men from the guild came to do the ploughing. Elizabeth soon learned how to plant and harvest the vegetables in the garden. She still fed the animals but left the milking to Amy Anne. Ever the stubborn one, Amy Anne insisted on helping and followed along behind the plough every day with a cloth seed sack slung over her shoulder. Her once soft white complexion turned a leathery tan; her once blond hair was almost bleached white from the sun. The two women who loved him the most patiently waited for Richard to return from the wars while Dr. Beaufort continued to quietly admire Elizabeth.

With the spring a new family came to Porlock and moved into the Hatherly's old cottage. They had been directed to speak with Amy Anne about the terms of the rental and Amy Anne welcomed Nicholas and Elizabeth White warmly to Porlock. She was especially drawn to Mrs. White, who was with child and expecting to give birth any day. For years Amy Anne had never understood why the good Lord had never blessed her with any more children after Richard was born; now that she was past the age of childbearing she could only look forward to grandchildren; even the two days each week that she spent with her students could not satisfy her maternal yearnings. In the meantime, she began to fuss over Mrs. White, sewing baby clothes for her and checking on her well-being whenever she was in town.

The Whites had migrated from Swanbourne in Buckinghamshire County, where they had found themselves living among a pocket of Yorkist supporters. Mr. White explained that being loyal to King Henry they were seen as traitors, and they had been living in fear ever since the Battle at Bosworth. With a child on the way they could not take any chances with their safety, so they decided to go west to find a more politically friendly environment in which to raise their child. After they were assured by everyone, they had met in Porlock that the town was loyal to the Lancastrian king, boasting of Porlock's own knight who was off fighting with King Henry, the Whites decided they would stay. The timing was perfect as the birth grew near and more travel would have been risky.

Mrs. White began to expose the women of Porlock to the more sophisticated customs of eastern England; she wore the latest London fashions and she loved to serve refreshments in the afternoons to entertain the ladies of Porlock. After Amy Anne had finished teaching her class one day, she finally accepted Mrs. White's invitation. When she arrived, Amy Anne was escorted to a table in front of the fire with a fine linen tablecloth and a tray of frosted cakes and fruit. As they sipped warm cider, they discussed the town of Porlock. Mr. White had invested in several businesses in town including Mr. Hartley's old shop where Amy Anne spent her childhood. The fact that the Whites were living in the Hatherly home and had taken over the Hartley family business made Amy Anne feel they were like family, and she wanted to treat them as such.

"Tell me about your son and his wife," said Mrs. White.

"He is not married to Elizabeth *yet*. He has been far too busy with the wars. I am hoping they will wed on his return."

"But they are *betrothed,* are they not?" asked Mrs. White.

"Yes, he has asked her to wait for him. He had no way of knowing that the wars would intervene," replied Amy Anne.

"It must be very difficult for her to wait for such a long time."

"My goodness, I waited much longer for my husband to ask for my hand. But it was well worth the wait, I assure you," said Amy Anne.

"My marriage was *arranged,*" said Mrs. White. "My parents picked Nicholas for me. I was such a stupid girl I probably would have ended up married to a penniless stable groom if left to my own devices."

"You mean that you didn't even *know* your husband when you married him?" Amy Anne asked. "Oh my, I could never have done that! I would have simply *died* if my parents had done that to me!"

"I am *glad* they chose for me," said Mrs. White. "I have been very happy. Nicholas is a very good provider."

She offered Amy Anne another cake.

"And how does a knight make a living? Is he paid to fight?" Mrs. White continued, seemingly very keen on the subject of wealth.

Amy Anne tried to explain. "From what I have read, a hundred years ago knights served their kings on loyalty alone. But their families would starve while they were out fighting for long periods of time. It was decided that the king would only call on them when they were needed, and he began paying them a fee for their service. It allowed them to return home to their families in times of peace."

"That's very interesting," said Mrs. White. "And what of Elizabeth's *father*? What did he do?"

Amy Anne was beginning to feel like she was being interrogated and it made her a bit uncomfortable. "Her father was a ship captain," said Amy Anne. "He was killed by pirates."

"That must be a dangerous occupation, but I suppose it pays a better wage than farming," was Mrs. White's reply.

"We have made a comfortable living from farming. It is hard, but it is honest work," said Amy Anne.

"I would much rather be married to a lord and live in a manor house with servants to tend to the chores. Wouldn't you?"

"Do you not love your husband, Mrs. White?" asked Amy Anne. The idea of an arranged marriage was troubling to her.

"Please, Amy, call me *Beth*. And love?" said Mrs. White. "I could just as well love a rich man as a poor one!"

"Well, *I* married for love. I would *never* have married for money," Amy Anne answered, who by now was becoming quite disenchanted with Mrs. White.

"Do you not wish your husband had ambitions to be more than just a farmer?"

Amy Anne suddenly decided she did not care to continue the conversation. She finished her cake and placed her napkin across her plate.

"Mrs. White, I do not think a man's profession is any measure of his worth. My husband was born a farmer, but he did good things with his life. He had great purpose!" retorted Amy Anne. "Many great men have come from humble beginnings!"

She thanked Mrs. White properly for her hospitality and excused herself. "I must get home before it gets dark," she said.

As Amy Anne was mounting her horse, Mrs. White came up and touched her arm. "I do hope I have not offended you my dear. I just chatter on sometimes without thinking how words sound once I have said them."

"No," replied Amy Anne. "You must forgive me. I have just recently lost my husband and my heart is still very broken. I loved him very much and he was a wonderful man."

"I am sure he was, Amy Anne."

"Good day, Mrs. White," was Amy Anne's reply as she rode off toward Porlock Hill.

As her horse walked along the road, she looked out over the serenity of the Porlock springtime and Amy's anger began to wane; she convinced herself that Mrs. White was just a stupid woman to be pitied because she knew not the beauty of true love. One thing was for sure; she was *not* anxious to ever have refreshments with her again! When she reached the top of Porlock Hill she could see the fields of the Snow farm, almost expecting to see Little John working behind the plough and a team of horses. She closed her eyes and imagined her husband's face and his smile again, the touch of his hands, the smell of his hair, the soothing sound of his breathing in the stillness of the night. No amount of money could buy that!

Chapter Forty-One "As Long as It Takes"

Elizabeth was outside feeding the animals when Amy Anne returned from her visit with Mrs. White. Amy Anne unsaddled her horse and turned him out.

"I am not feeling very well, Elizabeth," she said. "I am going in to lie down for a while before supper."

"Did you have too many sweet cakes at Mrs. White's house?"

"Maybe that's it. I just have a terrible ache in my stomach," said Amy Anne.

Elizabeth watched Amy Anne disappear into the house before she reluctantly retrieved the milk bucket from the nail on the fence. How she wished they could get rid of these horrible beasts and rescue her from her life as a dairy maid! How she hated milking! She sat down and noticed that the cow had been obviously lying in the bog at the bottom of the pasture and her udders were caked with foul smelling mud. Not wanting to go back to the house for a rag she wet her hands in the water barrel and attempted to rinse away the mud. She hated cows so much she could not even bring herself to drink milk anymore. She looked at her hands; there was no longer any point in trying to keep them soft and ladylike; her palms were beginning to callous, and her nails were always broken and dirty. *Richard! she thought to herself. Please come home!* She was so tired from all the farm work. Nursing her mother had been hard but at least she could stay inside out of the sun. Now her cheeks were peeling, and her lips were chapped and she was beginning to doubt the necessity of changing clothes when she only got them dirty again the next day.

Her mind continued to wander. Where was Richard now? Would he be home soon? She was beginning to have troubling doubts about their future together; was their betrothal official? Could he possibly marry someone else after all the years she had waited for him? Suddenly she realized Richard had never actually said he *loved* her even though he had implied it on several occasions. Maybe she should have returned to Barnstable with her mother, but how could she abandon Amy Anne now? It all seemed so hopeless. Why did life have to be so hard?

She finished the dreaded milking and returned to the house where she found Amy Anne lying on her bed looking very miserable.

"Goodness, how many cakes *did* you eat Amy?" Elizabeth asked.

"Only one," said Amy Anne. "I don't think that is the problem. My stomach has been feeling very queer lately."

"What else have you eaten besides Mrs. White's cakes?"

"Nothing *you* haven't eaten as well," said Amy Anne. "That can't be it."

"Do you want me to bring you some soup?"

"No. I think I will just rest. Maybe I will feel better tomorrow."

Elizabeth retired as well, crying tears into her pillow until she fell asleep.

By morning, Amy Anne looked much worse as she lay in her bed clinging to her chamber pot.

"Oh, Amy you don't look very well," remarked Elizabeth. "Whatever can I do for you?"

"Nothing please. I can't stand the thought of food or drink. I believe I have nothing left inside of me except bones," Amy said.

"At least let me bring you a clean chamber pot." Elizabeth said "And a cool cloth for your head. That always made Mother feel better."

When Elizabeth returned, she sat down on the edge of the mattress and began to sponge Amy's face. "Would you like me to brush your hair?"

"I don't think I can sit up just now," said Amy weakly.

Elizabeth was weary; after a restless night, tossing and turning over the question of Richard's love, she had to wake up to another sick woman to care for. And she still had to go out and tend to the animals. It was too much! *Where oh where is Richard? How did I get myself in this situation?* she thought but she would never tell Amy what she was thinking. She loved Amy, truly she did. She just felt so tired and discouraged she didn't think she could stand another minute!

"Would you like a cup of milk, Amy? That might soothe your upset stomach," she asked.

"Maybe later. Right now, I just want to rest." Amy Anne closed her eyes and Elizabeth tiptoed out of the room.

She put on her shawl to go out into the morning air; collecting the eggs and feeding the livestock before she started the dreaded milking. She wondered what would happen if she just skipped milking the beasts just once. Would they die? Would their udders burst wide open and bleed? She silently wished she could butcher them all and be done with it.

On her way back from the larder she noticed the roses on the little bush and decided to pick some for Amy Anne's bedside. This might cheer her up, she thought for she knew how Amy Anne loved flowers. She took them inside and put them in a little vase with some rainwater from the kitchen cask. When she brought them into Amy Anne's bedchamber and placed them on the table beside the bed Amy Anne opened her eyes and tried to smile.

"Here I have brought you some warm milk. You have to eat *something* Amy."

"Thank you, Elizabeth. You are very sweet. *Wherever* did you find the roses?"

"Just behind the house," replied Elizabeth, straightening Amy Anne's bedclothes.

"You mean the little bush by the kitchen porch?" Amy Anne asked with a confused look on her face.

"Yes," replied Elizabeth. "I thought they would cheer you up."

Amy Anne reached out and touched the flowers with her hand.

"You got *red* roses from the bush behind the house?"

"Yes, Amy. Why is that so strange?" Elizabeth began to think the fever was making Amy Anne delirious.

"It is very peculiar," said Amy Anne. "When I first moved into the house, John's father told me I was the only one who had been successful getting the rose bush to bloom at all. That first year it had *white* roses on it." She paused, as if to gain strength to go on. "The next spring the bush had *pink* blooms."

"And now it has *red* blooms," said Elizabeth. "Perhaps the plant hadn't matured yet. Perhaps it was going through some sort of *metamorphosis*."

"Possibly," said Amy Anne. "Except that when Little John was very ill, and the doctor had drained some blood from him to help rid his body of the fever I---"

She paused again, and Elizabeth waited for her to answer. "I poured Little John's blood into the ground under the roses."

Elizabeth's eyes widened. "Now you are scaring me, Amy! What are you saying? That Little John has come back in the form of a red rose?"

Amy Anne shook her head. "I don't know. Some things you can't explain away with logic."

"Let's change the subject. Would you like me to brush your hair now?"

"No," said Amy Anne. "I just want to rest. I don't care what I look like."

Elizabeth was getting very worried. Suddenly she knew what she needed to do.

"I am going to town to fetch Doctor Beaufort and don't argue with me, Amy! You are very ill. I will be back very soon."

She went outside and saddled a horse.

"Come now, you beast, behave yourself," she said when she climbed up on his back and started down the road.

"You must be good for me because *I* am the one who feeds you every day."

She held in the reins so tightly that the horse walked all the way to the doctor's house with his neck bowed, and she jumped down tying him up to the rail outside. Doctor Beaufort answered the door with his hair tousled and his face unshaven.

"Oh, I beg your pardon, Dr. Beaufort, for bothering you so early!" said Elizabeth.

"It's quite all right, Elizabeth. What is it?"

"Amy Anne is very sick. She can't keep anything on her stomach, and she has a very high fever. I am very worried about her."

"Let me make myself presentable and I will come with you. I must make one stop at the White's house first. Mrs. White has gone into labor. Why don't you come in and wait?"

"Oh no!" said Elizabeth. "I don't want to leave Amy Anne for very long. If you will just come when you have taken care of Mrs. White that would be fine."

"Please! I will just be a minute. Then we can ride back together."

Elizabeth went back to her horse and followed the doctor to the familiar cottage at the end of the street; the place that held so many happy memories of her father. When the doctor knocked at the door of her own house it seemed like a very strange thing to do.

Mr. White answered the door.

"How is our patient doing?" asked the doctor.

"You will have to ask her. I know nothing of such things." He looked at Elizabeth.

"I assume you have met Elizabeth Hatherly. There is illness in her house, and I must pay them a visit after I have checked in on your wife's progress."

"Is that Elizabeth I hear?" called Mrs. White from the bedchamber. "Come in my child! What's this about Amy Anne being ill?"

Elizabeth stepped into the bedchamber. Mrs. White was sitting up in the bed knitting baby clothes and didn't look at all in pain.

"She has been ill since she came home yesterday."

"Oh dear! Well, you must take the doctor to see her. My pains seem to have temporarily subsided. I haven't had one in over an hour," said Mrs. White.

Doctor Beaufort agreed. "First babies are sometimes very fickle; they can't seem to make up their minds whether they want to be born or not. I believe you still have awhile to wait Mrs. White. If you don't mind, I will ride out to check on Amy Anne and come straight back to you."

"Of course, doctor! And please give my condolences to Amy Anne!"

Elizabeth and the doctor rode out of town together.

"So, tell me some stories about Porlock."

"What kind of stories would you like to hear, Doctor Beaufort?"

"Please call me Robert. *Doctor Beaufort* sounds so impersonal. It always makes me look around for my father."

Elizabeth had wondered about his given name. *Robert.* It was a nice name. "So, your father was a doctor too?" she asked.

"Yes, he still is. He teaches at St. Bart's Hospital in London. That is where I received my training. It must run in the blood; all I ever wanted to be when I was a child was to be a doctor like my father."

"It must be a fascinating subject," said Elizabeth.

"Tell me about your father, the sea captain. There is much talk at the inn of him. He must have been a very interesting character."

Elizabeth was silent. She had rarely spoken of her father since his death.

"Unless it is too painful," apologized the doctor.

"No, I don't mind," said Elizabeth. "He was a very special man. I miss him very much."

"Did you ever sail with him on his ship? I expect that would have been very exciting for a young girl."

"No, Father never allowed that. He said it was too dangerous. But I used to play on the *Dove* when it was tied to the dock. He would teach me to tie knots and let me blow the boatswain's pipe and things like that. Wallace, his first mate, took me for a ride in the long boat all around the harbor once. My mother would always complain when I came home with a dirty dress from playing on the decks."

Elizabeth's mind drifted back into her precious memories.

"He would bring me presents from France like this," she put out her arm and showed him the silver bracelet on her wrist.

She chattered on until she realized they were already at the Snow farm, and she realized she had talked all the way.

"I am ever so sorry! I haven't let you say a thing! How rude you must think I am."

"Not at all," said the doctor. "I enjoyed your stories. You must tell me some more sometime."

He tied his horse to the fence and helped Elizabeth down from her saddle. His hand lingered on hers for just a moment until she pulled it away.

They found Amy Anne still burning with fever and now quite delirious. After the doctor examined her, he joined Elizabeth in the kitchen where she was preparing another cup of warm milk for Amy Anne. "She has an intestinal infection," he told her. "Most likely from something she has eaten."

"But we eat the same food, Doctor. How can it be that *she* is ill, and *I* am not?"

"Perhaps only her portion of the food was bad," said Dr. Beaufort. "What did she eat yesterday?"

"Only cakes at Mrs. White's. She refused to eat once she got home."

The doctor noticed the cup of milk sitting on the table. He picked it up and put his nose to it.

"This milk is bad. Where did it come from?"

"From the larder," said Elizabeth.

"Have you been drinking it as well?" he asked.

"No, Sir. I don't care for milk." Elizabeth was ashamed to tell him the thought of drinking the milk from the animals she hated nauseated her.

"Well, you must throw out the rest of it. It is contaminated! Throw out any cheese or cream you made with it as well. I want you to get as much clear broth down her as you can. We must keep her body hydrated with fluids."

Elizabeth was frozen with fear. She knew people died from bad food. Whatever would she do if she lost Amy Anne? The doctor was saying something, but his voice seemed distant, difficult to hear over the voices in her head. Her hands were trembling, and she began to cry.

"Will you be all right handling things all alone, Elizabeth?"

"Thank you, Doctor. I am sure everything will be all right. Richard is due to return any day. I only wish I had someone to care for the animals."

"I will see that you get some help. But are you quite sure you want to stay on here alone? Would you both be more comfortable staying in town?"

Elizabeth declined, shaking her head. "Thank you, no, Doctor," she said.

In her mind she remembered her last words to Richard: she had promised him she would wait *for as long as it takes*. She was trying to keep her word; she only prayed Richard would keep *his!*

Chapter Forty-Two "Passing Spirits"

Elizabeth went about throwing out the milk and butter in the larder and scrubbing out the buckets and pitchers with soap almost happily. *At least I won't have to milk those horrid cows any longer*, she was thinking to herself. She went back into the house and prepared the broth the doctor had ordered, taking it in to Amy Anne who was still weak and lapsing in and out of delirium.

"You must eat *something*, Amy," she urged when Amy Anne shook her head and pushed the cup away. "How do you expect to get well if you don't eat?"

"I can't keep it down, Elizabeth. My throat is sore from vomiting."

Elizabeth put the cup down and began to sponge Amy Anne's forehead again until Amy drifted off to sleep. She took the cup and poured the broth back into the pot then she wiped everything down in the kitchen and went to her bedchamber throwing herself on the bed. *God forgive me but I am so tired of caring for sick people!* she cried out silently but as soon as she realized what she was thinking she was ashamed. Amy Anne had been so good to her and her mother! *I'm just tired. Maybe I should sleep while Amy is sleeping. Then I will be in a better mood when she wakes up.*

She wasn't sure how long she had slept but the afternoon sunlight was coming in through the bedchamber window when she was awakened by knocking on the door. *Richard!* she immediately thought and jumped up only to find Doctor Beaufort standing at the door with a bucket of fresh milk in his hands.

"What shall I do with the milk?" he asked. "Shall I put it in the larder?"

"Doctor Beaufort, I thought you would send one of the men from town! I did not expect *you* to come yourself!" said Elizabeth.

"Can I not be a *doctor* and a *man* as well?" the doctor asked. "I'll have you know, Elizabeth, I spent a lot of time on my grandparents' farm, and I am quite knowledgeable in matters of farm work."

"Of course, I didn't mean that." She took the bucket. "I will put the milk away. You can check on Amy."

"I have fed all the animals for you."

"Thank you," she replied, realizing her hair must have looked awful and hoping she didn't have telltale marks on her face from the stitching on the coverlet.

"But what of Mrs. White's baby? Are you not needed in town?"

"Mrs. White delivered a fine baby girl an hour ago. I believe she said she is going to name her Martha. So, I am at your disposal, Elizabeth."

Elizabeth went outside to the larder. *What a funny man he is, this handsome young doctor*! she thought. Maybe things weren't so hopeless after all; maybe a little competition was just what Richard needed to declare his love for her! How sure he must be of himself after all this time without even so much as a letter! Did he not think she was attractive to other men? Then, she immediately felt terribly guilty and tried to clear her mind of such thoughts.

When she returned, she met the doctor coming out of Amy Anne's bedchamber. His expression was serious. He walked directly up to her and took her firmly by the shoulders. "Amy Anne is dead, Elizabeth," he said quietly, and she collapsed against him sobbing. He held her in his arms until she had cried herself dry of tears, pulling the stray strands of hair from her wet cheeks and rocking her back and forth like a child. While her ladylike conscience urged her to pull away from him, she could not. It had been so long since she had been cradled in a man's arms; Richard's farewells were but fleeting wisps in her memory for never had he held her for very long. This feeling was different, more like the embraces from her dear father; safe and secure, nurturing and warm, and she relished it and lingered there. When he leaned down putting his lips to her forehead and kissed her softly, she finally pulled away.

"I'm sorry, Elizabeth. I should not have done that," he said apologetically.

"No. It is fine. I am sorry I threw myself into your arms. It was most unladylike," said Elizabeth.

"On the contrary it was *most* ladylike, my dear. You have had the strength of two men, taking care of sick people and all the while doing the work about the farm. It is perfectly understandable that you would yield under such a weight when you have no one to turn to for support."

He is right! thought Elizabeth. She had no one now! She would have to return to Barnstable and the prospect of nursing her mother and her grandmother until they too died!

"I will help you, Elizabeth," said the doctor. "You won't have to do it all alone."

She looked at him and, for the first time, studied his face; the depth of his blue eyes and her reflection in them, the gentle waviness of his dark hair and the hint of a mustache above his upper lip. He was very handsome and very kind, and she found herself comparing his very real presence to Richard's rapidly fading memory.

"If you wish me to, I will see the priest when I get back to town and make arrangements for a coffin for Amy Anne," he said.

"Yes, I would appreciate that, *Robert,*" said Elizabeth.

She walked him to the door, and he kissed her hand. Then the young doctor rode back to town leaving Elizabeth alone in the house with Amy Anne's corpse.

Chapter Forty-Three "Elizabeth's Dilemma"

"I am so very tired of *burying* the people I love," said Elizabeth after Amy Anne had been laid to rest on the hill next to Little John. Robert had remained after the mourners had departed to care for the animals and Elizabeth sat on the fence talking to him as he milked the cows. He had been riding out to the farm every day and she was sure the entire town's tongues were wagging about it.

"You don't have to come every single day, Robert. You have far more important things to do."

The doctor laughed. "Are you worried about our reputations, Elizabeth?"

"Well, no. Yes, well, maybe," she stuttered.

"Well, I assure you I dispel any gossip I hear when I am in town. I am sure no one questions your virtue."

Elizabeth blushed. *No one except myself*, she thought. She was beginning to enjoy his company more than she cared to admit. She began preparing an occasional supper for him and they had spent several pleasant evenings by the fire, discussing a plethora of subjects ranging from farming to medicine. He always conducted himself in a most gentlemanly manner. It seemed as if they could talk for hours with no lack of topics. But she was acutely aware of how fast gossip could travel in Porlock. And what of Richard who could return at any moment? Her mind was filled with a thousand things over which she worried. Without Amy Anne the house seemed so large and empty; Elizabeth closed off Amy's bedchamber. Indeed, if not for the doctor's company Elizabeth was sure she would have gone quite mad! To occupy her time Elizabeth decided to take over teaching Amy Anne's classes and it did much to improve her anxiety. She had never envisioned herself as a schoolteacher, but she soon found herself enjoying the children immensely.

One day she was returning from the school just at the time that the doctor was leaving town on his way to the Snow farm to help with the milking.

"How are your classes going, Elizabeth?" he asked.

"Very well, Robert," she replied. "I am not sure I am as gifted at teaching as Amy Anne was, but the children are most understanding. They even teach *me* on occasion!"

He laughed. "It is too bad you have to ride such a long way every day. Have you had any more thoughts of moving into town?"

"I have thought about it. But the farm belongs to Richard, and I have an obligation to stay and keep it ready for when he returns."

"I am sure the men of the guild would keep the fields planted and the livestock cared for."

The doctor's face took on a slightly serious expression. The subject of Richard was rarely discussed between them, but it was very much on his mind. "And what will you do when he *does* return?"

"I am to marry him as I promised long ago. I must honor my pledge," she said the words coming out of her mouth with much difficulty.

"How long has it been since you have heard from him, Elizabeth? Has he written to you of his plans?" Robert knew he was treading on dangerous ground, but he could no longer keep silent. He loved this woman, and she gave every indication of loving him as well.

Elizabeth was silent for a moment. There was indeed a division in the chambers of her heart, and she had never spoken of it. There was affection for this man who had been so kind in her hours of need and yet there was still the dream of Richard. With every day that passed the dream was becoming hazy replaced by real life. "He has not written. I can only assume he is with King Henry and has no way to contact me."

Robert shook his head. "Elizabeth, forgive me, but in all this time he must have had the opportunity to send a message to you; there are messengers leaving London every day."

They had reached the farm and Elizabeth dismounted from her horse. Robert tied his horse and came up behind her, spinning her around by her shoulders. He kissed her deeply and held her tightly in his arms and Elizabeth succumbed to the emotion of the moment. Her entire body went limp, and she leaned against him for support. Then she pulled away suddenly and ran to the house. He let her go. He knew she felt the same as he did; he could tell by the way she kissed him.

He put her horse away and tended to the usual chores. Tempted to just ride back into town and leave Elizabeth alone to think on the words that had passed between them, he paused, looking up at the house not knowing what to do. *I have never told her that I love her*! he suddenly said to himself. *How can she possibly know if I don't tell her?*

He ran to the house and knocked on the door several times before she appeared. He could tell she had been crying by the still damp streaks across her cheeks. "I am sorry if I made you cry, Elizabeth," he said as she permitted him to enter the house.

She crossed the room and sat down in John's rocking chair, staring silently into the blackness of the cold fireplace. Robert followed her and fell to his knees at her feet.

"Elizabeth, I want to tell you something that I have been keeping to myself for a long time now."

Still Elizabeth uttered not a word.

"Elizabeth, I love you! I can't help the way I feel about you. What's more I think that you love me too but your honor in keeping your commitment to Richard has kept you from voicing it."

Elizabeth looked directly into his eyes and reached out her hand to stroke his forehead. He buried his face in her lap and he too began to cry. "Oh, Robert," she said softly. "I *do* love you! If I could take back my promise to Richard, I would this very minute! But how cruel would it be for a woman to reject a man when he is out fighting in the battlefield?"

"It is not a sin to break a betrothal, Elizabeth. It *is* a sin to marry one when you love another!"

"But what of his family? How disrespectful I would be if…."

"His family is gone, Elizabeth."

Robert raised his head and took her by the hands pulling her up to her feet. He kissed her again and she responded without restraint with all the pent-up feelings she had been keeping tucked away in the innermost recesses of her heart. He gathered her up and carried her to her bedchamber. There, in the shards of twilight that filtered through the curtain, Elizabeth became his and Robert became hers and by the time night fell they had become one being, emotionally joined forever. Promises were whispered in the dark and future plans were made that seemed, at that moment, possible. Not wanting to leave her but knowing he must, Robert kissed Elizabeth goodbye and stole away at midnight making his way quietly back to town through the back alleys to avoid the gossiping tongues of Porlock.

The next day Sir Richard returned home from the war.

Chapter Forty-Four "Farewell to Porlock"

The Battle at Bosworth Field put Henry Tudor on the throne but unfortunately had not put an end to the opposition from the Yorkist "white rose". Even though he squashed the rebellion at Stoke in 1487, raids continued on the Scottish border and in 1497 another fifteen thousand Cornish marched on London in defiance of his newly assessed war taxes. While victorious his armies were growing war-weary; it had now been years since they had seen their families. Richard had gained the favor of the king and had been promoted to a position in the Yeomen of the Guard who served as the king's private bodyguards. While honored by the king's confidence, he sorely missed his parents and Elizabeth; tired of the offensive London air he longed to see the green hills of Porlock and take a deep breath of the apple blossoms again. Finally, Henry set up a contingent plan, alternating leaves between his troops and Richard was granted a two week leave to go home.

He rode out of London in the early morn, dressed in his Tudor tunic and leaving his armor behind. It was an exhilarating feeling to ride without the heaviness of his shield and he urged his horse into a gallop as they passed through the countryside. He was happy to be going home; to be able to give his mother a proper hug and share his war stories with his father. Most importantly his mind was on marriage; he intended to marry Elizabeth as soon as he got home. Before he became a knight, he felt slightly unworthy of her hand but now with the wars behind him and now that he was a member of the most elite, the Yeoman of the Guard, he wanted his lady by his side!

It was almost sunset when he reached the crest of the hill above the farm. He reined in his horse and looked for a moment across his father's fields expecting to see him there as he usually was, squeezing every minute of daylight out of the day but his father was not in sight. As he drew nearer, he could see that the animals had been put away and fed and there was a lamp burning in the window of the house.

After he unsaddled his horse he approached the door, opening it quietly to surprise his mother. There, in his father's chair next to the fire sat Elizabeth doing needlework. She must have heard the floor creak with his step, and she looked up, on her face a look of shock.

"Richard!" she said. "You have come home!"

"Yes, my dear! The king granted us a two week leave." He crossed the room and took her by the hands, drawing her up into his arms. "We have time for a wedding before I have to return to London!"

Elizabeth was at a loss for words.

"Where are Mother and Father?" Richard asked looking around the house.

"Oh, Richard, there was no way for us to reach you...."

Richard released her from his arms and stared into her eyes.

"Elizabeth, what has happened? Why do you look so peculiar?"

"They are dead, Richard. *Both* of them," she replied.

Richard's face took a vacant look, and he shook his head. "It can't be true! Elizabeth, why are you telling me this?"

He sat down at the kitchen table and put his face into his hands.

Elizabeth followed him and put her arms around his shoulders. "It is true, Richard. I am so sorry."

After she had explained it all, he turned toward her and buried his face against her breasts. He began to cry while she cradled him and stroked his hair. It was a private beautiful moment and she realized what a privilege it was that he would share his grief with her.

"You went through all that and yet you waited for me," he murmured softly.

Elizabeth's guilt suddenly came upon her; there seemed to be a lump in her throat, and she could not speak.

"I love you so much, Elizabeth!" said Richard and it was her turn to cry although she wasn't exactly sure *who* she was crying *for.* He had finally said the words she had waited years to hear. She sat down beside him, and they continued to hold each other until their weeping subsided.

"Where is your mother?" he asked. "Tell me she didn't get sick too!"

"No," said Elizabeth. "She wanted to return to Barnstable after Tom died." Just as the words parted her lips, she realized Richard didn't know about Tom either!

"Tom too? What has happened around here? As soon as I go off to war, everyone dies!"

She related the story of the pirates and Wallace's escape. Richard shook his head in disbelief. At that moment he realized the immeasurable value of his friends and family. He looked at his Elizabeth realizing how incredibly strong and loyal she was, and he knew he never wanted to be separated from her ever again. Suddenly he stood up and seemed to take a deep breath and collect himself. "Get your shawl, Elizabeth. We are going to town."

"Why are we going to town?" she asked.

"We are going to find the priest who will marry us, so you can return to London with me!"

Elizabeth's heart was racing; she did not know what to say. She loved Richard, truly she did! But she also loved Robert. No matter what decision she made it was going to hurt one of them; there was no way out of her predicament. How could she leave Richard after he had lost his entire family? How could she love him when she had given herself to another? How could she break Robert's heart when he had been so good to her?

"You *are* still going to marry me aren't you, Elizabeth?" asked Richard.

Elizabeth retrieved her shawl and put out the lamp. "We should go before the priest retires for the night," she said quietly.

Chapter Forty-Five "The Letter"

Elizabeth was sitting at a small table in their living quarters within King Henry's castle. It was larger than the quarters of the other knights who did not have their families with them, but it was much smaller than the Snow farmhouse and it was colder and draftier within its walls of mortared stone. Elizabeth spent much of her time huddled near the fireplace to keep warm. Her appearance was much different than her last day in Porlock; when she first arrived at court she was expected to be properly dressed when she ventured into the public eye. Richard had purchased several colorful gowns and scarved-headdresses for her to wear which at one time in her life would have thrilled her but now gave her no pleasure at all now that her confinement had begun. She found it unpleasant outside in the foul air of London and was becoming more like her mother; often bedridden and morose at a time that should have brought happiness to her heart. The anticipation of pending motherhood was not a happy one for Elizabeth.

Richard had gone away again shortly after they had arrived in London; serving as His Majesty's personal bodyguard he had to be constantly at the king's side and she was again being left alone, this time in a cold stone tomb. It had been months since they had married in haste and left Porlock so abruptly. Now, with her husband gone and no idea of when he would return, she sat down to write a letter she had been meaning to write for so long; a letter she planned to mail secretly, away from the gossiping whispers at court and prying eyes of the king's servants. She was finally writing a letter to Robert to try to explain her impulsive behavior and ask his forgiveness for her betrayal.

Dear Robert, she began, *I have for a long time now wanted to write you and I hope this letter finds you happy and prosperous. I only wanted to try to explain why I left without saying goodbye to you; why I made the decision to marry Richard and how very difficult that decision was for me to make.*

One thing my father instilled in me for as long as I can remember was that of honor and keeping one's word. I believe that is why he stayed married to my mother until he died; he would have never broken his pledge of affection for her even when she was so very difficult to live with. He tried so very hard to make her happy!

Don't you see Robert that I had to keep my promise to Richard made so many years before? He had been true to me, and I owed him nothing less in return.

I will always remember you and I pray that you will someday be able to forgive me for hurting you. I truly loved you then as I love you now. Had we come into each other's lives earlier in time who can say what would have happened?

Affectionately Yours,

Elizabeth

She finished the letter and sealed it carefully in an envelope. She then covered herself in a long shawl that camouflaged her delicate condition and ventured out into the dark hallway where she kept herself in the shadows until she reached the castle gate.

The castle guard greeted her as she passed. "Good morning, M'Lady," he said.

"Good morning," she replied and hurried along, holding the letter under her shawl.

She went out into the street among the city peasants and held her skirts high above the dirty cobblestones as she made her way to the marketplace where she was confident she could find a messenger. When she found one, she dug some coins out of her pouch and put them in the man's dirty hands.

"Will you see that this gets to Porlock as soon as possible?" she asked. *Porlock*! she thought *how I miss you*! Memories of her father's ship tied up at the dock and of her as a little girl playing aboard the *Dove* flashed through her mind in slow motion.

The man quickly took the coins and put the letter in his pouch assuring her it would be delivered by the end of the week or as soon as he collected enough mail to make the trip profitable. There were no guarantees that the man would not take her money and throw her letter away, but she had to try. She wanted to scream at him *take me with you*! but she knew she would never see Porlock again.

She returned to their quarters and closed the door behind her. Crossing the room, she glanced at her image in the mirror on the wall and her heart plummeted at her reflection there; staring back at her was a matronly woman with child, whose complexion was sallow and withered from days spent in the darkness of the castle walls. She turned away from the mirror in disgust and threw herself on the bed. How disappointed her father would have been with her had he lived. She was glad her mother was back in Barnstable and would never know. It was a secret she would never tell a soul, not even her husband.

She could never admit to anyone that the paternity of her child was in question; *that secret she would take with her to her grave!*

Author's Note:

The story does not end here, however. What will be in store for Richard and Elizabeth in London under the new rule of Henry VIII? Will they ever again see Porlock? Will her shameful secret ever be revealed? Will Robert ever again be a part of Elizabeth's life? What lies in the future is a mystery to them but will be revealed in Volume Two in the series "An American Family" when the Snow family will find themselves preparing to leave England forever to explore a new world across the Atlantic. It is called *"Blood and Cobblestones"* and is set to be released next year.

J.A. Snow

Made in the USA
Las Vegas, NV
27 August 2022